*A Book Of*

# ORGANISATION DEVELOPMENT

**For**

**MPM Semester - III**

**As Per New Revised Syllabus, June 2014**

**Mrs. SAMITA KHER**

MA (Economics), MBS (HR)
Sinhgad Institute of Management
Pune.

**NIRALI PRAKASHAN**
**ADVANCEMENT OF KNOWLEDGE**

N2112

**Organisational Development**                    **ISBN 978-93-5164-053-0**

Third Edition    :    **August 2015**

©              :    **Author**

**Published By :**

**NIRALI PRAKASHAN**

Abhyudaya Pragati, 1312, Shivaji Nagar,

Off J.M. Road, PUNE – 411005

Tel - (020) 25512336/37/39, Fax - (020) 25511379

Email : niralipune@pragationline.com

## ☞ DISTRIBUTION CENTRES

**PUNE**

Nirali Prakashan    :    119, Budhwar Peth, Jogeshwari Mandir Lane, Pune 411002, Maharashtra
Tel : (020) 2445 2044, 66022708, Fax : (020) 2445 1538
Email : bookorder@pragationline.com, niralilocal@pragationline.com

Nirali Prakashan    :    S. No. 28/27, Dhyari, Near Pari Company, Pune 411041
Tel : (020) 24690204 Fax : (020) 24690316
Email :  dhyari@pragationline.com, bookorder@pragationline.com

**MUMBAI**

Nirali Prakashan    :    385, S.V.P. Road, Rasdhara Co-op. Hsg. Society Ltd.,
Girgaum, Mumbai 400004, Maharashtra
Tel : (022) 2385 6339 / 2386 9976, Fax : (022) 2386 9976
Email : niralimumbai@pragationline.com

## ☞ DISTRIBUTION BRANCHES

**JALGAON**

Nirali Prakashan    :    34, V. V. Golani Market, Navi Peth, Jalgaon 425001,
Maharashtra, Tel : (0257) 222 0395, Mob : 94234 91860

**KOLHAPUR**

Nirali Prakashan    :    New Mahadvar Road, Kedar Plaza, 1st Floor Opp. IDBI Bank
Kolhapur 416 012, Maharashtra. Mob : 9850046155

**NAGPUR**

Pratibha Book Distributors    :    Above Maratha Mandir, Shop No. 3, First Floor,
Rani Jhanshi Square, Sitabuldi, Nagpur 440012, Maharashtra
Tel : (0712) 254 7129

**DELHI**

Nirali Prakashan    :    4593/21, Basement, Aggarwal Lane 15, Ansari Road, Daryaganj
Near Times of India Building, New Delhi  110002
Mob :  08505972553

**BENGALURU**

Pragati Book House    :    House No. 1, Sanjeevappa Lane, Avenue Road Cross,
Opp. Rice Church, Bengaluru – 560002.
Tel : (080) 64513344, 64513355,Mob : 9880582331, 9845021552
Email:bharatsavla@yahoo.com

**CHENNAI**

Pragati Books    :    9/1, Montieth Road, Behind Taas Mahal, Egmore,
Chennai 600008 Tamil Nadu, Tel : (044) 6518 3535,
Mob : 94440 01782 / 98450 21552 / 98805 82331,
Email : bharatsavla@yahoo.com

niralipune@pragationline.com    |    www.pragationline.com

Also find us on 🅕 www.facebook.com/niralibooks

**Dedicated to my Parents**

*Smt. Annapurna Mahapatra*
*Late Shri Rabindranath Mahapatra*

# Foreword ...

Organisational Development ensures that all services and interventions are driven by excellence and quality services. In its essence, Organisational Development aims to complement the technical elements of development programs by focusing on inculcating a climate a climate and culture of innovation, change and productivity. It has been more responsive and practically relevant to organisation's needs to operate effectively in a highly complex and changing world.

It gives me immense pleasure to note that author Prof. Samita Kher has simplified the understanding of Organisational Development through the book. This book will be of great help to facilities, practitioners and post-graduate students. The author has incorporated interesting case-lets which will give an idea about the real life business situations to the students.

While going through this book, one cannot resist appreciating ardent efforts taken by the author.

My Best Wishes to the author for her present and future endeavors.

**Prof. M. N. Navale**
President
Sinhgad Technical Education Society

# Foreword ...

Organisational Development can help to provide a solution to a number of problems. It should be a core competence for anyone willing to bring about improvement in an organisation. To be effective, any organisational development intervention should be founded on a rigorous and systematic evidence base. The objective should be to combine the tools and techniques of quality improvement with effective organisation and leadership development. Organisational development should go beyond the limited techniques used by various well-known practitioners.

The book provides a key guide to leaders trying to engage their staff in changing their organisation by bringing together theory and experience. This is important so too often theory is neglected and there is inadequate reflection on experience. This book will be of great help to faculties, practitioners and post-graduate students.

I wish the author Prof. Samita Kher, success which is surely to follow.

**(Dr. Mrs. Sunanda Navale)**

Secretary

Sinhgad Technical Education Society

# Preface ...

Organisation Development is the process of aligning human capital strategy with the mission, vision, values, and strategy of the organisation. It includes organisation structure, supporting systems and processes, leadership development, succession planning, talent acquisition, and talent engagement (including design of reward and recognition systems). The overall theory is that a unity of what the organisation is and what it wishes to accomplish with that of the individual and his or her goals will propel the organisation to greater levels of performance.

By and large organisation development practice has been successful. It represents a planned attempt to use what is known about organisations and employee behaviour in the facilitation of organisation change. It stresses the management must recognise that people's emotions, attitude and perceptions play a large part in influencing their behaviour, specifically their willingness to undertake changes of which the outcomes may appear uncertain, risky or threatening. It addresses this fact by actively involving members of organisation in the change process.

The collaborative nature of OD implies that employees in the organisation who will be affected directly by the proposed change are actively involved in diagnosing and suggesting solutions to the problems. OD is an applied field of change that uses behavioural science knowledge to increase the capacity for change and to improve the functioning and performance of a human system. It is more than change management. It is about learning and improving in ways that make individuals, groups, organisations and ultimately the world better-off and more capable of managing change in the future. It is more than a bunch of interventions. It is an integrated theory and practice base aimed at increasing the effectiveness and efficiency of organisations.

The text is organised into five chapters providing a comprehensive coverage of all the vital aspects of Organisation Development. Chapters 1 to 4 provide an overview of OD, definitions of OD, history of OD, its underlying values, assumptions and beliefs, its theoretical and research foundations, importance of action research and an overview of OD interventions. Chapter 5 details Techno-structural interventions which include topics such as restructuring organisations, employee involvement, work design, performance management, developing talent, and managing workforce wellness.

A number of case studies have also been included in the textbook.

I acknowledge my debt to the work and writings of the pioneer practitioner- scholars.

I am grateful to Nirali Prakashan for giving me an opportunity to explore my knowledge and express this in the form of a textbook. I express my deep gratitude to Shri. Dineshbhai Furia and Shri. Jignesh Furia, my publishers and their staff for their cooperation and support. I would also like to thank Supriya Singh, for her kind collaboration in completing this book.

Any constructive comments for improving the contents will be warmly appreciated.

**Samita Kher**

# Syllabus ...

| Unit Number | Contents | Number of Sessions |
|:---:|:---|:---:|
| 1. | **Concept and Definition of OD:** Values and Assumptions, Importance, Evolution: Kurt Lewin, Robert Tanenbaum, McGregor, Herbert Shepard, Robert Blake. | 7 + 2 |
| 2. | **Foundations of OD:** Models and theories of Planed change, Systems Theory, Teams and Teamwork, Participation and Empowerment, Applied Behavioural Science, Parallel Learning Structures. | 7 + 2 |
| 3. | **The Process of Organisation Development:** Role of change agent. <br><br> Entering and Contracting, Diagnosing Organisations, Diagnosing Groups and Individuals, Collecting and Analysing Diagnostic Information, Feeding Back Diagnostic Information, Designing Interventions, Managing Change, Evaluating and Institutionalising Interventions | 7 + 2 |
| 4. | **Human Process Interventions:** Interpersonal and Group Process Approaches, Organisation Process Approaches. | 7 + 2 |
| 5. | **Techno-structural Interventions:** Restructuring Organisations, Employee Involvement, Work Design, Performance Management, Developing Talent, Managing Workforce Diversity and Wellness. | 7 + 2 |

# Contents ...

***

*Chapter* **1** ...

# Concept and Definition of Organisation Development

## *Contents ...*

## Learning Objectives ...

- To understand the concept of Organisational Development (OD)
- To be able to study the values and assumptions relating to Organisational Development
- To learn the objectives and importance of Organisational Development
- To examine the evolution of Organisational Development

## 1.1 Introduction

"Organisation" means the coming together of people and resources to form a unit. "Development" in its simplest form suggests change and growth. Organisation Development (OD) is a management field that focuses on helping organisations to develop their full potential. It is focused on improving the effectiveness of organisations and the people in those organisations.

OD is about collaborating with organisation leaders and their groups to create systemic change and root-cause problem-solving on behalf of improving productivity and employee satisfaction through improving the human processes through which they get their work done. Theory and practice of planned, systematic change in the attitudes, beliefs, and values of the employees is done through creation and reinforcement of long-term training programmes.

OD is action oriented. It starts with a careful organisation-wide analysis of the current situation and of the future requirements, and employs techniques of behavioural sciences such as behaviour modelling, sensitivity training, and transactional analysis. Its objective is to enable the organisation in adopting-better to the fast-changing external environment of new markets, regulations, and technologies.

Thus, Organisation Development is the process of improving organisations. The process is carefully planned and implemented to benefit the organisation, its employees and its stakeholders. The organisation can be an entire company, public agency, non-profit organisation, volunteer group - or a smaller part of a larger organisation.

## 1.2 Definition and Concept of Organisation Development

### Standard Definition of Organisation Development

The nature and needs of organisations are changing dramatically. Correspondingly, the profession of organisation development (OD) has been changing to meet the changing needs of organisations. So OD could be defined as *"the practice of changing people and organisations for positive growth."*

There is no single definition of organisation development. It may be most useful to consider several definitions of organisation development. For many years, the following definition was perhaps the standard definition for OD. It was developed in 1969 at a time when an organisation was considered to be much like a stable machine comprising interlocking parts.

- *"Organisation Development is an effort planned, organisation-wide, and managed from the top, to increase organisation effectiveness and health through planned interventions in the organisation's 'processes,' using behavioural-science knowledge."* **(Beckhard, "Organisation Development: Strategies and Models", Reading, MA: Addison-Wesley, 1969, p. 9)**

- *"OD is a response to change, a complex educational strategy intended to change the beliefs, attitudes, values and structure of organisations so that they can better adapt to new technologies, markets and challenges and the dizzying rate of change itself."* **(Bennis 1969)**

- *"OD can be defined as a planned and sustained effort to apply behavioural science for system improvement, using reflexive, self-analytic models."* **(Schmuck and Miles, 1971)**

**Recent Definitions of Organisation Development**

Today's organisations operate in a rapidly changing environment. Consequently, one of the most important assets for an organisation is the ability to manage change – and for people to remain healthy and authentic. Consider the following definition of OD:

*"Organisation Development is the attempt to influence the members of an organisation to expand their candidness with each other about their views of the organisation and their experience in it, and to take greater responsibility for their own actions as organisation members. The assumption behind OD is that when people pursue both of these objectives simultaneously, they are likely to discover new ways of working together that they experience as more effective for achieving their own and their shared (organisation) goals. And when that does not happen, such activity helps them to understand why and to make meaningful choices about what to do in light of this understanding."*

**(Neilsen, "Becoming an OD Practitioner", Englewood Cliffs, CA: Prentice-Hall, 1984, pp. 2-3.)**

Experts might agree that the following definitions of OD represent the major focus and thrust of many of today's OD practitioners.

*"Organisation development is a system-wide application of behavioural science knowledge to the planned development and reinforcement of organisation strategies, structures, and processes for improving an organisation's effectiveness."*

**(Cummings and Worley, "Organisation Development and Change", Sixth Edition, South-Western Publishing, 1993, p.2)**

*"OD is a planned process of change in an organisation's culture through the utilisation of behavioural science technologies, research and theory."* **(Burke, 1994)**

*"Organisation Development is a body of knowledge and practice that enhances organisation performance and individual development, viewing the organisation as a complex structure of systems that exist within a larger system, each of which has its own attributes and degrees of alignment. OD interventions in these systems are inclusive methodologies and approaches to strategic planning, organisation design, leadership development, change management, performance management, coaching, diversity, and work/life balance."*

**(Matt Minahan, MM & Associates, Silver Spring, Maryland)**

The authors agree that OD applies behavioural science to achieve planned change. They also agree that the objective of change is the total organisation or system to achieve increased organisation effectiveness and individual development. The OD programmes target organisation culture and processes.

**Cummings and Worley** emphasise achieving resemblance among the components of the organisation such as strategy, structure, culture and processes.

According to **Bennis**, *OD is both a response to change and an educational strategy intended to change beliefs, attitudes, values and organisation structure to make the organisation better to respond to the dynamic environment (Refer case: 1.1). OD alters people's behaviours by changing organisation work settings.*

---

**CASE: 1.1**

**Improving company performance by 'Being the Best'**

**The Challenge**

The UK's largest computer store and a major part of the Dixons Group, PC World is fully signed up to the group's "Being the Best" values: operating with integrity, giving outstanding service to customers, respecting their colleagues, continually seeking ways to improve performance, and working together to beat the competition. However, the extent that these values were lived by the staff in the stores made a significant difference to company performance.

**Key issues**

- Needing to create impact around the Being the Best values.
- Changing the culture of the organisation to improve company performance.

**The Solution**

- We explored with 10 strong teams what they would see, do and feel, and conversely what behaviours and ways of working would no longer occur if the values were really being lived.
- From these energetic discussions they have put together the "Being the Best" tool, using their own words. Teams then used these to assess their current behaviours against the aspiration and identify steps to close the gap.

**The Results**

- Within one year, three quarters of all stores have voluntarily participated in the programme with very positive outcomes
- We are currently looking at different approaches suitable for the leadership and central support teams.

---

All the authors agree with the desirability of creating self-renewing, "learning organisations." There is no set definition of OD and no agreement on the boundaries of the field i.e. what practices should be included and excluded.

*"Organisation Development (OD) is a long-term effort, led and supported by top-management to improve an organisation's visioning, empowerment, learning and problem-solving processes, through an ongoing, collaborative management of organisation culture, with special emphasis on the culture of intact work teams and other team configuration – using the consultant-facilitator role and the theory and technology of applied behavioural science, including action research." (French & Bell)*

## 1.3 Components of Organisation Development

The above definition includes essential components which are explained below:

### 1. Long-term Effort

Organisation development and change takes several years. Improvement is a continuous change. Various programmes and initiatives move the organisation to a higher level of effectiveness. It involves the investment of some time and money. OD is often organisation-wide, this investment is not insignificant and cannot therefore, be incurred too often.

### 2. Led and Supported by Top Management

Top management should lead and encourage the efforts to change. Organisation change is tough. It includes pain, uncertainty as well as setbacks. The initiative should be taken by top management towards improvement and they should remain committed to see it through. Many OD programmes fail as top management are not committed or become diverted from their duties. Thus, the management has to play a positive role by facilitating the agent's task not only in making an initial diagnosis but also in carrying it out.

### 3. Visioning Process

Visioning means creating a picture of the desired future. It includes how organisation members working together can make the picture a reality. The process through which organisation members develop a viable, rational and shared picture of the nature of the products and services offered by the organisations is called visioning. It involves the way the products and services will be produced and delivered to customers and what the organisation members expect from each other.

### 4. Empowerment Process

The leadership behaviours and human resource practices enable organisation members to develop and use their talent towards individual growth and organisation success. Here empowerment means involving large number of people in building the vision of tomorrow, developing the strategy for getting it and making it happen. Organisation should build its strategies, structure, processes and culture to make empowerment a fact of life.

### 5. Learning Process

**Peter Senge** describes a learning organisation as an "organisation where people continually expand their capacity to create the results they truly desire, where new and expensive patterns of thinking are nurtured, where collective aspiration is set free and where people are continually learning how to learn together." The learning process is a process of interacting, listening and self-examining process that facilitates individual, team and organisation learning.

### 6. Problem-Solving Process

It refers to the organisation's methods of dealing with the threats and opportunities in its environment. For example, managers may choose to solve the organisation's problems on their own or they might participate with subordinates in problem-solving and decision-making. This process refers to the ways organisation members diagnose situations, solve problems, make decisions and take actions on problems, opportunities and challenges. According to **Michael Beer** it is a process of "developing new and creative organisation solutions".

### 7. Ongoing Collaborative Management of the Organisation's Culture

Just as visioning, empowerment, learning and problem-solving processes are opportunities for collaboration in organisation development, so is managing the culture. It is important to manage the prevailing pattern of values, attitudes, beliefs, assumptions, expectations, activities, interactions, norms and sentiments. All these form an organisation's culture. Collaborative management of the culture means that everyone has a stake in making the organisation work. Collaborative management also means management through subordinate participation and power sharing rather than through the hierarchical imposition of authority.

### 8. Organisation Processes

Processes are how things get done and the importance of visioning, empowerment, learning and problem-solving. Processes are relatively easy to change. OD programmes make people stop doing things one way and make them start doing things a different way. When culture changes and people accept the new ways as the right ways then change becomes permanent.

### 9. Intact Work Teams and Other Configuration

Individuals and the total organisation function well when team functions well. Team culture can be collaboratively managed to ensure effectiveness. An intact team consists of superior and subordinates with a specific job to perform. In many organisations, intact work teams do not have a boss, they are self-directed teams. The members of such teams are trained in competencies such as planning, maintaining quality control and using management information. They also control performance appraisals, hiring, firing and training.

### 10. Consultant - facilitator Role

Many members of the organisation should be encouraged to increase their consultation skills and use these skills in various ways. It can help to run more effective meetings or counsel the peers. In the early years, the services of third-party consultant-facilitator were desirable. The third party person brings objectivity, neutrality and expertise to the situation.

### 11. Theory and Technology of Applied Behavioural Sciences

OD applies knowledge and theory. In addition to behavioural sciences such as psychology, sociology and so on, applied disciplines such as adult education, social work, economics and political science contribute to the practice of OD. It is the practical application of the science of organisations.

### 12. Action Research

Organisation development could be organisation improvement through participant action research. It is a process of diagnosing, taking action, re-diagnosing and taking new action. Action research includes three essential ingredients: the highly participative nature of OD, the consultant role of collaborator and co-learner, and the iterative process of diagnosis and action. Change occurs based on the actions taken. Leader, organisation members and OD practitioners work together to define and resolve problems and opportunities.

## 1.4 Values of Organisation Development

The field of Organisation Development rests on a foundation of values and assumptions about people and organisations. Values have always been an integral part of an OD package. Through the research and theories of behavioural scientists and from the experiences and observations of managers, values and assumptions are developed.

*Values are beliefs and are defined as: "Beliefs about what is desirable or 'good' (e.g., free speech) and what is an undesirable or a 'bad' (e.g., dishonesty)".*

*– (French and Bell, 1999)*

*A belief is a proposition about how the world works that the individual accepts as true; it is a cognitive fact for the person. (French and Bell, 1999).*

Values tend to be humanistic, optimistic and democratic. **Humanistic values** emphasise the importance of the individuals, to respect the whole person, to treat people with respect and dignity, to assume that everyone has intrinsic worth and view all people as having the potential for growth and development. They also emphasise development of people, beliefs such as trust and respect for the individual and feelings, open communication, empowerment, participation and contribution by all organisation members, collaboration and cooperation, appropriate uses of power, authentic interpersonal relations etc.

**Optimistic values** assume that people are basically good, that progress is possible and desirable in humans and that rationality, reason and goodwill are the tools for progressing.

While, **Democratic values** assert the sanctity of the individual, the fundamental human rights is to be free from arbitrary misuse of power, the importance of fair and equitable treatment for all and the need for justice through the rule of law and due process. It replaced authoritarian, autocratic and arbitrary management practices as well as the dysfunctions of bureaucracies.

The OD paradigm values human and organisation growth, collaborative and participative processes and a spirit of inquiry. The change agent may be directive in OD; however there is a strong emphasis on collaboration. The following briefly identifies the underlying values in most of OD efforts:

**(a) Respect the People:**

Individuals are perceived as being responsible, conscientious and caring. They should be treated with dignity and respect.

**(b) Trust and Support:**

An effective and healthy organisation is characterised by trust, authenticity, openness and a supportive climate.

**(c) Power and Equalisation:**

Effective organisations deemphasise hierarchical authority and control.

**(d) Confrontation:**

Problems should not be swept under the rug. They should be openly confronted.

**(e) Participation:**

The more people who will be affected by a change are involved in the decisions surrounding that change, the more they will be committed to implementing those decisions.

## 1.5 Basic Assumptions of Organisation Development

OD proceeds on the basis on certain assumptions. To implement the OD programme effectively, management support and the willingness of the people are prerequisites that there are many presuppositions for the programme to be carried out. *"Assumptions are beliefs that are regarded as so valuable and obviously correct that they are taken for granted and rarely examined or questioned" (French and Bell, 1999)*. The assumptions are discussed below in three levels:

**1. Assumptions about Individuals**

(a) It is assumed that individuals have needs for personal growth and development. OD is not being imposed upon them. They know that it is in their best interests and will enable them to satisfy their higher-order needs.

(b)   It is assumed that the capacity and capabilities of individuals are underutilised. They are capable of taking on more responsibility. When they undergo OD, they would improve further.

(c)   In essence, an individual's capacities, capabilities, values, beliefs and thinking will change making him/her altogether a different individual.

2.  **Assumptions about Groups**

(a)   It is assumed that there is less inter-personal trust and mutual support that can be enhanced through Organisation Development.

(b)   It is assumed when team spirit is fostered in groups, they would be ready to take on more responsibilities and with the identification of group goals with organisation goals and leadership, responsibilities can be widely shared.

(c)   There is need for developing a spirit of cooperation among groups.

(d)   In essence, cooperative groups having a high level of inter-personal trust and mutual support serve organisation interest better and OD can foster that spirit of cooperation.

3.  **Assumptions about Organisations**

(a)   OD enjoys the full and active support of the management. The change agent will initiate only at the behest of the management. Then, their support should be willingly forthcoming.

(b)   Cooperation among groups exists and therefore, inter-group relations are emphasised.

(c)   Conflicts and differences among people and groups, instead of working at cross purposes should prove mutually beneficial.

(d)   Any change in any part will not only affect that part but will also have an impact upon other parts.

Hence, OD represents a mutuality of interests – of people as well as the organisation and cooperation from groups and support from the management would facilitate turning the differences into enriched problem-solving.

Table 1.1 summarises the values and assumptions underlying Organisation Development:

**Table: 1.1: Summary of Assumptions underlying OD**

| ASSUMPTIONS | VALUES |
|---|---|
| **Individuals:** | **Individuals:** |
| People want to grow and mature and have much to offer that is not being used at work. | OD aims to overcome obstacles to the natural human tendency to grow, enabling employees to contribute more to the organisation. |
| Most employees desire the opportunity to contribute (they desire, seek and appreciate empowerment). | OD stresses open communication and treating employees with genuine dignity and respect. |

| ASSUMPTIONS | VALUES |
|---|---|
| **Groups:** | **Groups:** |
| Groups are critical to organisation success. | Hiding feelings or not being accepted by the group diminishes individual willingness to solve problems constructively. |
| Groups have powerful influences on individual behaviour. | |
| The complex roles to be played in groups require skill development. | Acceptance, collaboration, and involvement lead to expressions of feelings and perceptions. |
| **Organisation:** | **Organisation:** |
| Excessive controls, policies and rules are detrimental. | The ways groups are linked influence their effectiveness. |
| Conflict can be functional if properly channelled. | Change should start at the top and gradually be introduced through the rest of the organisation. |
| Individual and organisation goals can be compatible. | The group links the top and bottom of the organisation. |

*Source: Adapted from Hellriegel & Slocum, 1989, p. 800; Newstrom & Davis, 1997, p.41*

Thus, values and assumptions provide structure and stability for people as they attempt to understand the world around them.

## 1.6 Pre-requisites of Organisation Development

Successful organisation development can be challenging because it involves tackling issues associated with change and service improvement. The following pre-requisites are understood to help effective organisation development:

1. Establishing a focal point to coordinate and support organisation development activities.
2. Ensuring organisation development is placed within the organisation structure appropriately.
3. Being flexible and creative by using the approach to organisation development that best suits the organisation.
4. Taking steps to build the appropriate organisation skills and capacity.
5. Integrating organisation development into employee communications, staff development, team-working and other aspects of high-performance workplaces.

If managed well, it constitutes long-range effort to:

6. Improve the problem solving capacity of the organisation.
7. Foster effective management of the organisation culture.

8.   Improve the effectiveness of work groups/teams.

9.   Specially concerned with the development of organisation climate and culture (norms, values, power structure) including organisation change.

10.  Management and staff development to achieve corporate goals.

11.  The development of performance culture.

Organisation Development, wherever implemented, attempts to improve the overall effectiveness of the organisation.

## 1.7 Objectives of Organisation Development

OD aims at a higher quality of work life, productivity, adaptability and effectiveness. It seeks to change beliefs, attitudes, values, strategies, structures and practices to enable the organisation to better adapt to competitive actions, technological advances and the fast pace of other changes in the environment. The end-result is integration of individual and organisation goals.

**Stoner and Wankel** (1987) pointed out certain objectives of OD practitioners about people needs and aspirations as individuals and group members which are examined below:

### 1. Person

An individual is centrally important in OD. It is assumed that individuals have a natural desire for development and growth and they also have potential for growth. OD therefore, aims to develop self-awareness and self-acceptance among individuals. Awareness and acceptance of one's strengths and weaknesses are seen fundamental to one's growth. It is important to note that this awareness is in relation to the organisation tasks and goals, thus integrating self-development with organisation development.

### 2. Interpersonal

Organisation structure is intended to establish role relationships. Interpersonal relations therefore, are logical foundation bricks to develop effective interpersonal relationships. OD practitioners believe that these relationships need to be characterised by openness and free expression of feelings. Individuals need to be sensitised to this framework of interpersonal interactions.

### 3. Teams and Inter-teams

Individuals need to be accepted by their work group. OD aims at facilitating these work groups to deal with conflict and develop collaboration among them. OD practioners believe that the way co-ordination and cooperation exist within a work group (a team) would determine how the teams would interact with each other. The OD goal would be to facilitate the teams to interact in a win-win situation, through a consensus process than having win-lose situations among the departments. The latter can be harmful in the long-run.

### 4. Organisation

OD also aims to create enthusiasm in the entire organisation towards the goal-setting process by identifying internal strength to face the external challenges. These can be in terms of adaptive and proactive behaviour.

---

**CASE: 1.2**

**Pro Enviro-New Employment**

Following the announcement of the closure of a manufacturing plant, Pro Enviro were asked to design and deliver a series of workshops to assist the workforce in their quest for new employment. In order to do this they developed a set of sessions designed to prepare the operators and junior managers for the task of finding new roles.

While there are many such schemes for senior managers, this approach and support is much less common at the operator level. Working closely with the client, a set of aids was developed to support the employees through these difficult times. Many of the people involved had been with the company for many years and had little experience of working in other companies or the current job market.

The process consisted of a series of group and one to one workshops on how to develop an effective CV and prepare for an interview. The process is also designed to rebuild the individuals' self-confidence and reduce the stress associated with searching for new employment. Ongoing support and mentoring is provided to those that require it after completion of the programme.

All participants finished with a completed and comprehensive CV as well as renewed confidence in their own abilities. Within four weeks of completing the process 70% of the participants had found new employment.

The whole process takes between four and six weeks and because of its modular nature it can be undertaken with minimal disruption during the working day. During the process the company worked closely with the local Employment Services.

---

## 1.8 Importance of Organisation Development

The importance of organisation development is highlighted by the points given below:

### 1. For Achieving Organisation Goals

Profitability, productivity, morale and quality of work life are of concern to most organisations because they have to be achieved as organisation goals. There is an increasing trend to maximise an organisation's investment in its employees. Jobs that previously required physical dexterity now require more mental effort. Organisations need to "work smarter" and apply creative ideas. (Refer case 1.2).

## 2. Change in Work Force

The work force has also changed. Employees expect more from a day's work than simply a day's pay. They want challenge, recognition, a sense of accomplishment, worthwhile tasks and meaningful relationships with their managers and co-workers. When these needs are not met, performance declines.

## 3. Meet the Customer Demand

Today's customers' demands continually improving quality, rapid product or service delivery, fast turn-around time on changes, competitive pricing and other features that are best achieved in complex environments by innovative organisation practices.

## 4. Meet the Challenges

An effective organisation must be able to meet today's and tomorrow's challenges. Adaptability and responsiveness are essential to survive and succeed.

## 1.9 Evolution of Organisation Development

Over the past few decades, the theory of OD has grown larger and more diverse. The variety of new points of view and applications has increased, making it harder to define OD. Today, OD is being heavily influenced by other applied fields, such as human resource management, strategic management, organisation design, and organisation theory.

During the 1950s and 1960s, OD principles were relatively coherent, and focused mainly on the social side of organisations. Since OD was based on group dynamics, many human process interventions were implemented. The best known are T-groups, process consultation, and team building. The emphasis was on humanistic values promoting openness, trust, and collaboration.

In the 1970s, new concepts emerged, especially influenced by organisation theory and the human side of technology. Examples of this period are structural change, employee involvement, and work design. As a result, the traditional OD values favouring humanism expanded to include concerns for organisation effectiveness and bottom-line results.

In the 1980s, OD became a theory that many management consultants wanted to apply because it was relatively new, and successful. Consequently, more new concepts and opinions were aggregated to the current OD theory. Techniques for reward systems, career planning and development, and employee assistance programmes showed up. The tools of organisation theory and strategic management contributed to OD, along with organisation design, corporate culture, strategy formulation and implementation, self-designed organisations, and trans-organisation development. Besides, production concepts were incorporated, particularly process control and total quality management.

The 1990s was the decade when the applied disciplines were used broadly by OD practitioners. The addition of new concepts and methods implies that OD is growing. However, the field has lost much of its conceptual coherence and its identification with traditional values. Today, the field is known more by its techniques than its value orientation. OD practitioners have increasingly become involved with action learning. Like action research, the new perspectives involve collaboration between OD practitioners and organisation members in the process of changing. Thus, it is likely that OD will continue to expand conceptually in the future *(Cummings and Worley, 1993)*.

## 1.9.1 Robert Tannenbaum

Tannenbaum, whose humanist vision profoundly affected the field of organisation development for more than 50 years, died on March 15, 2003. But Tannenbaum's ideas were made more profound by his personal being. He held a Ph. D. in Industrial Relations from the School of Business at the University of Chicago in 1939. In 1942, he enlisted in the Navy serving as an officer in the Pacific teaching radar. Upon completion he was recruited by Neil Jacoby, a former University of Chicago professor who was dean of UCLA's College of Business Administration later called the Graduate School of Management. His first UCLA position was acting assistant professor and assistant research economist while his last, self-named, was professor of human systems development. Bootstrapping from deep-seated beliefs about the importance of personal consciousness and the capacities of people to grow themselves psychologically, with derivative payouts in interpersonal sensitivity, Tannenbaum's work was a forerunner contributor to considerations of human capital as a corporate asset. From the 1950s through the 1970s, he was instrumental in establishing UCLA's Graduate School of Management as a key centre of thought and practice in the fields of organisation development and leadership training. During this period he helped found the Western Training Lab, which promulgated a derivative of T-groups that became known as Sensitivity Training, and played an important role in the evolution of the NTL (National Training Laboratory) Institute of Applied Behavioural Science, which spearheaded the drive to utilise group dynamics as an important pedagogy for promoting increased awareness of self and impact on others as essential to team play in the corporate environment.

Robert Tannenbaum's intellectual work described organisation systems not as machines with interchangeable human parts, but as living communities that can be designed to enable people to grow and learn while achieving business goals. His writings, as well as his teaching and consulting, reflected the value he placed on people, and his belief that, to a great extent, leadership effectiveness derives from awareness of one's own basic assumptions about human nature and the testing out and revision of those assumptions.

His book, with Irving Weschler and Fred Massarik, *Leadership and Organisation* (1961), was significant in making the academic and practical argument for the use of group dynamics in developing leaders and teaching them how to operate effectively. His articles (with Warren Schmidt) "How to Choose a Leadership Pattern" (1958) and "Management of Differences" (1960) both set *Harvard Business Review* records for reprint requests and were reprinted in publications worldwide.

His charismatic impact created a demand that produced a second, post-UCLA, career – consulting and counselling executives and change agents on the use of self in facilitating organisation effectiveness. He was an active contributor to Pepperdine University's Master's Programme in Organisation Development; he led workshops for the NTL Institute, counselled with top executives and their spouses at his home office in Carmel, and continued professional writing. Among his jewels is an oral autobiography produced by David Russell (1987) as part of the Oral History Programme for the Humanistic Psychology Archive at the University of California, Santa Barbara and an edited book of readings (with Newton Margulies and Fred Massarik) written by people associated with the Behavioural Science, then Human Systems, now Human Resources and Organisation Behaviour group he founded at UCLA, titled *Human Systems Development*.

## 1.9.2 Kurt Lewin

Lewin is renowned for his field theory. The field theory is the "proposition that human behaviour is the function of both the person and the environment". This theory had a major impact on social psychology, supporting the notion that our individual traits and the environment interact to cause behaviour. His contributions in change theory, action research, and action learning earned him the title of the "father of organisation development."

Lewin is best known for his work in the field of organisation behaviour and the study of group dynamics. His research discovered that learning is best facilitated when there is a conflict between immediate concrete experience and detached analysis within the individual. His cycle of action, reflection, generalisation, and testing is characteristic of experiential learning.

While Lewin emphasised the importance of theory, he also believed that theories needed to have practical applications. He began applying his research to the war effort, working for the U.S. government. Lewin also established the Group Dynamics at Massachusetts Institute of Technology (MIT) and the National Training Laboratories (NTL).

Influenced by Gestalt psychology, Lewin developed a theory that emphasised the importance of individual personalities, interpersonal conflict, and situational variables.

In Lewin, Lippitt, and White study, school children were assigned to authoritarian, democratic, or laissez-fair leadership groups. It was demonstrated that democratic leadership was superior to authoritarian and laissez-faire leadership. These findings prompted a wealth of research on leadership styles.

Kurt Lewin contributed to Gestalt psychology by expanding on gestalt theories and applying them to human behaviour. He was also one of the first psychologists to systematically test human behaviour, influencing experimental psychology, social psychology, and personality psychology. He was a prolific writer, publishing more than 80 articles and eight books on various psychology topics.

Lewin is also known as the father of "modern social psychology", because of his pioneering work that utilised scientific methods and experimentation to look at social behaviour.

### 1.9.3 Douglas McGregor

Douglas McGregor, earned an M.A. and Ph.D. in psychology from Harvard University in 1933 and 1935 respectively. He was a Management Professor-Consultant working with Union Carbide, whose 1960 book *"The Human Side of Enterprise"* had a profound influence on management practices. In the book he identified an approach of creating an environment within which employees are motivated via authoritative, direction and control or integration and self-control, which he called theory X and theory Y, respectively. Theory Y is the practical application of Dr. Abraham Maslow's Humanistic School of Psychology, or Third Force psychology, applied to scientific management.

McGregor was the first behavioural scientist to address the transfer problem and to talk systematically about and to help implement the application of T-group skills in complex organisations. McGregor, Birny Mason Jr. and John Paul Jones established a small internal consulting group. This group used behavioural science knowledge to help line managers and their subordinates learn how to be more effective in groups. Jones' organisation was later called an "organisation development group".

### 1.9.4 Herbert Shepard

Herbert Shepard was a pioneering thinker in the Organisation Development movement, an engaging teacher and mentor of exceptional depth, scope and humility with a gift for recognising and nurturing the potential of others. He held faculty posts at several universities including M.I.T., where he received his doctorate in Industrial Economics. He founded and directed the first doctoral programme in Organisation Development at Case Western; developed a residency in administrative psychiatry at Yale University School of Medicine, and was also President of The Gestalt Institute of Cleveland.

Herb conducted the first large-scale experiments in Organisation Development, while at department of Esso Standard Oil in the late fifties, and served as principal consultant to TRW Systems in its pioneering work in the application of behavioural science to organisations and teams. He has published widely in this field and was chairman of the Douglas Memorial Award Committee of the Journal of Applied Behavioural Science. His research and pragmatic work made a significant contribution to our understanding of human behaviour and social systems from dyads (doctor-patient or consultant-client) to organisations (synergy, alternative dispute resolution, structure, building consensus and caring about the powerless). It opened the way for further developments in the psychology of teams, leadership and interpersonal compatibility; cognitive behaviour therapy, social cognitive theory (educational psychology); choice theory; principled negotiation, positive psychology and organisation development.

Shepard was heavily influenced by the writings of Kurt Lewin and others at NTL. He attended an NTL lab in 1950 and subsequently was a staff member in many of its programmes.

In 1958 and 1959 Shepard launched three experiments in organisation development at major Esso refineries: Bayonne, New Jersey; Baton Rouge, Louisiana and Bayway, Texas.

Herb advised clients of The Professional Development Institute and led executive seminars and workshops including "Managing in Turbulent Environment", since 1975.

## 1.9.5 Robert Blake

Dr. Robert R. Blake, was the co-founder of the renowned Managerial Grid Theory. He was a pioneer author and consultant who distinguished the "human side" of business leadership in the early 1950's, when the human resource development movement was in its infancy. With Dr. Jane S. Mouton, Dr. Blake formed Scientific Methods, Inc. (now Grid International, Inc.) in Austin, Texas in 1961, and co-authored, *The Managerial Grid*, a leadership theory that Harvard Business School still includes in their publication, *Business Classics: 15 Key Concepts for Managerial Success*. Blake's and Mouton's breakthrough approach included an empirical theory of behaviour with a learning methodology that truly effected fundamental change, promoting excellence in organisations through and with individuals. They developed a worldwide network of consultants, co-authored over 40 books and seminars, hundreds of articles, and consulted for governments, industries, and universities in 40 countries for almost four decades.

His professional life was divided between his passion for research and his passion for practical business applications. Growing up as a child during the depression, Dr. Blake always reflected on his time at Berea as truly memorable and inspiring. He then earned his M.A. degree in Psychology from the University of Virginia (1941). He received his Ph.D. in Psychology from the University of Texas at Austin (1947), where he continued as a tenured professor until 1964. Dr. Blake lectured at Harvard, Oxford, and Cambridge Universities, and worked on special extended assignments at the Tavistock Clinic, London, as a Fulbright Scholar (1949), where he participated in some of the breakthrough studies using psychoanalytic approaches in a group therapy setting. While working at Tavistock, he heard that National Training Laboratories was being established in Bethel, Maine, for the purpose of studying group behaviour. He reflected on those experiences throughout his career as being some of his richest learning experiences and a perfect complement to the psychoanalytic group therapy research done at Tavistock. The NTL years also occasioned his forming one of the most pivotal relationships of his professional career, with Dr. Herbert Shepard, an Exxon employee who also served on the faculty in Bethel. Blake and Shepard joined forces to conduct a ten-year study of the Exxon Corporation that served as the building block for Scientific Methods and the first real practical application for his theory and methodology. Dr. Blake was a Fellow of the American Psychological Association and a Diplomat in Industrial and Organisation Psychology. In 1992, he was chosen as a Management Laureate author; he also received an Honorary LL.D. from Berea College. Dr. Blake's writings were selected for inclusion in *Great Writers on Organisations* (Pugh, D.S. and Hickson, D.J.) and he was most recently acknowledged in *Outstanding Intellectuals of the 21st Century* (2003, 2nd ed.). Dr. Blake loved travelling with his family and spanned the globe numerous times, always exploring landmarks and cultures with enthusiasm. His passion for research never waned, even after retiring in 1997. Every conversation was an opportunity to study behaviour, every book, political event, or movie an opportunity for a new perspective for exploring Grid Theory. In 1995 he detailed crucial experiences at Bethel in an article in *Training and Development Journal* entitled, "Memories of HRD." He wrote that the future would look back on the field of HRD, "as crossing a great frontier, with the goal of bringing behavioural science applications into everyday use to better human activity in all their shapes and forms." Dr. Blake left an indelible mark by constantly exploring how human effectiveness emerges and how it might be enhanced.

---

**Case Study 1.3: General Motors – OD Efforts**

A classic example of how OD can change an organisation for the better is the initiative undertaken by General Motors Corp. at its Tarrytown, New York, auto assembly plant in the 1970s. By the late 1960s, Tarrytown had earned a reputation as one the least productive plants in the company. Labour relations and quality were at an all-time low, and absenteeism was rampant, when GM finally decided to take action.

Realising the seriousness of the situation, plant managers tried something new—they sought direct input from labourers about all aspects of the plant operations. Then they began to implement the ideas with success, sparking interest in a more comprehensive OD effort. Thus, in the early 1970s, GM initiated a quality-of-work-life (QWL) programme, an OD programme that integrates several types of interventions. The goal of QWLs is to improve organisation efficiency through employee well-being and participative decision-making.

In 1973, the union leaders signed a "letter of agreement" with management in which

---

both groups agreed to commit themselves to exploring specific OD initiatives that could improve the plant. The plant hired an outside consultant to oversee the change process. The initial research stage included a series of problem-solving training sessions, during which 34 workers from two shifts would meet for eight hours on Saturdays. Those meetings succeeded in helping plant managers to improve productivity. Therefore, in 1977 management increased the scope of the OD programme by launching a plant wide effort that included 3,800 managers and labourers.

Although the OD programme eventually cost GM more than $1.5 million, it paid off in the long run through greater productivity, higher quality, and improved labour relations. For example, the number of pending grievances plummeted from 2,000 in 1972 to only 32 by 1978. Absenteeism dropped as well, from more than seven percent to less than three percent. In fact, by the late 1970s the Tarrytown plant was recognised as one of the most productive and best run in the entire GM organisation.

## Points to Remember

- The definitions clarify the distinctive features of OD.
- Organisation Development is an applied behavioural science that is focused in the organisation as a system.
- It involves variety of planned strategies and efforts to benefit the organisation. Values are not static, they change over time.
- The field of Organisation Development rests on a foundation of values and assumptions about people and organisations. Values have always been an integral part of an OD package.
- OD proceeds on the basis on certain assumptions. To implement the OD programme effectively, management support and the willingness of the people are prerequisites that there are many presuppositions for the programme to be carried out.
- Assumptions are beliefs that are regarded as so valuable and obviously correct that they are taken for granted and rarely examined or questioned.
- OD aims at a higher quality of work life, productivity, adaptability and effectiveness. It seeks to change beliefs, attitudes, values, strategies, structures and practices to enable the organisation to better adapt to competitive actions, technological advances and the fast pace of other changes in the environment.
- Organisation Development must place high value on strong individuals, team and organisation performance coupled with people-oriented values.

## Questions for Discussion

1. Discuss the concept of Organisation Development. What should be the values and assumptions in the task of OD ?

2. Explain the main components of Organisation Development.

3. Discuss why Organisation Development is important.

4. Discuss the origin and current trends of Organisation Development.

# Foundations
# of
# Organisation Development

**Learning Objectives ...**

- To study the models and theories relating to planned change
- To understand the system theory of OD
- To learn the aspects relating to OD like teams and teamwork, participation and empowerment, applied behaviour science, parallel learning structures

## 2.1 Introduction

Organisation development is constructed based upon the foundations of organisation development theory and practice. Effective programmes of change are implemented by the practitioners of OD.

The field of Organisation Development is concerned with the performance, development and effectiveness of human organisations. OD is a work that focuses on how an organisation functions. In this chapter attempt has been made to explore important foundations of organisation development.

## 2.2 Models and Theories of Planned Change

Leading industry experts will need to continually review and provide new information relative to the change process and to our evolving society and culture. Successful change can be encouraged and facilitated for long-term success. There are many change theories and some of the most widely recognised are briefly discussed. The theories serve as a testimony to the fact that change is a real phenomenon.

### 2.2.1 Kurt Lewin's Three-Step Change Theory

One of the cornerstone models of understanding organisation change was developed by Kurt Lewin back in the 1950s. He introduced the three-step change model. This social scientist views behaviour as a dynamic balance of forces working in opposing directions. Driving forces facilitate change because they push employees in the desired direction. Restraining forces hinder change because they push employees in the opposite direction. Therefore, these forces must be analysed and Lewin's three-step model can help shift the balance in the direction of the planned change (Refer Fig. 2.1).

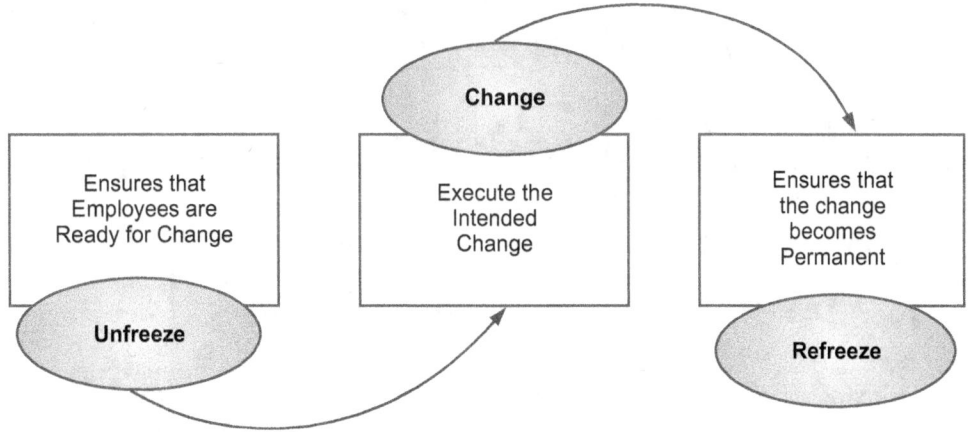

**Fig. 2.1: Lewin's Three-step Model**

According to Lewin, the **First Step** in the process of changing behaviour is to unfreeze the existing situation or *status quo*. The status quo is considered the equilibrium state. Unfreezing is necessary to overcome the strains of individual resistance and group conformity.

Unfreezing can be achieved by the use of three methods. First, increase in the driving forces that direct behaviour away from the existing situation or *status quo*. Second, decrease in the restraining forces that negatively affect the movement from the existing equilibrium. Third, finding a combination of the two methods listed above. Some activities that can assist in the unfreezing step include: motivating participants by preparing them for change, building trust and recognition for the need to change, and actively participating in recognising problems and brainstorming solutions within a group.

The **Second Step** in the process of changing behaviour is movement. In this step, it is necessary to move the target system to a new level of equilibrium. Three actions that can assist in the movement step include: persuading employees to agree that the *status quo* is not beneficial to them and encouraging them to view the problem from a fresh perspective, working together on a quest for new, relevant information, and connecting the views of the group to well-respected, powerful leaders that also support the change.

The **Third Step** of Lewin's three-step change model is refreezing. This step needs to take place after the change has been implemented in order for it to be sustained or "stick" over time. It is highly likely that the change will be short lived and the employees will revert to their old equilibrium (behaviours) if this step is not taken. It is the actual integration of the new values into the community values and traditions. The purpose of refreezing is to stabilise the new equilibrium resulting from the change by balancing both the driving and restraining forces. One action that can be used to implement Lewin's third step is to reinforce new patterns and institutionalise them through formal and informal mechanisms including policies and procedures.

Take an example of a man who is addicted to drugs and wants to quit consuming it, the three stage model says that he must unfreeze the old behaviour of consuming by believing that consumption of drugs is dangerous for his health and he must stop consuming it. The next step would be, by changing his behaviour from being non-addictive to drugs. Finally the non-addictive behaviour should remain permanent, which then becomes the new equilibrium point. Refreezing the desired behaviour requires establishing a new field of forces to support this new behaviour.

Lewin's model is very rational, goal and plan oriented. It does not take into account personal factors that can affect change. It attempts to analyse the forces (driving or restraining) that impacts change. The change looks good on paper, as it makes a rational sense, but when implemented the lack of considering human feelings and experiences can have negative consequences. There may be occasions when employees get so excited about a new change, that they bypass the feelings, attitudes, past input or experience of other employees. Consequently, they find themselves facing either resistance or little enthusiasm.

## 2.2.2 Lippitt's Phases of Change Theory

Ronald Lippitt, Jeanne Watson, and Bruce Westley extended Lewin's Three-Step Change Theory. They created a **Seven-Step Theory** that focuses more on the role and responsibility of the change agent than on the evolution of the change itself. Information is continuously exchanged throughout the process. The seven steps are:

**Phase 1:**  Diagnose the problem.

**Phase 2:**  Assess the motivation and capacity for change.

**Phase 3:**  Assess the resources and motivation of the change agent. This includes the change agent's commitment to change, power, and stamina.

**Phase 4:**  Choose progressive change objects. In this step, action plans are developed and strategies are established.

**Phase 5:**  The role of the change agents should be selected and clearly understood by all parties so that expectations are clear. Examples of roles are: cheerleader, facilitator, and expert.

**Phase 6:**  Maintain the change. Communication, feedback, and group coordination are essential elements in this step of the change process.

**Phase 7:**  Gradually terminate from the helping relationship. The change agent should gradually withdraw from their role over time. This will occur when the change becomes part of the organisation culture.

The framework proposed by Lippitt et al has a seven phase approach to the management of change, explicitly building on Lewin's model, and is shown in Case 2.1.

---

**Case 2.1: Lippitt, Watson and Westley's Phases of Planned Change**

1. Development of a need to change - the desire to change and to seek help from outside to do so ("**unfreezing**").

2. The establishment of a change relationship - establishing a working relationship between change agent and client.

   **3, 4, 5 changing:**

3. The clarification or diagnosis of the client system's problem - gathering and analysing data about the client system.

4. Examination of alternatives and establishing goals - translating diagnostic insights into alternative means of action and then into definite intentions to change in specific ways.

5. Transformation of intentions into actual change efforts - turning specified intentions into achievements.

---

> 6.  Generalisation and stabilisation of change - making the change remains a permanent and stable part of system ("**freezing**").
>
> 7.  Achieving a terminal relationship - leaving the client system non-dependent on the change agent.
>
> *(Adapted from Lippitt, Watson and Westley 1958:129-143).*

Lippitt, Watson, and Westley point out that changes are more likely to be stable if they spread to neighbouring systems or to subparts of the system immediately affected. Changes are better rooted. E.g. the individual meets other problems, in a similar way, several businesses adopt the same innovation, or the problem spreads to other departments of the same business. The more widespread imitation becomes, the more the behaviour is regarded as normal. Thus, the focus of seven-step change theory is on the change agent rather than change itself.

## 2.2.3 Edgar Schein's Change Theory

**Edgar Schein** provided further details for a more comprehensive model of change calling this approach "cognitive redefinition."

**Stage 1 – Becoming motivated to change (unfreezing)**

This phase of change is built on the theory that human behaviour is established by past observational learning and cultural influences. Change requires adding new forces for change or removal of some of the existing factors that are at play in perpetuating the behaviour. This unfreezing process has three sub-processes that relate to a readiness and motivation to change (Case 2.2).

---

**Case 2.2: Schein's Three-Stage Model of the Change Process**

**Stage 1: Unfreezing: Creating motivation and readiness to change through:**

(a)  Disconfirmation or lack of confirmation.

(b)  Creation of guilt or anxiety.

(c)  Provision of psychological safety.

**Stage 2: Changing through cognitive restructuring:** Helping the client to see things, judge things, feel things, and react to things based on a new point of view obtained through:

(a)  Identifying with a new role model, mentor, etc.

(b)  Scanning the environment for new relevant information.

**Stage 3: Refreezing:** Helping the client to integrate the new point of view into:

(a)  The total personality and the self concept.

(b)  Significant relationships.

---

- Disconfirmation where present conditions lead to dissatisfaction, such as not meeting personal goals. However, the larger the gap between what is believed and what needs to be believed for change to occur, the more likely the new information will be ignored.

- Previous beliefs now being seen as invalid creates "survival anxiety." However, this may not be sufficient to prompt change if learning anxiety is present.

- Learning anxiety triggers defensiveness and resistance due to the pain of having to unlearn what had been previously accepted. Three stages occur in response to learning anxiety: denial; scapegoating and passing the buck; and manipulation and bargaining.

- It is necessary to move past the possible anxieties for change to progress. This can be accomplished by either having the survival anxiety be greater than the learning anxiety or preferably, learning anxiety could be reduced.

### Stage 2 – Change what needs to be changed (unfrozen and moving to a new state)

Once there is sufficient dissatisfaction with the current conditions and a real desire to make some change exists, it is necessary to identify exactly what needs to be changed. Three possible impacts from processing new information are: words take on new or expanded meaning, concepts are interpreted within a broader context, and there is an adjustment in the scale used in evaluating new input.

A concise view of the new state is required to clearly identify the gap between the present state and that which is being proposed. Activities that aid in making the change include imitation of role models and looking for personalised solutions through trial-and-error learning.

### Stage 3 – Making the change permanent (refreezing)

Refreezing is the final stage where new behaviour becomes habitual, which includes developing a new self-concept and identity and establishing new interpersonal relationships.

In "Transforming Managers for Organisation Change," Paul O'Neill (1990) summarises the work of Edgar Schein, which was built on the earlier work of Kurt Lewin, in developing a model for organisation change. Schein's model features three stages of change:

(a) **Unfreezing:** Workers are motivated to unlearn current behaviours and attitudes.

(b) **Changing:** Workers learn about new behaviours and attitudes.

(c) **Refreezing:** Workers are supported as they integrate their new behaviours and attitudes into routine activities.

## 2.2.4 Ralph Kilmann's Total System Change

Ralph Kilmann has tested this model at AT&T, Eastman Kodak, Ford, General Electric, General Goods and Xerox with good results. It is a comprehensive change model which specifies the critical leverage points for organisation change. This model has five sequential stages:

**Stage 1:** Initiating the programme entails securing commitment from top management.

**Stage 2:** Diagnosing the problems requires a thorough analysis of the problems and opportunities facing the organisation.

**Stage 3:** Scheduling the "tracks". When the tracks function properly, it makes the organisation to be successful. Kilmann's five tracks are:

    (a)   the culture track.

    (b)   the management skills track.

    (c)   the team-building track.

    (d)   the strategy-structure track and

    (e)   the reward system track.

**Stage 4:** Implementing the "tracks".

**Stage 5:** Evaluating the results.

Change programme takes one to five years to complete. Interventions include training programmes, problem-solving sessions and critique of current practices and procedures. Each track mentioned above provides improvements for the organisation. The culture track enhances trust, communication, information sharing and willingness to change among members. The management-skills track provides all management personnel with new ways of coping with complex problems and hidden assumptions. The team-building track infuses the new culture and updated management skills into each work unit, thereby instilling cooperation organisation – wide so that complex problems can be addressed with all the expertise and information available. The strategy-structure track develops either a completely new or a revised strategic plan for the firm. Then the divisions, departments, work groups, jobs and all resources are aligned with new strategic direction. The reward system track establishes a performance – based reward system that sustains all improvements by officially sanctioning the new culture, the use of updated management skills and cooperative team efforts within and among all work groups.

## 2.2.5 The Burke – Litwin Model of Organisation Change

Organisation change is a kind of chaos. The Burke-Litwin Model integrates a range of factors that provides some guidance to understand how organisation works amidst this chaos (Refer figure 2.2). They distinguished between transformational factors and transactional factors.

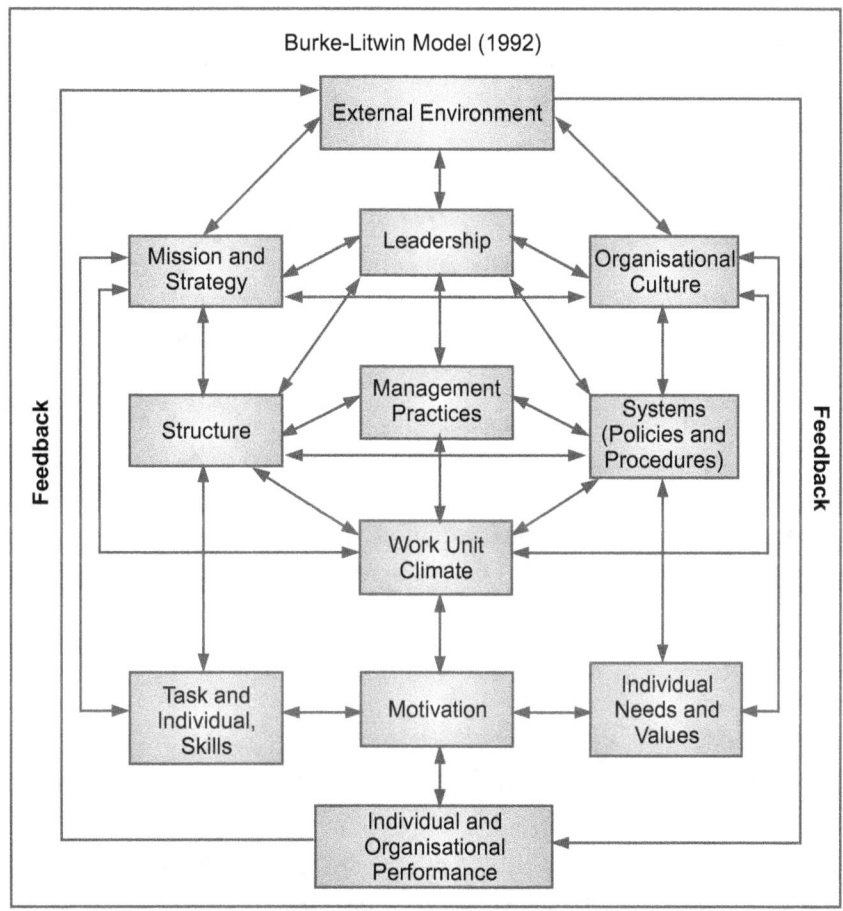

**Fig. 2.2: Burke-Litwin Model of Organisation Change**

**Source:** *W. Warner Burke, Organisation Development, 2d ed. (Figure 7.1), p. 128, 1994 by Addison-Wesley Publishing Company, Inc.*

The authors have distinguished between transformational factors and transactional factors. The transactional factors are structure, management practices, systems (policies and procedures) and work unit climate. The authors call transactional factors as *first-order change* and transformational factors as second-order change. The transformational factors are mission and strategy, leadership and organisation culture. The first-order change goes by many different labels: transactional, evolutionary, adaptive, incremental or continuous change. While the second-order change goes by many different labels: transformational, revolutionary, radical or discontinuous change. Organisation Development programmes give more emphasis to second-order change. These transactional and transformational factors together affect motivation, which in turn affects performance. The feedback loop in the Fig. 2.2 indicates that organisation performance directly effects the external environment.

The Burke-Litwin model also distinguishes between *organisation climate* and *organisation culture*. Organisation climate is defined as people's perceptions and attitudes about the organisation – whether it is a good or bad place to work, friendly or unfriendly, hard-working or easy-going and so on. On the other hand, *organisation culture* is defined as deep-seated assumptions, values and beliefs that are enduring, often unconscious and difficult to change. Changing culture is much more difficult than changing climate.

The premise of the Burke-Litwin model is this: OD interventions directed toward structure, management practices and systems (policies and procedures) result in first-order change; interventions directed toward mission and strategy, leadership and organisation culture result in second-order change.

The model also makes a distinction between transactional and transformational leadership styles. Transactional leaders are "leaders who guide or motivate their followers in the direction of established goals by clarifying role and task requirements." Transformational leaders are "leaders who inspire followers to transcend their own self-interest for the good of the organisation and who are capable of having a profound and extraordinary effect on their followers."

The factors involving first-order change: changing structure, management practices and systems cause changes in work unit climate, which changes motivation and in turn, individual and organisation performance. Transactional leaders are required to make this change in organisation climate.

On the other hand is second-order change: change mission and strategy, leadership styles and organisation culture. Interventions directed towards these factors transform the organisation and cause a permanent change in organisation culture, which produces changes in individual and organisation performance.

This model is a bit complex. Some organisation changes may be initiated by leadership or internal factors rather than the external environment.

## 2.2.6 Porras and Robertson Model of Organisation Change

Jerry Porras and Peter Robertson (1992) maintained that "change in the individual organisation members' behaviour is the core of organisation change." The basic premise is that OD interventions alter features of the work setting causing changes in individuals' behaviours, which in turn lead to individual and organisation improvement.

Organisation change occurs only when individuals change their behaviour and these behaviour changes happen when elements of the work setting have been modified by OD interventions. Work setting plays a central role in this model and consists of four factors: organising arrangements, social factors, physical setting and technology.

OD interventions focus on goals, strategies and rewards which will affect organising arrangements. Interventions that focus on culture, management style and interaction processes will affect social factors. Interventions affecting technology are job design and work flow design.

---

**Case 2.3: "Succeeding in a Changing World"**

Convocation Address by Azim Premji, Chairman, Wipro Corporation at the Convocation of Indian Institute of Management, Ahmedabad on March 23, 2002 on "*Succeeding in a Changing World*".

It is a great privilege to be with you here today and participate in this very important occasion in your life. It has been a real challenge for you to get to this point. You are among the select few to enter and graduating from this prestigious institution. Today will always remain a very memorable day in your lives, marking the threshold to the world of your careers and dreams.

The Indian Institute of Management at Ahmedabad pioneered the concept of management institutes in India. It is known not only for its standards of academic excellence, but also for the moving spirit of Professor Ravi Mathai, who began this institute against all odds and set its foundation.

I compliment all the members of the faculty, the management and the excellent students who have been constantly working hard towards making it such an outstanding institution, not only in India but also around the world. As an Indian, I feel proud that we have an institution like the Indian Institute of Management.

Institutions such as these have an important role to play when a sea of change surrounds us. They can become lighthouses, showing the way and pointing out the hazards. While change and uncertainty have always been a part of life, what has been shocking over the last year has been both the quantum and suddenness of change. For many people who are cruising along on placid waters, the wind was knocked out of their sails. The entire logic of doing business was turned on its head. Not only business, but also every aspect of human life has been impacted by the change. What lies ahead is even more dynamic and uncertain.

---

I would like to use this opportunity to share with you some of our own guiding principles for staying afloat in a changing world. This is based on our experiences in Wipro. I hope you find them useful.

First, be alert for the first signs of change. Change descends on every one equally; it is just that some realise it faster. Some changes are sudden but many others are gradual. While sudden changes get attention because they are dramatic, it is the gradual changes that are ignored till it is too late. You must have all heard of story of the frog in boiling water. If the temperature of the water is suddenly increased, the frog realises it and jumps out of the water. But if the temperature very slowly increases, one degree at a time, the frog does not realise it till it boils to death. You must develop your own early warning system, which warns you of changes and calls your attention to it. In the case of change, being forewarned is being forearmed.

Second, anticipate change even when things are going right. Most people wait for something to go long way before they think of change. It is like going to the doctor for a check up only when you are seriously sick, or thinking of maintaining your vehicle only when it breaks down. The biggest enemy of future success is past success. When you succeed you feel that you must be doing something right for it to happen. But when the parameters for success change, doing the same things may or may not continue to lead to success. Guard against complacency all the time.

Complacency makes you blind to the early signals from the environment that something is going wrong.

Third, always look at the opportunities that change represents. Managing change has a lot to do with our own attitude towards it. It is the proverbial half full or half empty glass approach. For every problem that change represents, there is an opportunity lurking in disguise somewhere. It is up to you to spot it before someone else does.

Fourth, do not allow routines to become chains. For many of us it is the routine we have got accustomed to that obstructs change. Routines represent our own zones of comfort. There is a sense of predictability about them. They have structured our time and even our thoughts in a certain way. While routines are useful, do not let them enslave you. Deliberately break out of them from time to time.

Fifth, realise that fear of the unknown is natural. With changes comes a feeling of insecurity. Many people believe that brave people are not afflicted by this malady. The truth is different. Every one feels the fear of the unknown. Courage is not the absence of fear but the ability to manage fear without getting paralysed. Feel the fear, but move on regardless of the fear.

Sixth, keep renewing yourself. This prepares you to anticipate change and be ready for it when it comes. Constantly ask yourself what new skills and competencies will be needed.

Begin working on them before it becomes necessary and you will have a natural advantage. The greatest benefit of your education lies not only in what you have learnt, but in knowing how to learn. Formal education is the beginning of the journey of learning. Yet I do meet youngsters who feel that they have already learnt all there is to learn. You have to constantly learn about people and how to interact effectively with them. In the world of tomorrow, only those individuals and organisations will succeed who have.

Seventh, surround yourself with people who are open to change. If you are always in the company of cynics, you will soon find yourself becoming like them. A cynic knows all the reasons why something cannot be done. Instead, spend time with people who have a "can-do" approach. Choose your advisors and mentors correctly. Pessimism is contagious, but then so is enthusiasm. In fact, reasonable optimism can be an amazing force multiplier.

Eighth, play to win. I have said this many times in the past. Playing to win is not the same as cutting corners. When you play to win, you stretch yourself to your maximum and use all your potential. It also helps you to concentrate your energy on what you can influence instead of getting bogged down with the worry of what you cannot change. Do your best and leave the rest.

Ninth, respect yourself. The world will reward you on your successes. Success requires no explanation and failure permits none. But you need to respect yourself enough so that your self-confidence remains intact whether you succeed or fail. If you succeed 90 percent of the time, you are doing fine. If you are succeeding all the time, you should ask yourself if you are taking enough risks. If you do not take enough risks, you may also be losing out on many opportunities. Think through but take the plunge. If some things do go wrong, learn from them. I came across this interesting story some time ago:

One day a farmer's donkey fell down into a well. The animal cried piteously for hours as the farmer tried to figure out what to do. Finally he decided the animal was old and the well needed to be covered up anyway; it just wasn't worth it to retrieve the donkey. He invited all his neighbours to come over and help him. They all grabbed a shovel and began to shovel dirt into the well. At first, the donkey realised what was happening and cried horribly. Then, to everyone's amazement, he quieted down. A few shovel loads later, the farmer finally looked down the well and was astonished at what he saw. With every shovel of dirt that hit his back, the donkey was doing something amazing. He would shake it off and take a step up. As the farmer's neighbours continued to shovel dirt on top of the animal, he would shake it off and take a step up. Pretty soon, everyone was amazed as the donkey stepped up over the edge of the well and trotted off!

Life is going to shovel dirt on you, all kinds of dirt. The trick is not to get bogged down by it. We can get out of the deepest wells by not stopping, and by never giving up! Shake it off and take a step up!

Tenth, inspite of all the change around you, decide upon what you will never change-your core values. Take your time to decide what they are but once you do, do not compromise on them for any reason. Integrity is one such value. There can be no compromises, no gray. It is either black or white. And when you are in doubt the answer is simple: just don't do it.

Finally, we must remember that succeeding in a changing world is beyond just surviving. It is our responsibility to create and contribute something to the world that has given us so much. We must remember that many have contributed to our success, including our parents and others from our society. All of us have a responsibility to utilise our potential for making our nation a better place for others, who may not be as well endowed as us, or as fortunate in having the opportunities that we have got. Let us do our bit, because doing one good deed can give multiple benefits not only for us but also for many others.

Let us end my talk with a small story I came across some time back, which illustrates this very well.

This is a story of a poor Scottish farmer whose name was Fleming. One day, while trying to make a living for his family, he heard a cry for help coming from a nearby bog. He dropped his tools and ran to the bog. There, mired to his waist in black muck, was a terrified boy, screaming and struggling to free himself. Farmer Fleming saved the boy from what could have been a slow and terrifying death. The next day, a fancy carriage pulled up to the Scotsman's sparse surroundings. An elegantly dressed nobleman stepped out and introduced himself as the father of the boy farmer Fleming had saved.

"I want to repay you," said the nobleman. "You saved my son's life." "No, I can't accept payment for what I did," the Scottish farmer replied, waving off the offer. At that moment the farmer's own son came to the door of the hovel.

"Is that your son ?" the nobleman asked: "Yes," the farmer replied proudly. "I'll make you a deal. Let me take him and give him a good education. If he's anything like his father, he'll grow up to be a man you will be proud of."

And that he did. In time, farmer Fleming's son graduated from St. Mary's Hospital Medical School in London, and went on to become known throughout the world as the noted Sir Alexander Fleming, the discoverer of Penicillin. Years afterward, the nobleman's son was stricken with pneumonia. What saved him ? Penicillin. This is not the end. The nobleman's son also made a great contribution to society. For the nobleman was none other than Lord Randolph Churchill. And his son's name was Winston Churchill.

Let us use all our talent, competency and energy for creating peace and happiness for the nation. I wish you all the best for success that lies ahead of all of you.

## 2.3 Systems Theory

The second foundation of organisation development is systems theory. It views organisations as open systems in active exchange with their environments. "A System study asks: How and why does this system as a whole function as it does ?" Fagen defines system as *"a set of objects together with relationships between the objects and between their attributes."* Hanne says, *"a system is an arrangement of interrelated parts. The words arrangement and interrelated describe interdependent elements forming an entity that is the system. Thus, when taking a systems approach, one begins by identifying the individual parts and then seeks to understand the nature of their collective interaction."* Systems theory enforces the concept that the organisation is able to function only because of the interdependence of its parts. It has been particularly useful in the organisation diagnosis and intervention strategies stages of the organisation development process.

Organisations are open systems. Studying such systems leads to a good understanding of organisations. The characteristics of an open system are discussed below:

**1. Input-throughput-output Mechanisms:** Systems take inputs from the environment in the form of energy, information, money, people, raw materials and so on. They do something to the inputs via throughput, conversation or transformation processes that change the inputs and they export products to the environment in the form of output. Each of these three system processes must work well if the system is to be effective and survive.

David Nadler, associated at Delta Consulting Group developed a congruence model which depicts the organisation as an *input-throughput-output-system*. The three major input factors are: *Environment, Resources and History*. The environment imposes constraints and opportunities about what the organisation can and cannot do. Resources available to the organisation are capital, people, knowledge and technology. History, consists of memories of past successes, failures, important events and critical decisions that still influence behaviour today.

*Outputs* are performance at the total organisation level, unit/group level and individual level. Elements of the organisation per se are *labelled strategy*, what the organisation is trying to accomplish and how it plans to do it; *work*, the tasks people perform to create products and service markets; people, which includes skills, knowledge, perceptions and the workforce's expectations; formal organisation which includes formal structures, processes and systems for performing the work and *informal organisation*, which includes the organisation culture, informal rules and understandings and how things really work.

The congruence model's value is an analytical tool for assessing the characteristics and functioning of each of the elements and evaluating the goodness of fit or how well the elements go together.

2. **System is Described by a Boundary:** Whatever is inside the boundary is the system and what is outside the boundary is the environment. A good rule of thumb for drawing the boundary is that more energy exchange occurs within the boundary than across the boundary. Boundaries of open systems are permeable, in that they permit exchange of information, resources and energy between a system and environment.

3. **Open Systems have Purposes and Goals:** The purpose must align with purposes or needs of the environment. For instance, an organisation's goal will be reflected in its outputs and if the environment does not want these outputs the organisation will cease to exist.

4. **Information is Important to Systems:** Feedback is information from the environment about the system performance. Systems require two types of feedback, negative and positive. Negative feedback measures whether or not the output is on course with the purpose and goals. Positive feedback measures whether or not the purpose and goals are aligned with environmental needs. Systems are bombarded by all kinds of information. Some are useful, but most is not useful. Systems "code" useful information and incorporate it.

5. **Open Systems are Steady State:** Systems achieve a steady state or equilibrium point and seek to maintain this equilibrium against troublesome forces, either internal or external. As Katz and Kahn say: "the basic principle is the preservation of the character of the system." Systems tend to get more elaborated, differentiated, specialised and complex over a period of time, this process is called   differentiation. With increased differentiation, increased integration and coordination are necessary.

6. **System is Equifinality:** The principle that there are multiple ways to arrive at a particular outcome or state systems have multiple paths to goals. Subsystems exist within larger systems. These subsystems can be arranged into a hierarchy of systems moving from less important to more important.

The important applications of systems theory in organisation development are:

1.   Socio-technical System Theory (STS)

2.   Open Systems Planning

Socio-technical system theory was developed by Eric Trist, Fred Emery and others at the Tavistock Institute in the 1950s. The thesis of STS is that all organisations comprises of two interdependent systems, a social system and a technical system and that changes in one system affects the other system. To achieve high productivity and employee satisfaction, organisations must optimise both systems. STS is the principle conceptual foundation for efforts in work redesign and organisation restructuring.

Open systems planning entails:

(a)   Scanning the environment to determine the expectations of external organisations and stakeholders.

(b)   Developing scenarios of possible futures both realistic and ideal.

(c)   Developing action plans to ensure that a desirable future occurs.

Most of the OD practitioners engaged in redesign projects use a combination of socio-technical systems theory and open systems planning.

### Open Systems Thinking

Open systems thinking is required for creating learning organisations. Learning organisations can cope effectively with rapidly changing environmental demands. Peter Senge believes that five disciplines must be mastered to create a learning organisation: personal mastery, mental models, building shared vision, team learning and systems thinking.

## 2.4 Teams and Teamwork

Work teams are the building blocks of any organisation. Teams must manage their culture, processes, systems and relationships if they are to be effective. Teams and teamwork are part of the foundation of organisation development. Theory, research and practice attest to the central role teams play in organisation success. The act of empowering individuals into teams creates extraordinary effects on performance and satisfaction. Effective teams produce results far beyond the performance of unrelated individuals.

### Importance of Team

1.   Most individual behaviour is rooted in the socio-cultural norms and value of the work teams. If the team, as a team, changes those norms and values, the effects on individual behaviour are immediate and lasting.

2.   Many tasks are very complex and cannot be performed by individuals, people must work together to accomplish them.

3.   Teams create synergy i.e., the sum of the efforts of team members is far greater than the sum of the individual efforts of people working alone. Synergy is a principal reason teams are so important.

4.   Teams satisfy people's needs for social interaction, status, recognition and respect. Teams nurture human nature.

Team building activities are now a way of life for many organisations. Teams hold team-building meetings, people are trained in group dynamics and group problem-solving skills and individuals are trained as group leaders and group facilitators. The team performs at increasingly higher levels, they achieve synergy and teamwork becomes more satisfying for team members.

Larson and Lafasto found eight characteristics present in a team to become successful, they are as follows:

(a) A clear, elevating goal.

(b) A results-driven structure.

(c) Competent team members.

(d) Unified commitment.

(e) A collaborative climate.

(f) Standards of excellence.

(g) External support and recognition and

(h) Principled leadership.

All the above features are required for superior team performance. When any one feature is lost, team performance declines. Larson and Lafasto also found that the most frequent cause of team failure was letting personal or political agendas take superiority over the clear and elevating team goal.

According to Jon Katzenback and Douglas Smith, a key feature of high performance teams is discipline. Groups become teams through disciplined action. They shape a common purpose, agree on performance goals, define a common working approach, develop high levels of complementary skills and hold themselves mutually accountable for results. It is hard work for groups to become teams, but hard work is required to create a high-performance organisation.

According to Johanson, Sibbet, Benson, Martin, Mittman and Saffo, a team room should be designed; a room filled with tools, gadgets and furniture to help teams to be more effective. As the key goal is to help teams make better decisions, therefore, the room provides a variety of decision-support tools, including computer workstations.

Thus, teams have always been an important foundation of OD. There is a growing awareness of the teams unique ability to create synergy, respond quickly and flexibly to problems.

## 2.5 Participation and Empowerment

Participation in OD programmes is not restricted to elites or the top people; it is extended broadly throughout the organisation. Increased participation and empowerment have always been central goals and fundamental values of the field. These pillars of OD practice are validated by both research and practice. The research demonstrated that most people desire increased involvement and participation. Further, involvement and participation energise greater performance, produce better solutions to problems and greatly enhance acceptance of decisions. Researchers on group dynamics in the 1940s found that group dynamics work to overcome resistance to change, increase commitment to the organisation, reduce stress levels, and generally make people feel better about themselves and their work. Participation is a powerful miraculous substance – it is good for people and performance.

To empower is to give someone power, which is done by giving individuals the authority to make decisions, to contribute their ideas, to exert influence, and to be responsible. Participation is an especially effective form of empowerment. Participation enhances empowerment and empowerment in turn enhances performance and individual well-being. Autonomous work groups, quality circles, team building, survey feedback, quality of work life programmes, search conferences and the culture audit are all predicted on the belief that increased participation will lead to better solutions. OD interventions are methods for increasing participation. The entire field of OD is about empowerment (Refer Case 2.1).

James Belasco presents numerous examples in which leaders reap extraordinary gains by empowering their employees. He believes that:

(a)    Only massive changes will suffice to keep organisations viable in the future.

(b)    People will not naturally embrace the needed changes and

(c)    Empowerment is the key to getting people to want to participate in change.

The four-step model by Belasco to describe empowerment process is:

1.    Preparation                    2.    Create tomorrow

3.    Vision and                    4.    Change

One of the most important step of empowerment is vision – a coherent, credible picture of the desired future. According to Belasco, developing a clear vision, devising a strategy to achieve the vision, and unleashing the intelligence and energy of the workforce to accomplish the vision are what empowerment is all about.

---

**Case 2.4: A Better Idea**

Donald Peterson describes the organisation redesign for Ford Motor Company in his book "A Better Idea". Peterson was President, CEO and Chairman of Ford during the turnaround of that 3,70,000 – person company from one that was losing money and market share to one that produced high-quality products, made big profits and created the Ford Taurus, one of the best-selling cars in American history. The primary vehicle for the turnaround was employee involvement, participation and empowerment. In the early 1980s, Ford launched programmes in EI (Employee Involvement), participative management training for supervisors, employee involvement teams, and total quality management. The net effect was a significant change in the company's culture from being a top-down, autocratic, functionally oriented company to one that gave responsibility and power to cross-functional teams at all levels of the organisation. Ford became a different company and a much more successful company, by empowering its employees.

---

Tom Peters and Nancy Austin say that excellent companies pay attention to four things: customer, innovation, people and leadership. The challenge for leaders is to empower employees so that they create great customer relations and continuous innovation. Peter offers the following prescriptions for achieving flexibility by empowering people: involve everyone in everything, use self-managing teams, listen/celebrate/recognise, spend time lavishly on recruiting, train and retrain, provide incentive pay for everyone, provide an employment guarantee, simply/reduce structure, reconceive the middle manager's role and eliminate bureaucratic rules and humiliating conditions. This advice is powerful, practical and rational.

Open-book management approach encourages every employee of a company to think like an owner of the business and then start to act like one. Open-book management rests on several simple principles:

(a)  Every employee in an open-book company seeks and learns to understand the company's financial along with all other numbers that are critical to tracking the business performance.

(b)  Employees assume that whatever else they do, part of their job is to move those numbers in the right direction and

(c)  Employees have a direct stake in the company's success.

Thus, participation/empowerment works.

## 2.6 Applied Behavioural Science

Applied behavioural science is the basis of OD. Since 1947, by convention, applied behavioural science, as a singular noun, has come to denote special applications of the behavioural sciences, rooted in the psycho-dynamic tradition of studying and changing behaviour. The elements of action research are assumed to be within this meaning. After the establishment of National Training Laboratories (NTL) in USA in 1947, under the influence of Kurt Lewin, the term "applied behavioural science" was adopted to indicate the study and modification of behaviour by involving people concerned to confront the psychodynamic issues in which they were involved, generally using sensitivity training or T-Groups (Training Groups) approach.

Applied Behavioural Science is different from behavioural science or social science. Firstly, Applied Behavioural Science must deal with group or social issues (individual issues as part of a group in which several individuals interact with one another on significant issues. Secondly, it must use human process interventions, as contrasted with administrative or purely structural changes. Applied Behavioural Science interventions are concerned with human processes like socialisation, communication, decision making, problem-solving, conflict, collaboration, change of norms and values, etc. Thirdly, it uses a scientific problem solving approach in its interventions.

Organisation Development (OD) is the systematic application of behavioural science knowledge at various levels, such as group, inter-group, organisation, etc., to bring about planned change. It is also the application of behavioural science knowledge practices and skills in ongoing systems in collaboration with system members. OD as a behavioural science is concerned with:

(a)   The health of the organisation.

(b)   Organisation effectiveness.

(c)   The organisation's capacity to solve problems.

(d)   The organisation's ability to adapt, change or of self-renewal.

(e)   The organisation's ability to create a high quality of life for its employees.

Although human behaviour in organisations is far from an exact science, lawful patterns of events produce effectiveness and ineffectiveness. OD practitioners know about these patterns through research and theory.

## 2.7 Parallel Learning Structures

Parallel learning structures are a foundation of OD because they are prevalent in so many different OD programmes. The quality of work life programmes of the 1970s and 1980s used parallel structures composed of union leaders, managers and employees. Most socio-technical systems redesign efforts and open systems planning programmes use parallel structures. High performance organisations often use parallel structures to coordinate self-directed teams.

Parallel learning structures are specially created in organisation structures for planning and guiding change programmes. According to Gervasa Bushe and Abraham Shani, parallel learning structures are a mechanism to facilitate innovation in large bureaucratic organisations where the forces of inertia, hierarchical communication patterns and standard ways of addressing problems inhibit learning, innovation and change. In essence, parallel structures are a vehicle for learning how to change the system and then leading the change process. The authors describe the idea as follows; *"We offer the team parallel learning structure as a generic label to cover intervention where a structure is created that operates parallel with the formal hierarchy and structure and has the purpose of increasing an organisation's learning (creation and implementation of new thoughts and behaviours of employees"*. A parallel learning structure consists of a steering committee and a number of working groups that studies what changes are needed, makes recommendations for improvement and monitors the change efforts. It should be a microcosm (a little world) of the larger organisation, i.e., it should have representatives from all parts of the organisation. One or more top executives should be members of the steering committee to give the parallel structure authority, legitimacy and influence.

Thus, parallel learning structures are often the best way to initiate change in large bureaucratic organisations, especially when the change involves a fundamental shift in the organisation's method of work and/or culture. Parallel structures help people break free of the normal constraints imposed by the organisation, engage in genuine inquiry and experimentation and initiate needed changes.

## Points to Remember

- Organisation models can be useful in helping one to understand the dynamics of action taken and organisation members behaviour in an organisation.

- Lewin's model illustrates the effects of forces that either promote or inhibit change. Specifically, driving forces promote change while restraining forces oppose change. Hence, change will occur when the combined strength of one force is greater than the combined strength of the opposing set of forces.

- The "Burke-Litwin model" examines organisation change and performance. It provides a link between an assessment of the wider institutional context and the nature and process of change within an organisation. As a leader, one must feast on the opportunity of having clear data and truly listen and involve members in organisation development and change endeavour. There is no right or wrong theory to change management. It is not an exact science. However, through the ongoing research and studies by the industry's leading experts, a clearer picture of what it takes to lead a change effort effectively will continue to emerge. It is important that one must continually review and consider how our changing society and culture will require fresh insight on the appropriate change process.

## Questions For Discussion

1. Discuss the exercise of Organisation Development with reference to the following aspects:

    (a) Models of Change Management

    (b) Team and Team work

2. Compare the various models of change management.

3.    Explain the Systems Theory and Team and Parallel Learning structures.

4.    Write Short Notes on:

(a)    Behavioural Science

(c)    Participation and Empowerment

✱✱✱

*Chapter* **3**...

# The Process of Organisation Development

## Contents ...

### Learning Objectives ...

- To understand the process of organisational development
- To study the role of change agents in organisational development

## 3.1 Introduction

Organisation development can be taken as a process of changing people and other related aspects of an organisation. It consists of many sub-processes or steps. OD is a long process. It is not necessary that all organisations may involve all the steps with same results from OD strategy.

Organisational Development (OD) is a field of research, theory, and practice dedicated to increasing the knowledge and effectiveness of people to accomplish more successful organisational change and performance.

OD is a process of continuous diagnosis, action planning, implementation and evaluation, with the aim of transferring knowledge and skills to organisations to improve their capacity for solving problems and managing future change.

## 3.2 The Role of Change Agent in OD Process

The individual or group that undertakes the task of implementing and managing change in an organisation is known as a change agent. Change agents can be internal, such as managers or employees who are appointed to oversee the change process. In many innovative companies, managers and employees alike are being trained to develop the needed skills to oversee change. Change agents also can be external, such as consultants from outside the firm.

For major organisation-wide changes, companies frequently will hire external change agents. Because these consultants are from the outside, they are not bound by the firm's culture, politics, or traditions. Therefore, they are able to bring a different perspective to the situation and challenge the existing system. This can be a disadvantage, however, because external change agents lack an understanding of the company's history, operating procedures, and personnel.

To set right their limited familiarity with the organisation, external change agents usually are paired with an internal coordinator from the human resources department.

These two then work together with line management. In very large firms, the organisation sometimes has its own in-house change specialist. This person replaces the external consultant and works directly with the organisation's management team to facilitate change efforts.

## 3.2.1 Types of Change Agent

Although little research has explored what type of change agent is most effective in a given situation, some research has identified different types of change agents according to their characteristics and methods of implementing change. These include the following types.

### 1. Outside Pressure Type

These change agents work to change systems from outside the organisation. They are not members of the company they are trying to change and use various pressure tactics such as mass demonstrations, civil disobedience, and violence to accomplish their objectives. Typically, they offer options that are more radical than the community might accept. This usually results in the possibility of examining many different change alternatives.

### 2.  People-Change-Technology Type

The focus of activity for this type of change agent is the individual. The change agent may be concerned with employee morale and motivation, including absenteeism, turnover, and the quality of work performed. The methods used include job enrichment, goal setting, and behaviour modification. The major assumption underlying this orientation is that if individuals change their behaviour, the organisation will also change, providing enough people within the organisation change. A manager can certainly assume the role of people-change-technology type and often do.

### 3.  Analysis-for-the-Top Type

The focus of this change agent is on changing the organisational structure so as to improve output and efficiency. The change agent uses operations research, systems analysis, policy studies, and other forms of analytical approaches to change the organisation's structure or technology. For example, the change might include introducing computerised information-processing systems. Many managers assume this role when implementing change.

### 4.  Organisation-Development Type

These change agents focus their attention on internal processes such as intergroup relations, communication, and decision making. Their intervention strategy is often called a cultural change approach, because they thoroughly analyse the culture of the targeted organisation. This approach grew out of such areas as sensitivity training, team building, and survey feedback. Many managers assume the role of organisation-development type when implementing change.

## 3.2.2 Change Agent Roles

There are at least three distinct roles that change agents play: consulting, training, and research. A manager can and often does perform each of these functions. An outside change agent can perform these activities as well.

### 1.  Consulting

As a consultant, the manager places employees in touch with data from outside the organisation or helping organisation members to generate data from within the organisation. The overall purpose is to help employees find solutions to problems through analysis of valid data.

### 2.  Training

In addition to performing the role of consultant, the manager may function as a trainer. Here the manager helps organisation members learn how to use data to effect change. The manager, or outside change agent if one is used, has a dual purpose as trainer: (1) to help organisation members derive implications for action from the present data and (2) to provide organisation members with a new set of skills—the ability to retrieve, translate, and use new data to solve future problems. Several companies have hired outside consultants to instruct organisation members on how to improve the overall operation of their firms.

### 3. Research

Finally, and closely associated with the previous role, the manager may assume the role of researcher. As researcher, the manager may train organisation members in the skills needed for valid evaluation of the effectiveness of action plans that have been implemented. Furthermore, as part of the overall intervention strategy, the manager will design an evaluation component that can be used in solving not only the current problem but also future problems.

## 3.2.3 Characteristics of Successful Change Agent

After an extensive review of the literature, several researchers have identified a set of ten factors characteristic of effective change agent. These factors briefly defined in the following list, refer to the way in which change agents manage change rather than to any personal characteristics they may possess. In many cases, the plant manager performs the role of change agent. However, the change agent can be an internal change specialist, corporate office administrator (often called a "trouble shooter"), or outside consultant whose expertise is in implementing change.

### 1. Hemophily

The more similar the change agent and employees are, the more likely it is that the change agent will be successful. Similarity between the change agent and organisation members results in acceptance of the change agent by the employees and understanding of the employees by the change agent.

### 2. Empathy

This is the skill of understanding the feelings of another person. Empathy leads to improved communication and understanding between the change agent and organisation members.

### 3. Linkage

This refers to the extent to which the change agent and organisation members are tied together in collaborative activities. The greater the collaborative involvement (the tighter the linkage), the more likely the change agent will be successful.

### 4. Proximity

This refers to the physical and psychological closeness of the change agent and organisation members. The greater the proximity between the change agent and the organisation members, the more likely the change agent will be successful. Increasing proximity makes it easier to develop collaborative linkages. Proximity also facilitates the development of empathy between change agent and organisation members. Proximity has relevance to open door policy and the visibility of the change agent during working hours.

### 5. Structuring

This factor refers to the ability of the change agent and organisation members to clearly plan and organise their activities concerning the change effort. A clearly designed change effort is more likely to be understood and implemented by the employees.

### 6. Capacity

This factor is a characteristic of the organisation. It refers to the company's capability of providing the resources needed for a successful change effort. A successful change effort requires an adequate amount of resources.

### 7. Openness

This characteristic refers to the degree to which the change agent and organisation members are willing to hear, respond to, and be influenced by one another. The preceding six factors can all facilitate the development of such openness or, when absent, they can hinder the development of openness between the change agent and organisation members.

### 8. Reward

This refers to the nature and variety of potential positive outcomes of the change effort that might accrue to the change agent and organisation members. Change efforts should be designed so that the employees are rewarded for changing.

### 9. Energy

This refers to the amount of physical and psychological effort the change agent and organisation members are able and willing to expend on the change effort. When day-to-day problems are so pressing that they sap all of the employee's energy, it diminishes the energy they can devote to the change effort.

### 10. Synergy

This characteristic refers to the positively reinforcing effects that each of the preceding nine factors has on one another. More specifically, synergy involves the variety of people, resources, energies, and activities involved in interacting in the change effort that mutually support success.

## 3.3 Process of Organisational Development

### 3.3.1 Entering and Contracting

Entering and contracting are the initial activities of the OD process, They set the parameters, for the phase of planned change that follow: diagnosing, planning and implementing change, and evaluating and institutionalising it. Organisational entry involves clarifying the organisational issue or presenting problem, determining the relevant client, and selecting an OD practitioner. Developing an OD contract focuses on making a good decision about whether to proceed and allows both the client and the OD practitioner to clarify expectations about how the change process will unfold. Contracting involves setting mutual expectations, negotiating time and resources, and developing ground rules for working together.

### 3.3.2 Diagnosing Organisations, Groups and Individual Jobs

The next step presents background information for diagnosing organisations, groups, and individual jobs. Diagnosis is a collaborative process, involving both managers and consultants in collecting pertinent data, analysing them, and drawing conclusions for action planning and intervention. Diagnosis may be aimed at discovering the causes of specific problems, or it may be directed at assessing the organisation or department to find areas of future development. Diagnosis provides the necessary practical understanding to devise interventions for solving problems and improving organisation effectiveness.

Diagnosis is based on conceptual frameworks about how organisations function. Such diagnostic models serve as road maps by identifying areas to examine and questions to ask in determining how an organisation or department is operating.

The comprehensive model (Fig. 3.1) presented here views organisations as open systems. The organisation serves to coordinate the behaviours of its departments. It is open to exchanges with the larger environment and is influenced by external forces. As open systems, organisations are hierarchically ordered; that is, they are composed of groups, which in turn are composed of individual jobs. Organisations also display five key systems properties: inputs, transformations, and outputs; boundaries; feedback; equifinality and alignment.

An organisation level diagnostic model is described as under. It consists of environmental inputs; a set of design components called a strategic orientation; and a variety of outputs; such as performance, productivity, and stakeholder satisfaction. Diagnosis involves understanding each of the parts in the model and then assessing how the elements of the strategic orientation align with each other and with the inputs. Organisation effectiveness is likely to be high when there is good alignment.

Group diagnostic models take the organisation's design as the primary input: examine goal clarity, task structure, group composition, performance norms, and group functioning as the key design components and list group performance and member quality of work life as the outputs. As with any open-systems model, the alignment of these parts is the key to understanding effectiveness.

At the individual job level, organisation design, group design, and characteristics of each job are the salient inputs. Task variety, task significance, task identity, autonomy, and feedback work together to produce outputs of work satisfaction and work quality.

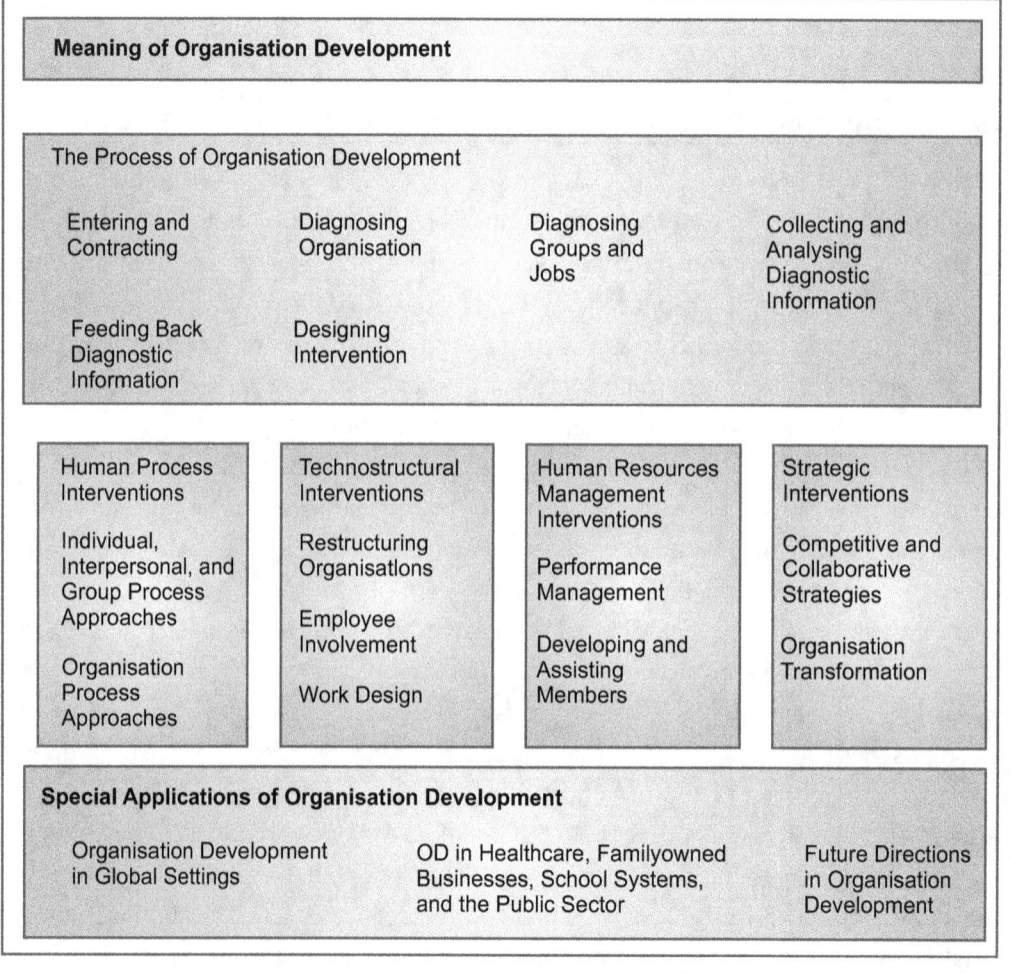

**Meaning of Organisation Development**

**The Process of Organisation Development**

| Entering and Contracting | Diagnosing Organisation | Diagnosing Groups and Jobs | Collecting and Analysing Diagnostic Information |

Feeding Back Diagnostic Information　Designing Intervention

| Human Process Interventions | Technostructural Interventions | Human Resources Management Interventions | Strategic Interventions |

Individual, Interpersonal, and Group Process Approaches

Organisation Process Approaches

Restructuring Organisations

Employee Involvement

Work Design

Performance Management

Developing and Assisting Members

Competitive and Collaborative Strategies

Organisation Transformation

**Special Applications of Organisation Development**

Organisation Development in Global Settings

OD in Healthcare, Familyowned Businesses, School Systems, and the Public Sector

Future Directions in Organisation Development

**Fig. 3.1: Overview of the Organisation Development**

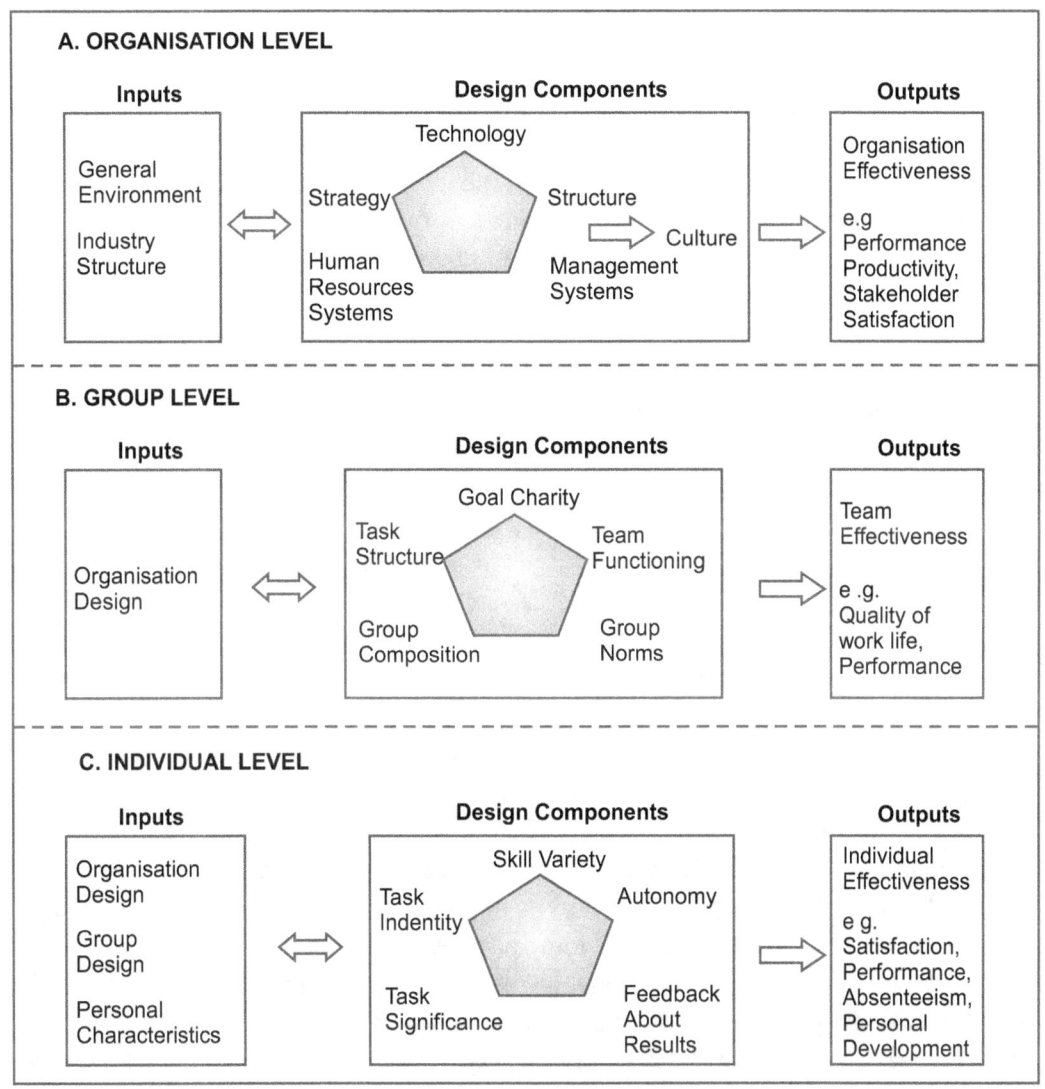

**Fig. 3.2: Comprehensive Model for Diagnosing Organisational System**

**What is Diagnosis?**

Basically diagnosis is the process of understanding how the organisation is currently functioning, and it provides the information necessary to design change interventions. It generally follows from successful entry and contracting, which set the stage for successful diagnosis. Those processes help OD practitioners and client members jointly determine organisational issue to focus on how to collect and analyse data to understand them, and how to work together to develop action steps from the diagnosis.

First, the values and ethical beliefs that underlie OD suggest that both organisation members and change agents should be involved in discovering the determinants of current organisational effectiveness. Similarly, both should be involved actively in developing appropriate intervention and implementing them. For example, a manager might seek OD help to reduce absenteeism in his department. The manager and an OD consultant jointly might decide to diagnose the cause of the problem by examining company absenteeism records and by interviewing selected employees, about possible reasons for absenteeism. Alternatively, they might examine employee loyalty and discover the organisational elements that encourage people to stay. Analysis of those data could uncover determinants of absenteeism or loyalty in the department, thus helping the manager and the practitioner to develop an appropriate intervention to address the issue. The choice about how to approach the issue of absenteeism and the decisions about how to address it are made jointly by the OD practitioner and the manager.

Second, the medical model of diagnosis also implies that something is wrong with the patient and that one needs to uncover the cause of the illness. In those cases where organisations do have specific problems, diagnosis can be problem-oriented, seeking reasons for the problems, On the other hand, as suggested by the absenteeism example above, the practitioner and the client may choose one of the newer views of organisation change and frame the issue positively. Additionally, the client and OD practitioner may be looking for ways to enhance the organisation's existing functioning. Many managers involved with OD are not experiencing specific organisational problems. Here, diagnosis is development-oriented. It assesses the current functioning of the organisation to discover areas for future development. For example, a manager might be interested in using OD to improve a department that already seems to be functioning well. Diagnosis might include an overall assessment of both the task-performance capabilities of the department and the impact of the department on its individual members. This process seeks to uncover specific areas for future development of the department's effectiveness.

In organisation development, diagnosis is used more broadly than medical definition would suggest. It is a collaborative process between organisation members and the OD consultant to collect pertinent information, analyse it, and draw conclusions for action planning and intervention. Diagnosis may be aimed at uncovering the causes of specific problems, focused on understanding effective processes, or directed as assessing the overall functioning of the organisation or department to discover areas for future development. Diagnosis provides a systematic understanding of organisations so that appropriate interventions may be developed for solving problems and enhancing defectiveness.

The technology appears well-supported and aligned with the structure. The production process is craft-based and deliberately ambiguous. The functional structure promotes specialisation and professionalisation of skills and knowledge. Specific tasks, that require flexibility and adaptability from the organisation are given, a wide berth. Although a divisional structure overlays Steinway's corporate activities, the piano division's structure is functional but not rigid, and there appears to be a cultural willingness to be responsive to the craft and the artists they serve.

In addition, the concert bank programme is important for two reasons. First, it builds loyalty into the customer and ensures future demand. Second, it is a natural source of feedback on the instruments themselves, keeping the organisation close to the artist's demands and emerging trends in sound preferences. Finally, the well-developed human resources system supports the responsive production and marketing functions as well as the global nature of the enterprise.

Steinway's culture of quality and responsiveness promotes coordination among the production tasks, serves as a method for socializing and developing people and establishes methods for moving information around the organisation. Clearly, any change effort at Steinway will have to acknowledge this role and design an intervention accordingly. The strong culture will either sabotage or facilitate change depending on how the change process aligns with the culture's impact on individual behaviour.

Based on this understanding of the Steinway organisation, at least two intervention possibilities are suggested. First, in collaboration with the client, the OD practitioner could suggest increasing Steinway's clarity about its strategy. In this intervention, the practitioner would want to talk about formalising—rather than changing—Steinway's strategy because the culture would resist such an attempt. However, there are some clear advantages to be gained from a clearer sense of Steinway's future goals, its businesses, and the relationships among them. Second, Steinway could focus on increasing the integration and coordination of its structure, measurement systems, and human resources systems. The difficulty of retaining key production personnel warrants continuously improved retention systems as well as efforts to codify and retain key production knowledge in case workers do leave. This would apply to the marketing and distribution functions as well since they control an important interface with the customer.

There are several different methods for collecting and analysing diagnostic data. Because diagnosis is an important step that occurs frequently in the planned change process, a working familiarity with these techniques is essential (Fig. 3.3). Methods of data collection include questionnaires, interviews, observation, and unobtrusive measures (Figure 3). Methods of analysis include qualitative techniques, such as content and force-field analysis, and quantitative techniques, such as the determination of mean, standard deviation, correlation coefficient, as well as difference tests.

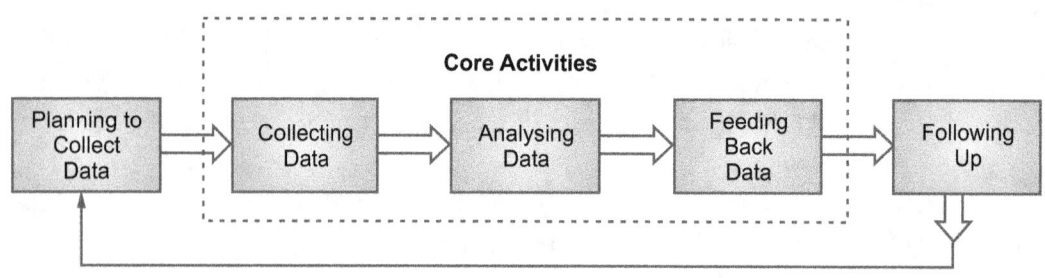

**Fig. 3.3: The Data Collection and Feedback Cycle**

**Table 3.1 Shows a Comparison of Different Methods and Data Collection.**

| Method | Major Advantages | Major Potential Problems |
|---|---|---|
| **Questionnaires:** | 1. Responses can be quantified and easily summarized<br>2. Easy to use with large samples<br>3. Relatively inexpensive<br>4. Can obtain large volume of data | 1. Non-empathy<br>2. Predetermined questions/missing issues<br>3. Overinterpretation of data<br>4. Response bias |
| **Interviews:** | 1. Adaptive—allows data collection on a range of possible subjects<br>2. Source of 'rich' data<br>3. Empathic<br>4. Process of interviewing can build rapport | 1. Expense<br>2. Bias in interviewer responses<br>3. Coding and interpretation difficulties<br>4. Self-report bias |
| **Observations:** | 1. Collects data on behaviour, rather than reports of behaviour<br>2. Real time, not retrospective<br>3. Adaptive | 1. Coding and interpretation difficulties<br>2. Sampling inconsistencies<br>3. Observer bias and questionable reliability<br>4. Expense |
| **Unobtrusive measures:** | 1. Non-reactive - no response bias<br>2. High face validity<br>3. Easily quantified | 1. Access and retrieval difficulties<br>2. Validity concerns<br>3. Coding and interpretation difficulties. |

### 3.3.3 Feeding Back Diagnostic Information

The process of feeding back data to a client system is mentioned. It is concerned with identifying the content of the data to be fed back and designing a feedback process that ensures ownership of the data. Feeding back data is a central activity in almost any OD program. If members own the data, they will be motivated to solve organisational problems. A special application of the data collection and feedback process is called survey feedback. It is one of the most accepted processes in organisation development, enabling practitioners to collect diagnostic data from a large number of organisation members and to feed back that information for purposes of problem-solving. Survey feedback highlights the importance of contracting appropriately with the client system, establishing relevant categories for data collection, and feeding back the data as necessary steps for diagnosing organisational problems and developing interventions for resolving them.

Perhaps the most important step in the diagnostic process is feeding back diagnostic information to the client organisation. Although the data may have been collected with the client's help, the OD practitioner often organises and presents them to the client. Properly analyzed and meaningful data can have an impact on organisational change only if organisation members can use the information to devise appropriate action plans. A key objective of the feedback process is to be sure that the client has ownership of the data.

As shown in Fig. 3.4, the success of data feedback depends largely on its ability to arouse organisational action and to direct energy toward organisational problem-solving. Whether feedback helps to energize the organisation depends on the content of the feedback data and on the process by which they are fed back to organisation members.

**Determining the Content of the Feedback**

In the course of diagnosing the organisation, a large amount of data is collected. In fact, there is often more information than the client needs or can interpret in a realistic period of time. If too many data are fed back, the client may decide that changing is impossible. Therefore, OD practitioners need to summarise the data in ways that enable clients to understand the information and draw action implications from it. The techniques for data analysis can improve this task. Additional criteria for determining the content of diagnostic feedback are described below.

Several characteristics of effective feedback data have been described in the literature. They include the following nine properties:

**(i) Relevant**

Organisation members are likely to use feedback data for problem-solving when they find the information meaningful. Including managers and employees in the initial data collection activities can increase the relevance of the data.

**(ii) Understandable**

Data must be prevented to organisation members in a form that is readily interpreted. Statistical data, for example, can be made understandable through the use of graphs and charts.

### (iii) Descriptive

Feedback data need to be linked to real organisational behaviours if they are to arouse and direct energy. The use of examples and detailed illustrations can help employees gain a better feel for the data.

### (iv) Verifiable

Feedback data should be valid and accurate if they are to guide action. Thus, the information should allow organisation members to verify whether the findings really describe the organisation. For example, questionnaire data might include information about the sample of respondents as well as frequency distributions for each item or measure. Such information can help members verifying whether the feedback data accurately represent organisational events or attitudes.

### (v) Timely

Data should be fed back to members as quickly as possible after being collected and analysed. This will help ensure that the information is still valid and is linked to members' motivations to examine it.

### (vi) Limited

Because people can easily become overloaded with too much information, feedback, data should be limited to what employees can realistically process at one time.

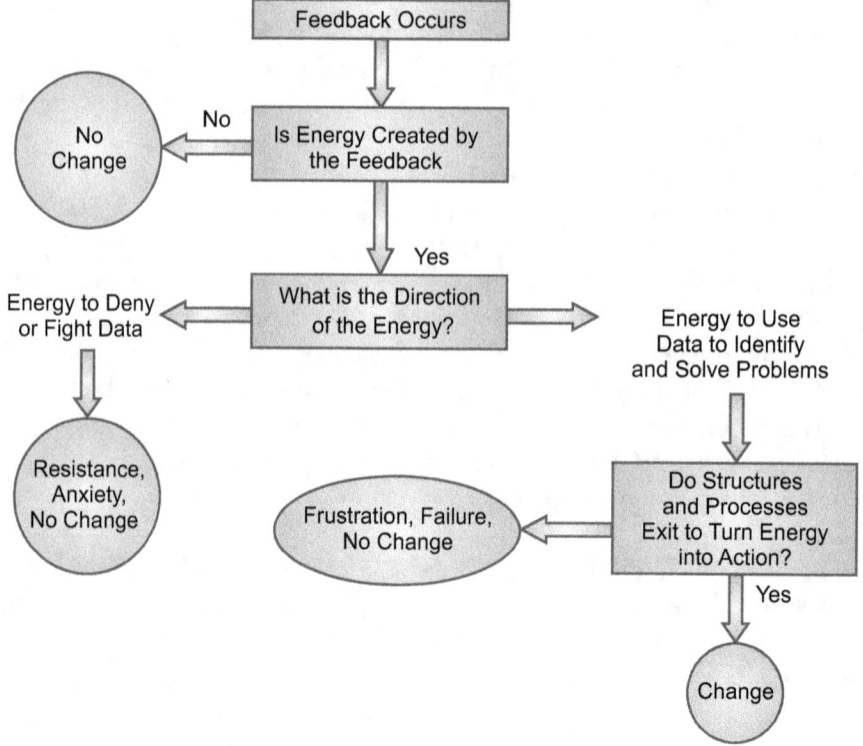

**Fig. 3.4: Possible Effect of Feedback**

### 3.3.4 Designing Interventions

An organisation development intervention is a sequence of activities, actions, and events intended to help an organisation improve its performance and effectiveness. Intervention design, or action planning, derives from careful diagnosis, and is meant to resolve specific problems and to improve particular areas of organisational functioning identified in the diagnosis. OD intervention vary from standardized programmes that have been developed and used in many organisations to relatively unique programmes tailored to a specific organisation or department.

**What are Effective Interventions?**

The term intervention refers to a set of sequenced planned actions or events, intended to help an organisation increase its effectiveness. Interventions purposely disrupt the status quo; they are deliberate attempts to change an organisation or subunit toward a different and more effective state. In OD, three major criteria define an effective intervention (a) the extent to which it fits the needs of the organisation; (b) the degree to which it is based on causal knowledge of intended outcomes; and (c) the extent to which it transfers change-management competence to organisation members.

The first criterion concerns the extent to which the intervention is relevant to the organisation and its members. Effective interventions are based on valid information about the organisation's functioning; they provide organisation members with opportunities to make free and informed choices and they gain members' internal commitment to those choices.

The second criterion of an effective intervention involves those of outcomes. Because interventions are intended to produce specific results, they must be based on valid knowledge that those outcomes actually can be produced. Otherwise there is no scientific basis for designing an effective OD intervention.

The third criterion of an effective intervention involves the extent to which it enhances the organisation's capacity to manage change. The values underlying OD suggest that following an intervention, organisation members should be better able to carry out planned change activities on their own, From active participation in designing and implementing the intervention they should gain knowledge and skill in managing change. Competence in change management is essential in today's environment, where technological, social, economic and political changes are rapid and persistent.

**How to Design Effective Interventions**

Designing OD interventions requires paying careful attention to the needs and dynamics of the change situation and crafting a change program that will be consistent with previously described criteria of effective interventions. Current knowledge of OD interventions provides only general prescriptions for change. There is scant precise information or research about how to design interventions or how they can be expected to interact with organisational conditions to achieve specific results. Moreover, because the ability to implement most OD interventions is highly dependent on the skills and knowledge of the change agent, the design of an intervention will depend to some extent on the expertise of the practitioner.

Two major sets of contingencies that can affect intervention success are those having to do with the change situation (including the practitioner) and those related to the target of change. Both kinds of contingencies need to be considered in designing interventions.

### (a) Contingencies Related to the Change Situation

Researchers have identified a number of contingencies present in the change situation that can affect intervention success. These include individual differences among organisation members (for example, needs for autonomy), organisational factors (for example, management style and technical uncertainty), and dimensions of the change process itself (for example, degree of top-management support). Unless these factors are taken into account, designing an intervention will have little impact on organisational functioning or, worse, it may produce negative results.

They include situational factors that must be considered in designing any intervention:

(i) the organisation's readiness for change, (ii) its change capability, (iii) its cultural context which exerts influence on members, and (iv) the change agent's skills and abilities.

### (b) Contingencies related to Target of Change

Researchers have identified two key contingencies related to change target that can affect intervention success: (i) the organisational issues that the intervention is intended to resolve, and the level of organisational system at which the intervention is expected to have a primary impact.

The following four interrelated issues that are key targets of OD interventions: (as shown in Fig. 3.5).

### 1. Strategic Issues

Organisations need to decide what products or services they will provide and the markets in which they will compete, as well as how to relate to their environments and how to transform themselves to keep pace with changing conditions. These strategic issues are among the most critical facing organisations in today's changing and highly competitive environments.

OD methods aimed at these issues are called strategic interventions. The methods are among the most recent additions to OD and include integrated strategic change, mergers and acquisitions, alliance and network development, and organisation learning.

### 2. Technology and Structure Issues

Organisations must decide how to divide work into departments and then how to coordinate among those departments to support strategic directions. They also must make decisions about how to deliver products or services and how to link people to tasks. OD methods for dealing with these structural and technological issues are called technostructural interventions and include OD activities relating to organisation design, employee involvement and work design.

### 3.  Human Resources Issues

These issues are concerned with attracting competent people to the organisation, setting goals for them, appraising and rewarding their performance, and ensuring that they develop their careers and manage stress. OD techniques, aimed at these issues are called human resources management interventions.

### 4.  Human Process Issues

These issues have to do with social processes occurring among organisation members, such as communication, decision-making, leadership, and group dynamics. OD methods focusing on these kinds of issues are called human process interventions: included among them are some of the most common OD techniques, such as conflict resolution and team-building.

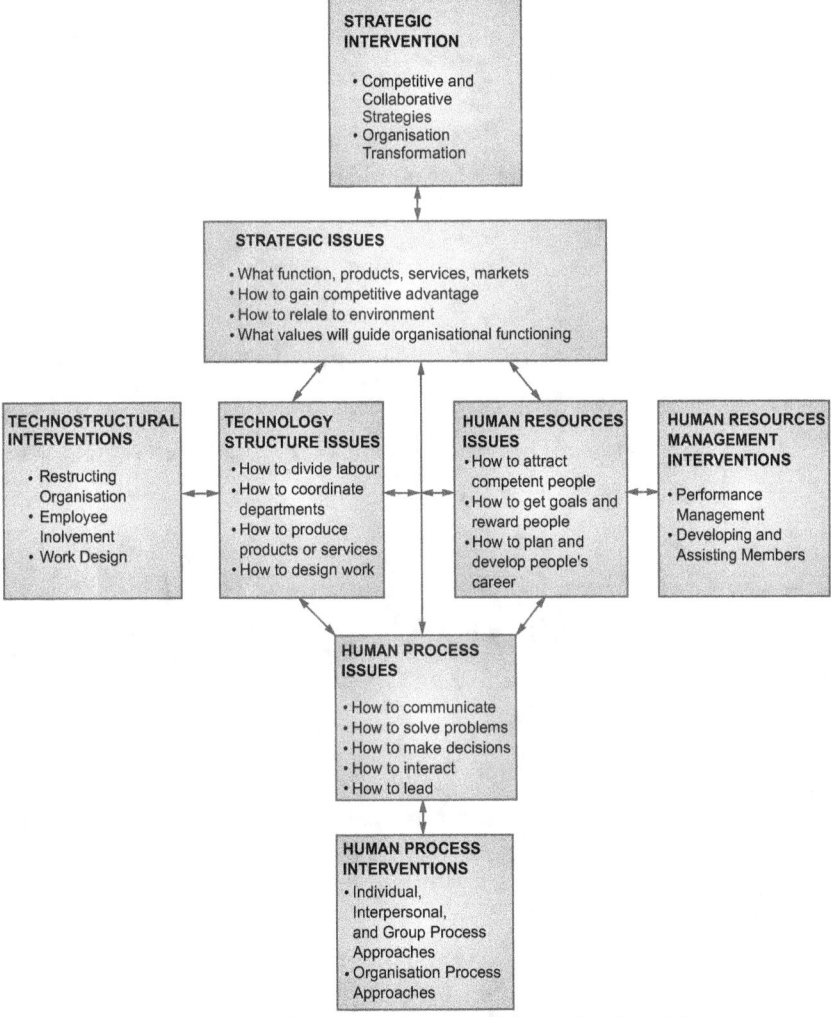

**Fig. 3.5: Types of Interventions and Organisational Issues**

In line with system theory, these organisational issues are interrelated and need to be integrated with each other. For example, decisions about gaining competitive advantage need to fit with choices about organisation structure, setting goals for and rewarding people, communication and problem-solving.

Intervention design must create change methods appropriate to the organisational issues identified in diagnosis. Moreover, because the organisational issues are themselves linked together, OD interventions similarly need to be integrated with one another. For example, a goal-setting intervention that tries to establish motivating goals may need to be integrated with supporting interventions, such as a reward system that links pay to goal achievement. The key point is to think systemically. Interventions aimed at one kind of organisational issue will invariably have repercussions on other kinds of issues. Careful thinking about how OD interventions affect the different kinds of issues and how different change programmes might be integrated to bring about more coherent impact on organisational functioning.

## 5. Organisational Level System

Besides facing interrelated issues, organisations function at different levels: individual, group, organisation, and transorganisation. Thus, organisational levels are targets of change in OD. For example, some technostructural interventions affect mainly individuals and groups (for example, work design), whereas others impact primarily the total organisation (for example, structural design). It is important to emphasise that only the primary level affected by the intervention is identified. Many OD interventions also have a secondary impact on the other levels. For example, structural design affects mainly the organisation level, but it can have an indirect effect on groups and individuals because it sets the broad parameters for designing work groups and individual jobs. Again, practitioners need to think systemically. They must design interventions to apply to specific organisational levels, address the possibility of cross-level effects, integrate interventions affecting different levels to achieve overall success. For example, an intervention to create self-managed work teams may need to be linked to organisation-level changes in measurement and reward system to promote team-based work.

## 3.3.5 Managing Change

After diagnosis reveals the causes of problems or identifies opportunities for development, organisation members begin planning and subsequently leading and implementing the changes necessary to improve organisation effectiveness and performance. A large part of OD is concerned with interventions for improving organisations. Change can vary in complexity from the introduction of relatively simple processes into a small work group to transforming the strategies and design features of the whole organisation.

## Overview of Change Activities

The OD literature has directed considerable attention at leading and managing change. Much of the material is highly prescriptive, advising managers about how to plan and implement organisational changes. For example, one study suggested that successful managers in continuously changing organisations: (1) provide employees with clear responsibility and priorities, including extensive communication and freedom to improvise; (2) explore the future by experimenting with a wide variety of low-cost probes; and (3) link current projects to the future with predictable (time-paced rather than event-paced) intervals and choreographed transition procedures.

Traditionally, change management has focused on identifying sources of resistance to change and offering ways to overcome them. Other contributions have challenged the focus on resistance and have been aimed at creating visions and desired futures, gaining political support for them, and managing the transition of the organisation toward them. Still others have described the learning practices and leader behaviours that accelerate complex change.

The diversity of practical advice for managing change can be organised into five major activities, as shown in Figure 3.6. The activities contribute to effective change management and are listed roughly in the order in which they typically are performed. Each activity represents a key element in change leadership. The first activity involves *motivating change* and includes creating a readiness for change among organisation members and helping them address resistance to change. Leadership must create an environment in which people accept the need for change and commit physical and psychological energy to it. Motivation is a critical issue in starting change because ample evidence indicates that people and organisations seek to preserve the status quo and are willing to change only when there are compelling reasons to do so. The second activity is concerned with *creating a vision* and is closely aligned with leadership activities. The vision provides a purpose and reason for change and describes the desired future state. Together, they provide the "why" and "what" of planned change.

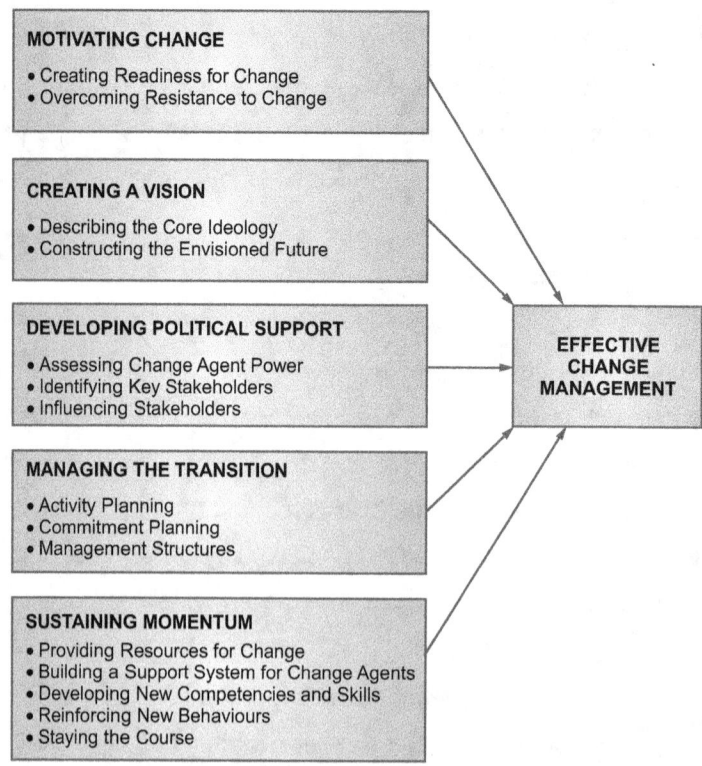

**Fig. 3.6: Activities Contributing to Effective Change Management**

The third activity involves *developing political support* for change. Organisations are composed of powerful individuals and groups that can either block or promote change, and leaders and change agents need to gain their support to implement changes. The fourth activity is concerned with *managing the transition* from the current state to the desired future state. It involves creating a plan for managing the change activities as well as planning special management structures for operating the organisation during the transition. The fifth activity involves *sustaining momentum* for change so that it will be carried to completion. This includes providing resources for implementing the changes, building a support system for change agents, developing new competencies and skills, and reinforcing the new behaviours needed to implement the changes.

Each of the activities is important for managing change. Although little research has been conducted on their relative contributions, organisational leaders must give careful attention to each activity when planning and implementing organisational change. Unless individuals are motivated and committed to change, getting movement on the desired change will be extremely difficult. In the absence of vision, change is likely to be disorganised and diffused. Without the support of powerful individuals and groups, change may be blocked and possibly sabotaged. Unless the transition process is managed carefully, the organisation will have difficulty functioning while it moves from the current state to the future state. Without efforts to sustain momentum for change, the organisation will have problems carrying the changes through to completion. Thus, all five activities must be managed effectively to realise success.

In the following sections of this chapter, we discuss more fully each of these change activities, directing attention to how leaders contribute to planning and implementing organisational change.

## 1. Motivating Change

Organisational change involves moving from the known to the unknown. Because the future is uncertain and may adversely affect people's competencies, worth, and coping abilities, organisation members generally do not support change unless compelling reasons convince them to do so. Similarly, organisations tend to be heavily invested in the status quo, and they resist changing it in the face of uncertain future benefits. Consequently, a key issue in planning for action is how to motivate commitment to organisational change. As shown in Figure 10.1, this requires attention to two related tasks: creating readiness for change and overcoming resistance to change.

### (a) Creating Readiness for Change

One of the more fundamental axioms of OD is that people's readiness for change depends on creating a felt need for change. This involves making people so dissatisfied with the status quo that they are motivated to try new work processes, technologies, or ways of behaving. Creating such dissatisfaction can be difficult, as anyone knows who has tried to lose weight, stop smoking, or change some other habitual behaviour. Generally, people and organisations need to experience deep levels of hurt before they will seriously undertake meaningful change. For example, IBM, GM, and Sears experienced threats to their very survival before they undertook significant change programmes.

### (b) Overcoming Resistance to Change

Change can generate deep resistance in people and in organisations, thus making it difficult, if not impossible, to implement organisational improvements. At a personal level, change can arouse considerable anxiety about letting go of the known and moving to an uncertain future. People may be unsure whether their existing skills and contributions will be valued in the future, or may have significant questions about whether they can learn to function effectively and to achieve benefits in the new situation.

At the organisation level, resistance to change can come from three sources. *Technical resistance* comes from the habit of following common procedures and the consideration of sunk costs invested in the status quo. *Political resistance* can arise when organisational changes threaten powerful stakeholders, such as top executive or staff personnel, or call into question the past decisions of leaders. Organisation change often implies a different allocation of already scarce resources, such as capital, training budgets, and good people.

Finally, *cultural resistance* takes the form of systems and procedures that reinforce the status quo, promoting conformity to existing values, norms, and assumptions about how things should operate.

## 2. Creating a Vision

The second activity in leading and managing change involves creating a vision of what members want the organisation to look like or become. It is one of the most popular yet least understood practices in management. Generally, a vision describes the core values and purpose that guide the organisation as well as an envisioned future toward which change is directed. It provides a valued direction for designing, implementing, and assessing organisational changes. The vision also can energise commitment to change by providing members with a common goal and a compelling rationale for why change is necessary and worth the effort. However, if the vision is seen as impossible or promotes changes that the organisation cannot implement, it actually can depress member motivation.

Compelling visions are composed of two parts: (1) a relatively stable identity or core ideology that describes the organisation's core values and purpose, and (2) an envisioned future with bold goals and a vivid description of the desired future state that reflects the specific change under consideration.

### (a) Describing the Core Ideology

The fundamental basis of a vision for change is the organisation's core ideology. It describes the organisation's core values and purpose and is relatively stable over time. *Core values* typically include three to five basic principles or beliefs that have stood the test of time and best represent what the organisation stands for. Although the vision ultimately describes a desired future, it must acknowledge the organisation's historical roots—the intrinsically meaningful core values and principles that have guided and will guide the organisation over time. Core values are not "espoused values"; they are the "values in use" that actually inform members what is important in the organisation. The retailer Nordstrom, for example, has clear values around the importance of customer service; toymaker Lego has distinct values around the importance of families; and the Disney companies have explicit values around wholesomeness and imagination. These values define the true nature of these firms and cannot be separated from them. Thus, core values are not determined or designed; they are discovered and described through a process of inquiry.

### (b) Constructing the Envisioned Future

The core ideology provides the context for the envisioned future. Unlike core values and purpose, which are stable aspects of the organisation and must be discovered, the envisioned future is specific to the change project at hand and must be created. The envisioned future varies in complexity and scope depending on the changes being considered. A relatively simple upgrading of a work group's word-processing software requires a less complex envisioned future than the transformation of a government bureaucracy.

### 3. Developing Political Support

From a political perspective, organisations can be seen as loosely structured coalitions of individuals and groups having different preferences and interests. For example, shop-floor workers may want secure, high-paying jobs, and top executives may be interested in diversifying the organisation into new businesses. The marketing department might be interested in developing new products and markets, and the production department may want to manufacture standard products in the most efficient ways.

These different groups or coalitions compete with one another for scarce resources and influence. They act to preserve or enhance their self-interests while managing to arrive at a sufficient balance of power to sustain commitment to the organisation and achieve overall effectiveness.

Given this political view, attempts to change the organisation often threaten the balance of power among groups, thus resulting in political conflicts and struggles. Individuals and groups will be concerned with how the changes affect their own power and influence, and they will act accordingly. Some groups will become less powerful; others will gain influence. Those whose power is threatened by the change will act defensively and seek to preserve the status quo. For example, they may try to present compelling evidence that change is unnecessary or that only minor modifications are needed. On the other hand, those participants who will gain power from the changes will push heavily for them, perhaps bringing in seemingly impartial consultants to legitimize the need for change. Consequently, significant organisational changes are frequently accompanied by conflicting interests, distorted information, and political turmoil.

Managing the political dynamics of change includes the following activities: assessing the change agent's power, identifying key stakeholders, and influencing stakeholders.

### (a) Assessing Change Agent Power

The first task is to evaluate the change agent's own sources of power. This agent may be the leader of the organisation or department undergoing change, or he or she may be the OD consultant if professional help is being used. By assessing their own power base, change agents can determine how to use it to influence others to support changes. They also can identify areas in which they need to enhance their sources of power. The key sources of personal power in organisations (in addition to one's formal position) are: knowledge, personality, and others' support. Knowledge bases of power include having expertise that is valued by others and controlling important information.

OD professionals typically gain power through their expertise in organisational change. Personality sources of power can derive from change agents' charisma, reputation, and professional credibility. Charismatic leaders can inspire devotion and enthusiasm for change from subordinates. OD consultants with strong reputations and professional credibility can wield considerable power during organisational change. Others' support can contribute to individual power by providing access to information and resource networks. Others also may use their power on behalf of the change agent. For example, leaders in organisational units undergoing change can call on their informal networks for resources and support, and encourage subordinates to exercise power in support of the change.

### (b) Identifying Key Stakeholders

Having assessed their own power bases, change agents should identify powerful individuals and groups with an interest in the changes, such as staff groups, unions, departmental managers, and top-level executives. These key stakeholders can thwart or support change, and it is important to gain broad-based support to minimise the risk that a single interest group will block the changes. As organisations have become more global, networked, and customer focused, and change has become more strategic, it is also important to identify key external stakeholders. Customers, regulatory agencies, suppliers, and the local community, for example, can exert considerable influence over change.

Identifying key stakeholders can start with the simple question, "Who stands to gain or to lose from the changes?" Once stakeholders are identified, creating a map of their influence may be useful. The map could show relationships among the stakeholders in terms of who influences whom and what the stakes are for each party. This would provide change agents with information about which people and groups need to be influenced to accept and support the changes.

### (c) Influencing Stakeholders

This activity involves gaining the support of key stakeholders to motivate a critical mass for change. There are at least three major strategies for using power to influence others in OD: playing it straight, using social networks, and going around the formal system.

The strategy of playing it straight is very consistent with an OD perspective, and thus it is the most widely used power strategy in OD. It involves determining the needs of particular stakeholders and presenting information about how the changes can benefit them. This relatively straightforward approach is based on the premise that information and knowledge can persuade people about the need and direction for change. The success of this strategy relies heavily on the change agent's knowledge base. He or she must have the expertise and information to persuade stakeholders that the changes are a logical way to meet their needs.

The second power strategy, using social networks, is more foreign to OD and involves forming alliances and coalitions with other powerful individuals and groups, dealing directly with key decision makers, and using formal and informal contacts to gain information. In this strategy, change agents attempt to use their social relationships to gain support for changes. They use the individual power base of others' support to gain the resources, commitment, and political momentum needed to implement change.

The power strategy of going around the formal system is probably least used in OD and involves purposely circumventing organisational structures and procedures to get the changes made. Existing organisational arrangements can be roadblocks to change, and working around the barriers may be more expedient and effective than taking the time and energy to remove them.

## 4. Managing the Transition

Implementing organisation change involves moving from an existing organisation state to a desired future state. Such movement does not occur immediately but, as shown in Figure 10.3, instead requires a transition period during which the organisation learns how to implement the conditions needed to reach the desired future. Beckhard and Harris pointed out that the transition may be quite different from the present state of the organisation and consequently may require special management structures and activities. They identified three major activities and structures to facilitate organisational transition: activity planning, commitment planning, and change-management structures.

A fourth set of activities involves managing the learning process during change.

## (a) Activity Planning

Activity planning involves making a road map for change, citing specific activities and events that must occur if the transition is to be successful. It should clearly identify, temporally orient, and integrate discrete change tasks, and it should explicitly link these tasks to the organisation's change goals and priorities. Activity planning also should gain top-management approval, be cost effective, and remain adaptable as feedback is received during the change process.

**Fig. 3.7: Organisation Change as a Transition State**

## (b) Commitment Planning

This activity involves identifying key people and groups whose commitment is needed for change to occur and formulating a strategy for gaining their support. Although commitment planning is generally a part of developing political support, discussed above, specific plans for identifying key stakeholders and obtaining their commitment to change need to be made early in the change process.

## (c) Change-Management Structures

Because organisational transitions tend to be ambiguous and to need direction, special structures for managing the change process need to be created. These management structures should include people who have the power to mobilize resources to promote change, the respect of the existing leadership and change advocates, and the interpersonal and political skills to guide the change process. Alternative management structures include the following:

- The chief executive or head person manages the change effort.
- A project manager temporarily is assigned to coordinate the transition.
- A steering committee of representatives from the major constituencies involved in the change jointly manage the project.
- Natural leaders who have the confidence and trust of large numbers of affected employees are selected to manage the transition.
- A cross section of people representing different organisational functions and levels manages the change.

## 5. Sustaining Momentum

Once organisational changes are under way, special attention must be directed to sustaining energy and commitment for implementing them. The initial excitement and activity of changing often dissipate in the face of practical problems of trying to learn new ways of operating. A strong tendency exists among organisation members to return to old behaviours and well-known processes unless they receive sustained support and reinforcement for carrying the changes through to completion.

The following five activities can help to sustain momentum for carrying change through to completion: providing resources for change, building a support system for change agents, developing new competencies and skills, reinforcing new behaviours, and staying the course.

### (a) Providing Resources for Change

Bringing about organisation change generally requires additional financial and human resources, particularly if the organisation continues day-to-day operations while trying to change itself. These extra resources are needed for such change activities as training, consultation, data collection and feedback, and special meetings. Extra resources also are helpful to provide a buffer as performance drops during the transition period. Organisations can underestimate seriously the need for special resources devoted to the change process. Significant organisational change invariably requires considerable management time and energy, as well as the help of consultants. A separate "change budget" that exists along with capital and operating budgets can earmark the resources needed for training members in how to behave differently and for assessing progress and making necessary modifications in the change program. Unless these extra resources are planned for and provided, meaningful change is less likely to occur.

### (b) Building a Support System for Change Agents

Organisation change can be difficult and filled with tension, not only for participants but for change agents as well. They often must give members emotional support, but they may receive little support themselves. They often must maintain "psychological distance" from others to gain the perspective needed to lead the change process. This separation can produce considerable tension and isolation, and change agents may need to create their own support system to help them cope with such problems. A support system typically consists of a network of people with whom the change agent has close personal relationships—people who can give emotional support, serve as a sounding board for ideas and problems, and challenge untested assumptions.

### (c) Developing New Competencies and Skills

Organisational changes frequently demand new knowledge, skills, and behaviours from organisation members. In many cases, the changes cannot be implemented unless members gain new skills. For example, employee-involvement programmes often require managers to learn new leadership styles and new approaches to problem solving. Change agents must ensure that such learning occurs. They need to provide multiple learning opportunities, such as traditional training programmes, on-the-job counselling and coaching, and experiential simulations, covering both technical and social skills. Because it is easy to overlook the social component, change agents may need to devote special time and resources to helping members gain the social skills required to implement changes.

### (d) Reinforcing New Behaviours

In organisations, people generally do those things that bring them rewards. Consequently, one of the most effective ways to sustain momentum for change is to reinforce the kinds of behaviours needed to implement the changes. This can be accomplished by linking formal rewards directly to the desired behaviours. Equally important are the intrinsic rewards that people can experience through early success in the change effort. Achieving identifiable early successes can make participants feel good about themselves and their behaviours, and thus reinforce the drive to change.

### (e) Staying the Course

Change requires time, and many of the expected financial and organisational benefits from change lag behind its implementation. If the organisation changes again too quickly or abandons the change before it is fully implemented, the desired results may never materialise. There are two primary reasons that managers do not keep a steady focus on change implementation. First, many managers fail to anticipate the decline in performance, productivity, or satisfaction as change is implemented.

Organisation members need time to practice, develop, and learn new behaviours; they do not abandon old ways of doing things and adopt a new set of behaviours overnight. Moreover, change activities, such as training, extra meetings, and consulting assistance, are extra expenses added onto current operating expenditures. There should be little surprise, therefore, that effectiveness declines before it gets better. However, perfectly good change projects often are abandoned when questions are raised about short-term performance declines. Patience and trust in the diagnosis and intervention design work are necessary.

Second, many managers do not keep focused on a change because they want to implement the next big idea that comes along. When organisations change before they have to, in response to the latest management fad, a "flavour-of-the-month" cynicism can develop. As a result, organisation members provide only token support to a change under the (accurate) notion that the current change won't last. Successful organisational change requires persistent leadership that does not waver unnecessarily.

## 3.3.7 Evaluating and Institutionalising Intervention

*Evaluation* is concerned with providing feedback to practitioners and organisation members about the progress and impact of interventions. Such information may suggest the need for further diagnosis and modification of the change program, or it may show that the intervention is successful. *Institutionalisation* is a process for maintaining a particular change for an appropriate period of time. It ensures that the results of successful change programmes persist over time.

Evaluation processes consider both the implementation success of the intended intervention and the long-term results it produces. Two key aspects of effective evaluation are measurement and research design. The persistence of intervention effects is examined in a framework showing the organisation characteristics, intervention dimensions, and processes contributing to institutionalisation of OD interventions in organisations.

### 1. Evaluating Organisation Development Interventions

Assessing OD interventions involves judgements about whether an intervention has been implemented as intended and, if so, whether it is having desired results. Managers investing resources in OD efforts increasingly are being held accountable for results—being asked to justify the expenditures in terms of hard, bottom-line outcomes. More and more managers are asking for rigorous assessment of OD interventions and are using the results to make important resource allocation decisions about OD, such as whether to continue to support the change program, to modify or alter it, or to terminate it and try something else. Traditionally, OD evaluation has been discussed as something that occurs after the intervention.

There are two distinct types of OD evaluation: one intended to guide the implementation of interventions and another to assess their overall impact. The key issues in evaluation are measurement and research design.

### Implementation and Evaluation Feedback

Most discussions and applications of OD evaluation imply that evaluation is something done after intervention. It is typically argued that once the intervention is implemented, it should be evaluated to discover whether it is producing the intended effects. For example, it might be expected that a job enrichment program would lead to higher employee satisfaction and performance. After implementing job enrichment, evaluation would involve assessing whether these positive results indeed did occur.

This after-implementation view of evaluation is only partially correct. It assumes that interventions have been implemented as intended and that the key purpose of evaluation is to assess their effects. However, in many, if not most, organisation development programmes, implementing interventions cannot be taken for granted. Most OD interventions require significant changes in people's behaviours and ways of thinking about organisations, but they typically offer only broad prescriptions for how such changes are to occur.

Consequently, we should expand our view of evaluation to include both *during-implementation* assessments about if and how well changes are actually being implemented and *after- implementation* evaluation of whether they are producing expected results.

Both kinds of evaluation provide organisation members with feedback about interventions. Evaluation aimed at guiding implementation may be called *implementation feedback*, and assessment intended to discover intervention outcomes may be called *evaluation feedback*. Fig. 3.8 shows how the two kinds of feedback fit with the diagnostic and intervention stages of OD.

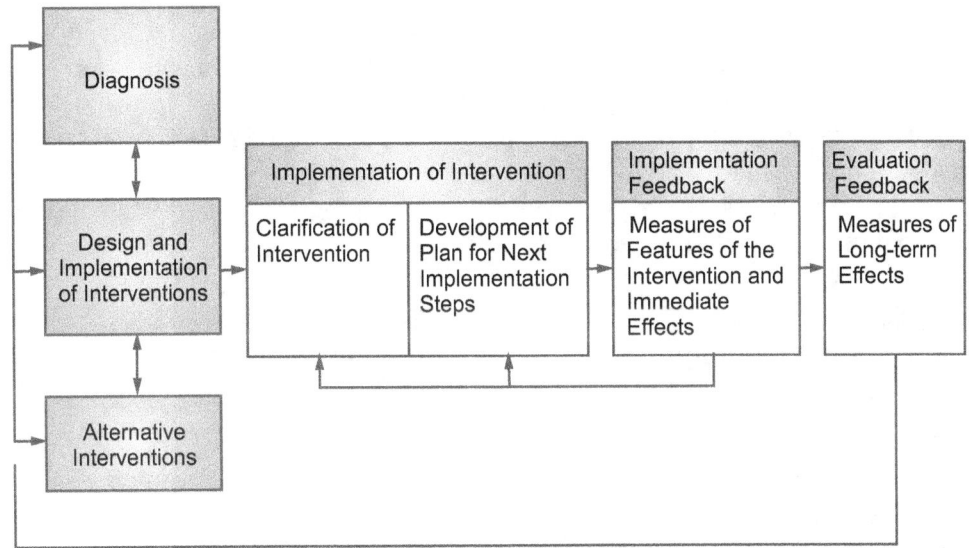

**Fig. 3.8: Implementation and Evaluation Feedback**

In most cases, the chosen intervention provides only general guidelines for organisational change, leaving managers and employees with the task of translating those guidelines into specific behaviours and procedures. Implementation feedback informs this process by supplying data about the different features of the intervention itself, perceptions of the people involved, and data about the immediate effects of the intervention. These data, collected repeatedly and at short intervals, provide a series of snapshots about how the intervention is progressing. Organisation members can use this information, first, to gain a clearer understanding of the intervention (the kinds of behaviours and procedures required to implement it) and, second, to plan for the next implementation steps. This feedback cycle might proceed for several rounds, with each round providing members with knowledge about the intervention and ideas for the next stage of implementation.

Once implementation feedback informs organisation members that the intervention is sufficiently in place and accepted, evaluation feedback begins. In contrast to implementation feedback, it is concerned with the overall impact of the intervention and with whether resources should continue to be allocated to it or to other possible interventions. Evaluation feedback takes longer to gather and interpret than does implementation feedback.

It typically includes a broad array of outcome measures, such as performance, job satisfaction, productivity, and turnover. Negative results on these measures tell members either that the initial diagnosis was seriously flawed or that the wrong intervention was chosen. Such feedback might prompt additional diagnosis and a search for a more effective intervention. Positive results, on the other hand, tell members that the intervention produced expected outcomes and might prompt a search for ways to institutionalise the changes, making them a permanent part of the organisation's normal functioning.

The evaluation feedback includes all the data from the satisfaction and performance measures used in the implementation feedback. Because both the immediate and broader effects of the intervention are being evaluated, additional outcomes are examined, such as employee absenteeism, maintenance costs, and reactions of other organisational units not included in job enrichment. The full array of evaluation data might suggest that after one year from the start of implementation, the job enrichment programme is having the expected effects and thus should be continued and made more permanent.

## (a) Measurement

Providing useful implementation and evaluation feedback involves two activities: selecting the appropriate variables and designing good measures.

### • Selecting Appropriate Variables

Ideally, the variables measured in OD evaluation should derive from the theory or conceptual model underlying the intervention. The model should incorporate the key features of the intervention as well as its expected results.

The job-level diagnostic model suggests a number of measurement variables for implementation and evaluation feedback. Whether the intervention is being implemented could be assessed by determining how many job descriptions have been rewritten to include more responsibility or how many organisation members have received cross training in other job skills. Evaluation of the immediate and long-term impact of job enrichment would include measures of employee performance and satisfaction over time. Again, these measures would likely be included in the initial diagnosis, when the company's problems or areas for improvement are discovered.

Measuring both intervention and outcome variables is necessary for implementation and evaluation feedback. Unfortunately, there has been a tendency in OD to measure only outcome variables while neglecting intervention variables altogether. It generally is assumed that the intervention has been implemented, and attention, therefore, is directed to its impact on such organisational outcomes as performance, absenteeism, and satisfaction. As argued earlier, implementing OD interventions generally takes considerable time and learning. It must be empirically determined that the intervention has been implemented; it cannot simply be assumed. Implementation feedback serves this purpose, guiding the implementation process and helping to interpret outcome data.

Outcome measures are ambiguous without knowledge of how well the intervention has been implemented.

- **Designing Good Measures**

Each of the measurement methods has advantages and disadvantages. Many of these characteristics are linked to the extent to which a measurement is operationally defined, reliable, and valid. These assessment characteristics are discussed below.

(i) **Operational Definition:** A good measure is operationally defined; that is, it specifies the empirical data needed, how they will be collected and, most important, how they will be converted from data to information. They consist of specific computational rules that can be used to construct measures for each of the behaviours. Most of the behaviours are reported as rates adjusted for the number of employees in the organisation and for the possible incidents of behaviour. These adjustments make it possible to compare the measures across different situations and time periods.

(ii) **Reliability:** Reliability concerns the extent to which a measure represents the "true" value of a variable—that is, how accurately the operational definition translates data into information.

(iii) **Validity:** Validity concerns the extent to which a measure actually reflects the variable it is intended to reflect.

## (b) Research Design

In addition to measurement, OD practitioners must make choices about how to design the evaluation to achieve valid results. The key issue is how to design the assessment to show whether the intervention did in fact produce the observed results. This is called *internal validity*. The secondary question of whether the intervention would work similarly in other situations is referred to as *external validity*.

Given the problems inherent in assessing OD interventions, practitioners have turned to *quasi-experimental research designs*. These designs are not as rigorous and controlled as are randomized experimental designs, but they allow evaluators to rule out many rival explanations for OD results other than the intervention itself. Although several quasi-experimental designs are available, those with the following three features are particularly powerful for assessing changes:

- **Longitudinal Measurement:** This involves measuring results repeatedly over relatively long time periods. Ideally, the data collection should start before the change program is implemented and continue for a period considered reasonable for producing expected results.
- **Comparison Unit:** It is always desirable to compare results in the intervention situation with those in another situation where no such change has taken place. Although it is never possible to get a matching group identical to the intervention group, most organisations include a number of similar work units that can be used for comparison purposes.
- **Statistical Analysis:** Whenever possible, statistical methods should be used to rule out the possibility that the results are caused by random error or chance. Various statistical techniques are applicable to quasi-experimental designs, and OD practitioners should apply these methods or seek help from those who can apply them.

## 2. Institutionalising Organisational Changes

Once it is determined that changes have been implemented and are effective, attention is directed at institutionalising the changes—maintaining them as a normal part of the organisation's functioning for an appropriate period of time. In complex and uncertain environments, some changes are only part of a long journey of organisation adaptation.

Innovating new products is not a one-time change but a continuous process that must be implemented over and over again. Other changes, such as the process for appraising performance, need to persist.

### Institutionalisation Framework

Figure 3.9 presents a framework that identifies organisation and intervention characteristics and institutionalisation processes affecting the degree to which change programmes are institutionalised. The model shows that two key antecedents—organisation and intervention characteristics—affect different institutionalisation processes operating in organisations. These processes, in turn, affect various indicators of institutionalisation. The model also shows that organisation characteristics can influence intervention characteristics. For example, organisations having powerful unions may have trouble gaining internal support for OD interventions.

### Organisation Characteristics

Fig. 3.9 shows that the following three key dimensions of an organisation can affect intervention characteristics and institutionalisation processes:

1. **Congruence:** This is the degree to which an intervention is seen as being in harmony with the organisation's managerial philosophy, strategy, and structure; its current environment; and other changes taking place. When an intervention is congruent

with these dimensions, the probability is improved that it will be supported and sustained. Congruence can facilitate persistence by making it easier to gain member commitment to the intervention and to diffuse it to wider segments of the organisation. The converse also is true: Many OD interventions promote employee participation and growth. When applied in highly bureaucratic organisations with formalised structures and autocratic managerial styles, participative interventions are not perceived as congruent with the organisation's managerial philosophy.

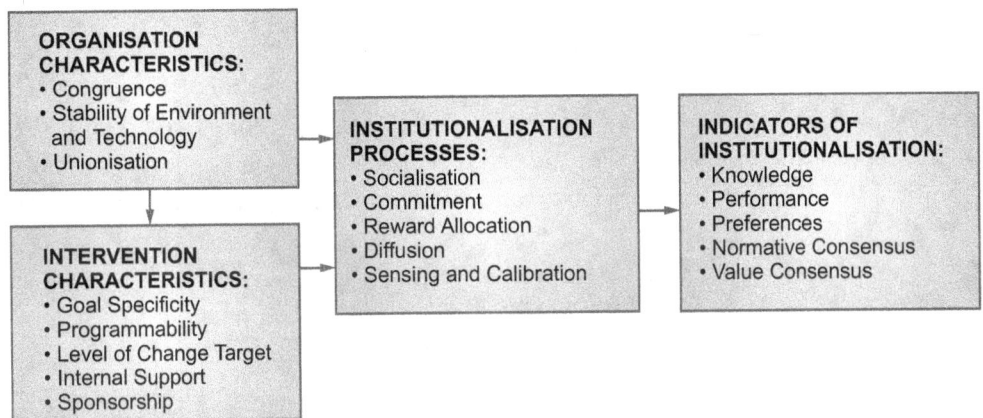

**Fig. 3.9: Institutionalisation Framework**

2.  **Stability of Environment and Technology:** This involves the degree to which the organisation's environment and technology are changing. The persistence of change is favoured when environments are stable. Under these conditions, it makes sense to embed the change in an organisation's culture and organisation design processes. On the other hand, volatile demand for the firm's products or services can lead to reductions in personnel that may change the composition of the groups involved in the intervention or bring new members on board at a rate faster than they can be socialised effectively.

3.  **Unionisation:** Implementation of interventions may be more difficult in unionised settings, especially if the changes affect union contract issues, such as salary and fringe benefits, job design, and employee flexibility. For example, a rigid union contract can make it difficult to merge several job classifications into one, as might be required to increase task variety in a job enrichment program. It is important to emphasise, however, that unions can be a powerful force for promoting change, particularly when a good relationship exists between union and management.

**Intervention Characteristics**

The following five major features of OD interventions can affect institutionalisation processes:

1. **Goal Specificity:** This involves the extent to which intervention goals are specific rather than broad. Specificity of goals helps direct socialising activities (for example, training and orienting new members) to particular behaviours required to implement the intervention. It also helps operationalise the new behaviours so that rewards can be linked clearly to them. For example, an intervention aimed only at increasing product quality is likely to be more focused and readily put into operation than a change program intended to improve quality, quantity, safety, absenteeism, and employee development.

2. **Programmability:** This involves the degree to which the changes can be programmed or the extent to which the different intervention characteristics can be specified clearly in advance to enable socialisation, commitment, and reward allocation. For example, job enrichment specifies three targets of change: employee discretion, task variety, and feedback. The change program can be planned and designed to promote those specific features.

3. **Level of Change Target:** This concerns the extent to which the change target is the total organisation, rather than a department or small work group. Each level of organisation has facilitators and inhibitors of persistence. Departmental and group change are susceptible to countervailing forces from others in the organisation. These can reduce the diffusion of the intervention and lower its ability to impact organisation effectiveness. However, this does not preclude institutionalising the change within a department that successfully insulates itself from the rest of the organisation. Such insulation often manifests itself as a subculture within the organisation. Targeting the intervention toward wider segments of the organisation, on the other hand, can also help or hinder change persistence. A shared belief about the intervention's value can be a powerful incentive to maintain the change, and promoting a consensus across organisational departments exposed to the change can facilitate institutionalisation. But targeting the larger system also can inhibit institutionalisation. The intervention can become mired in political resistance because of the "not invented here" syndrome or because powerful constituencies oppose it.

4. **Internal Support:** This refers to the degree to which there is an internal support system to guide the change process. Internal support, typically provided by an internal consultant, can gain commitment for the changes and help organisation members implement them. External consultants also can provide support, especially on a temporary basis during the early stages of implementation. For example, in many interventions aimed at implementing high-involvement organisations, both external and internal consultants provide change support. The external consultant typically brings expertise on organisational design and trains members to implement

the design. The internal consultant generally helps members relate to other organisational units, resolve conflicts, and legitimize the change activities within the organisation.

5. **Sponsorship:** This concerns the presence of a powerful sponsor who can initiate, allocate, and legitimise resources for the intervention. Sponsors must come from levels in the organisation high enough to control appropriate resources, and they must have the visibility and power to nurture the intervention and see that it remains viable. There are many examples of OD interventions that persisted for several years and then collapsed abruptly when the sponsor, usually a top administrator, left the organisation. There also are numerous examples of middle managers withdrawing support for interventions because top management did not include them in the change program.

## Institutionalisation Processes

The following five institutionalisation processes that can directly affect the degree to which OD interventions are institutionalised:

1. **Socialisation:** This concerns the transmission of information about beliefs, preferences, norms, and values with respect to the intervention. Because implementation of OD interventions generally involves considerable learning and experimentation, a continual process of socialisation is necessary to promote persistence of the change program. Organisation members must focus attention on the evolving nature of the intervention and its ongoing meaning. They must communicate this information to other employees, especially new members of the organisation. Transmission of information about the intervention helps bring new members onboard and allows participants to reaffirm the beliefs, norms, and values underlying the intervention. For example, employee involvement programmes often include initial transmission of information about the intervention, as well as retraining of existing participants and training of new members. Such processes are intended to promote persistence of the programme as new behaviours are learned and new members introduced.

2. **Commitment:** This binds people to behaviours associated with the intervention. It includes initial commitment to the program, as well as recommitment over time. Opportunities for commitment should allow people to select the necessary behaviours freely, explicitly, and publicly. These conditions favour high commitment and can promote stability of the new behaviours. Commitment should come from several organisational levels, including the employees directly involved and the middle and upper managers who can support or thwart the intervention. In many early employee involvement programmes, for example, attention was directed at gaining workers' commitment to such programmes. Unfortunately, middle managers were often ignored and considerable management resistance to the interventions resulted.

3.  **Reward Allocation:** This involves linking rewards to the new behaviours required by an intervention. Organisational rewards can enhance the persistence of changes in at least two ways. First, a combination of intrinsic and extrinsic rewards can reinforce new behaviours. Intrinsic rewards are internal and derive from the opportunities for challenge, development, and accomplishment found in the work. When interventions provide these opportunities, motivation to perform should persist. This behaviour can be further reinforced by providing extrinsic rewards, such as money, for increased contributions. Because the value of extrinsic rewards tends to diminish over time, it may be necessary to revise the reward system to maintain high levels of desired behaviours. Second, new behaviours will persist to the extent that rewards are perceived as equitable by employees. When new behaviours are fairly compensated, people are likely to develop preferences for those behaviours. Over time, those preferences should lead to normative and value consensus about the appropriateness of the intervention. For example, many employee involvement programmes fail to persist because employees feel that their increased contributions to organisational improvements are unfairly rewarded. This is especially true for interventions relying exclusively on intrinsic rewards. People argue that an intervention that provides opportunities for intrinsic rewards also should provide greater pay or extrinsic rewards for higher levels of contribution to the organisation.

4.  **Diffusion:** This refers to the process of transferring changes from one system to another. Diffusion facilitates institutionalisation by providing a wider organisational base to support the new behaviours. Many interventions fail to persist because they run counter to the values, purpose, or identity of the larger organisation. Rather than support the intervention, the larger organisation rejects the changes and often puts pressure on the change target to revert to old behaviours. Diffusion of a change to other organisational units reduces this counter-implementation force. It tends to lock in behaviours by providing normative consensus from other parts of the organisation. Moreover, the act of transmitting institutionalised behaviours to other systems reinforces commitment to the changes.

5.  **Sensing and Calibration:** This involves detecting deviations from desired intervention behaviours and taking corrective action. Institutionalised behaviours invariably encounter destabilizing forces, such as changes in the environment, new technologies, and pressures from other departments to nullify changes. These factors cause some variation in performances, preferences, norms, and values. To detect this variation and take corrective actions, organisations must have some sensing mechanism. Sensing mechanisms, such as implementation feedback, provide information about the occurrence of deviations. This knowledge can then initiate corrective actions to ensure that behaviours are more in line with the intervention. For example, if a high level of job discretion associated with a job enrichment

intervention does not persist, information about this problem might initiate corrective actions, such as renewed attempts to socialize people or to gain commitment to the intervention.

## Indicators of Institutionalisation

Institutionalisation is not an all-or-nothing concept but reflects degrees of persistence in a change. The extent to which the following factors are present or absent indicates the degree of institutionalisation:

1. **Knowledge:** This involves the extent to which organisation members have knowledge of the behaviours associated with an intervention. It is concerned with whether members know enough to perform the behaviours and to recognise the consequences of that performance. For example, job enrichment includes a number of new behaviours, such as performing a greater variety of tasks, analysing information about task performance, and making decisions about work methods and plans.

2. **Performance:** This is concerned with the degree to which intervention behaviours are actually performed. It may be measured by counting the proportion of relevant people performing the behaviours. For example, 60% of the employees in a particular work unit might be performing the job enrichment behaviours described above. Another measure of performance is the frequency with which the new behaviours are performed. In assessing frequency, it is important to account for different variations of the same essential behaviour, as well as highly institutionalised behaviours that need to be performed only infrequently.

3. **Preferences:** This involves the degree to which organisation members privately accept the organisational changes. This contrasts with acceptance based primarily on organisational sanctions or group pressures. Private acceptance usually is reflected in people's positive attitudes toward the changes and can be measured by the direction and intensity of those attitudes across the members of the work unit receiving the intervention. For example, a questionnaire assessing members' perceptions of a job enrichment program might show that most employees have a strong positive attitude toward making decisions, analysing feedback, and performing a variety of tasks.

4. **Normative Consensus:** This focuses on the extent to which people agree about the appropriateness of the organisational changes. This indicator of institutionalisation reflects how fully changes have become part of the normative structure of the organisation. Changes persist to the degree members feel that they should support them. For example, a job enrichment program would become institutionalised to the extent that employees support it and see it as appropriate to organisational functioning.

5. **Value Consensus:** This is concerned with social consensus on values relevant to the organisational changes. Values are beliefs about how people ought or ought not to behave. They are abstractions from more specific norms. Job enrichment, for example, is based on values promoting employee self-control and responsibility. Different behaviours associated with job enrichment, such as making decisions and performing a variety of tasks, would persist to the extent that employees widely share values of self-control and responsibility.

## Points to Remember

- **Organisation development** can be taken as a process of changing people and other related aspects of an organisation. It consists of many sub-processes or steps.
- The individual or group that undertakes the task of initiating and managing change in an organisation is known as a change agent.
- **Types of Change Agent:**
  1. Outside Pressure Type
  2. People-Change-Technology Type
  3. Analysis-for-the-Top Type
  4. Organisation-Development Type
- **Change Agent Roles**
  1. Consulting
  2. Training
  3. Research
- **Characteristics of Successful Change Agent**
  1. Hemophily
  2. Empathy
  3. Linkage
  4. Proximity
  5. Structuring
  6. Capacity
  7. Openness
  8. Reward
  9. Energy
  10. Synergy
- **Process of Organisational Development**
  1. Entering and Contracting
  2. Diagnosing Organisations, Groups and Individual Jobs

3.  Collecting and Analysing Diagnostic Information
4.  Feeding back Diagnostic Information
5.  Designing Interventions
6.  Managing Change
7.  Evaluating and Institutionalising Intervention

## Questions for Discussion

1.  Discuss briefly the steps involved in the process of organisational development.
2.  Describe the role of change agent in organisational development.
3.  What are the characteristics of a change agent?
4.  Explain the types of change agent.
5.  Describe the comprehensive model of diagnosing organisational system.
6.  Discuss the characteristics of effective feedback data for organisational development process.

✱✱✱

*Chapter* **4**...

# Human Process Interventions

## Contents ...

## 4.1 Introduction

Human process interventions derive mainly from the disciplines of psychology and social psychology and the applied fields of groups dynamic and human relations". **DeSimone** and **Werner** defined that *"Human process-based interventions are directed at improving interpersonal, intragroup and intergroup relation"*. Human process includes the following numerous steps such as: Process consultation, third –party interventions, team building, organisation confrontation meeting, intergroup relations interventions and large group intervention. OD programmes focused more on interpersonal dynamics and social relation. The purpose of the change is to make the company achieve the full potential of productivity and profitability, to be able to solve its own problems. According to Neumann, Kellner, Shepherd human process interventions focus on improving communication, interaction and leadership, gain the skills and understanding to identify, resolve conflicts and solve problem through process consultation and Third-party intervention.

Human Process Interventions also follow team building interventions through helps the development of organisational success. Including team building knowledge to solve problems in the organisation, team building help team members feel less pressure, devise solution to problem. Team buildings also need to trust and support members in order to help members more creative ideas to help complete the group's task, increase understanding, improvement and increased ability about interpersonal behaviour.

## 4.2 Types of Human Process Interventions

These interventions are aimed at the social processes occurring within organisations (Cummings and Worley 1997). These can be of two types:

*   Interpersonal and group process approaches, for example, T-groups, process consultation, third party interventions, team building and the like.
*   Organisation process approaches, for example, organisation confrontation meeting, inter-group relations interventions, large group interventions, etc.

## 4.3 Interpersonal and Group Process Approaches

Process Interventions are in OD skill used by OD practitioners, whether managers or OD professions, to help work groups become more effective. The purpose of process interventions is to help the work group become more aware of the way it operates and the way its members work with one another. The work group uses this knowledge to develop its own problem-solving ability. Process interventions, then, aim at helping the work group to become more aware of its own processes, including the way it operates, and uses this knowledge to solve its own problems.

The manager practicing process intervention observes individuals and teams in action and helps them learn to diagnose and solve their own problems. The manager refrains from telling them how to solve their problems but instead asks questions, focuses their attention on how they are working together, teaches or provides resources where necessary and listens. The major advantages is that teams becomes more independent to solve problems.

Now we will discuss change programmes relating to interpersonal relations and group dynamics. These change programmes are among the earliest ones devised in OD and represent attempts to improve people's working relationships with one another.

The interventions are aimed at helping group members assess their interactions are devise more effective ways of working together. These interventions represent a basic skill requirement for an OD practitioner.

Interpersonal relationships and group dynamics, involve four types of interventions:

1.   T-group.
2.   Process consultation.
3.   Third-party intervention.
4.   Team building.

## 4.3.1 T-Group or Sensitivity Training

T-Group training emphasises learning by means of an unstructured group experience. It attempts to apply behavioural science concepts in the design and conduct of the experiences which the members of the group undergo. The origin of T-Group (T stands for training) is relatively recent. It was in 1947 that National Training Laboratory in the US began pioneering work in the development of T-Group training. In contrast to other training techniques, T-Group training is more concerned with the dynamics of inter-personal relationships in the "here and now" experiences of group members in a laboratory situations. The emphasis is on learning about group dynamics, social change theory and human interaction patterns - all the behavioural science phenomena which provide the framework for managerial decisions and actions. Managers are trained in small face-to-face discussion groups to be more sensitive to the underlying processes of individual and group behaviour.

The objective of this training method is to gain insight and to increase one's sensitivity to:

- One's own behaviour.
- The behaviour of others.
- The effect of one's own behaviour on others.
- Factors that help or hinder group interaction and effectiveness.

Each T-Group consists of about 10-15 members in a learning group who continue to meet throughout the course. The group is basically unstructured, without any agenda or specific subject for discussion or a clearly defined leader. It remains the focus of the group's emotional experiences and intra-group transactions. The trainer acts as a facilitator or climate setter. **Chris Argyris** defines T-Group Training as a group experiences designed to provide maximum opportunity for the individuals involved to expose their behaviour, give and receive feedback, experiment with new behaviours and develop a permanent awareness and acceptance of themselves and others.

All T-Groups discuss such issues as: what to do; how to spend the time; how to distribute power, control and influence; how to develop standards and a climate which permits maximum learning; how to develop group goals and a sense of group progress and how to keep the group process within bounds. In the early stages of laboratory experience, the group may express considerable hostility towards the trainer and in some situations this hostility may turn inward towards one of the group members.

The T-Group, as a vehicle for learning, utilises:

(a) Activities involving interaction between the individuals.

(b) Systematic feedback and analysis of information regarding what happened in the current situation.

(c)   Situations confronted by the group members for which old ways of behaving do not provide adequate answers and hence the need for 'new behaviour'.

(d)   Reformulation of concepts and values based on an analysis of the participant's current experiences.

**Benne, Bradford and Ronald Lippitt** list the goals of the laboratory method as follows:

1.   One hoped for outcome for the participant is increased awareness of and sensitivity to emotional reactions and expression in himself and in others.

2.   Another desired objective is greater ability to perceive and to learn from the consequences of his actions through attention to feelings, his own and others. Emphasis is placed on the development of sensitivity to cues furnished by the behaviour of others and ability to utilise "feedback" in understanding his own behaviour.

3.   The staff also attempts to stimulate the clarification and development of personal values and goals consonant with a democratic and scientific approach to problems and personal decision and action.

4.   Another objective is the development of concepts and theoretical insights which will serve as tools in linking personal values, goals and intention to actions consistent with these inner factors and with the requirements of the situation. One important source of valid concepts is the findings and methodologies of the behavioural sciences.

5.   All laboratory programmes foster the achievement of behavioural effectiveness in transactions with one's environment. The learning of concepts, the setting of goals, the clarification of values and even the achievement of valid insight into self, are sometimes far ahead of the development of the performance skills necessary to expression in actual social transactions. For this reason, laboratory programmes normally focus on the development of behavioural skills to support better integration of interactions and actions.

The T-Group is a powerful learning laboratory where individuals gain insights into the meaning and consequences of their own behaviour, the meaning and consequences of others behaviours and the dynamic and processes of group behaviour. These insights are coupled with growth of skills in diagnosing and taking more effective interpersonal and group action. Thus, the T-Group can give individuals the basic skills necessary for more competent action taking in the organisation.

Uses of T-Group relative to OD are varied, but they are particularly appropriate to introducing key members of the organisation to group and interpersonal process issues and for enhancing basic skills relevant to group and interpersonal dynamics. The most frequently used T-Group format is the "stranger" lab composed of people from a variety of organisations. For example, a one-week T-Group experience might involve three trainers and 30-36 participants, all strangers to each other at the beginning of the lab.

Thus, T-Group learning provides numerous insights and skills of importance to successful OD efforts and to effective organisation functioning.

## 4.3.2 Process Consultation

This intervention focuses on interpersonal relationships and social dynamics occurring in work groups. A process consultant helps group members diagnose group functioning and devise appropriate solutions to process problems, such as dysfunctional conflicts, poor communication and effective norms. The aim is to help members gain the necessary skills and to identify and solve problems themselves.

Process consulting requires the OD Practitioner to analyse a business and figures out strategies for improving its day-to-day operations and overall functioning. Succeeding in this diagnostic usually requires an individual, who is adept at problem solving, is creative and has excellent interpersonal skills. Some common responsibilities of this job include observing business operations, identifying problem areas, developing practical solutions, executing changes and assisting employees throughout the process. The consulting process involves the practitioner meeting the members of the department and work teams observing the interaction, problem identification skills, solving procedures etc. He feeds back the team with the information collected through observations, coaches and counsels individuals and groups in moulding their behaviour.

Before improvements can begin, it's important for a OD Practitioner to first observe a business's operations. This practice typically involves things like monitoring employee performance, investigating organisational habits and determining overall efficiency. In addition, an individual might get feedback from both employees and supervisors to get a feel for a business. After a period of observation, the OD practitioner will need to identify the primary problem areas of a business. For example, he might decide that a company's warehouse is disorganised, and that getting products from shelves is unnecessarily difficult. In another instance, he might discover that ineffective employee scheduling is hurting a company's production. Being effective at this job requires a person to find specific flaws and take note of them.

1. **Process Identification:** Many companies think they know their processes — manufacturing, sales, accounting, building services. But it is just this solo mentality that causes processes to lose their customer-centric approach. Instead of defining processes based on the company's understanding, they must be defined by the customer's understanding. Walking through customer experiences helps the reviewer identify those trigger points that can make or break success. These then form the basis for process identification.

2.  **Information Gathering:** There is a large volume of information that should be obtained before trying to learn the intricacies of a process. Primary among these is identifying who the true process owners are — the ones who can effect change. Their buy-in and agreement throughout the analysis is paramount. Additional information that should be obtained includes the objectives of the process, risks to the process, key controls over those risks, and measures of success for the process.

3.  **Process Mapping:** This involves sitting with each employee and having him or her describe what it is they do. This information is recorded using a sticky-note method. Each step in the process is recorded on a sticky-note and built in front of the individual completing the work. This allows them to interactively ensure the final map matches their understanding of their work. The final process maps are developed using flowcharting software. Time flows down the page, and each individual involved is represented by a separate column. In this manner, a simple map can result from a complicated process.

4.  **Analysis:**   Analysis must really occur throughout the review. While defining the processes, the reviewer may determine that objectives are not in line with the processes in place. In gathering information, it may become apparent that measures of success do not correspond to department objectives. These are just some of the examples of ongoing analysis. However, there are some specific examples of analysis that can be completed once maps are done. These include identifying unnecessary approvals, isolating rework, removing duplicate forms, eliminating useless holdfiles, and investigating decision requirements that lead to no discernable result. In and of them, no single incident is necessarily wrong. But each must be analysed in the context of the map to ensure it supports the objectives.  When done correctly, Business Process Mapping should lead everyone to a better understanding of what the company is trying to achieve, a realigned sense of purpose, and a number of suggestions that can streamline operations while increasing customer satisfaction.

### 4.3.3 Third-Party Intervention

This change method is a form of process consultation aimed at dysfunctional interpersonal relations in organisations. Interpersonal conflict may derive from substantive issues, such as disputes over work methods or from interpersonal issues, such as miscommunication. The third-party intervener helps people resolve conflicts through such methods as problem solving, bargaining and conciliation.

Third-party intervention focuses on conflicts arising between two or more people within the same organisation. Conflict is inherent in groups and organisations and can arise from a variety of sources, include differences in personality, task orientation, and perceptions among group members, as well as competition for scarce resources. To emphasise that conflict is neither good nor bad per se is important.

Conflict can enhance motivation and innovation and lead to greater understanding of ideas and views. On the other hand, it can prevent people from working together constructively, destroying necessary task interactions among group members. Consequently, third-party intervention is used primarily in situations in which conflicts significantly disrupts necessary task   interactions and work relationships among members.

Third-party intervention varies considerably depending on the kind of issues underlying the conflict.

Conflict can arise over substantive issues, such as work methods, pay rates, and conditions of employment; or it can emerge from interpersonal issues, such as personalities and misperceptions. When applied to substantive issues, conflict resolution interventions often involve resolving labour-management disputes through arbitration and mediation. The methods used in such substantive interventions require considerable training and expertise in law and labour relations and generally are not considered part of OD practice. For example, when union and management representatives cannot resolve a joint problem, they can call upon the Federal Mediation and Conciliation Service to help them resolve the conflict. In addition, "alternative dispute resolution" (ADR) practices increasingly are offered in lieu of more expensive and time-consuming court trials. Conflicts also may arise at the boundaries of the organisation, such as between suppliers and the company or between a company and a public policy agency.

When conflict involves interpersonal issues, however, OD has developed approaches that help control and resolve it. These third- party interventions help the parties interact with each other directly, facilitating their party diagnosis of the conflict and how to resolve it. That ability to facilitate conflict resolution is a basic skill in OD and applies to all of the process interventions. Consultants, for example, frequently help organisation members resolve interpersonal conflicts that invariably arise during process consultation and team building.

Third-party consultation interventions cannot resolve all interpersonal conflicts in organisations, nor should they. Many times, interpersonal conflicts are not severe or disruptive enough to warrant attention.

At other times, they imply may burn themselves out. Evidence also suggests that other methods may be more appropriate under certain conditions. For example, managers tend to control the process and outcomes of conflict resolution actively when they are under heavy time pressures, when the disputants are not expected to work together in the future, and when the resolution of the dispute has a broad impact on the organisation. Under those conditions, the third party may resolve the conflict unilaterally with little input from the conflicting parties.

## 4.3.4 Team Building

Team development and group processes interventions aim at improving different aspects of a group performance, such as goal setting, development of interpersonal relations among team members, role clarification and analysis, decision making, problem solving, and communities of practice, among other. One of the most important objectives of team building interventions relies on improving interdependency of team members. The underlying premise is that the aggregated value of the team is much greater than any individual. According to **Robbins**, *"Team building is applicable where group activities are interdependent. The objective is to improve the coordination efforts of members, which will result in increasing the team's performance".*

The use of teams in organisations is not a new phenomenon, but use of and attention to work teams and their functioning has increased over the past several decades. Organisations have implemented new forms of teams, such as self-directed work teams, virtual teams and cross-functional teams. These new types of teams combined with the complexity of work today frequently requires increased collaboration and problem solving in a global environment, mean that organisations rely heavily on teams for their success and must devote attention to the effectiveness of their teams. The effective functioning of groups and teams is central to the effective functioning of organisations. In addition, teams not only play a central role in an organisation's effectiveness, but they also play a central role in the accomplishment and implementation of organisation change such as shifts in strategy. Leaders often fail to pay much attention to team effectiveness not knowing how to develop the team or assuming that the team will work things out on its own.

Many practitioners and scholars find it instructive to distinguish between a group and a team. **Katzenbach and Smith** define a team as *"a small number of people with complementary skills who are committed to a common purpose, performance goals, and approach for which they hold themselves mutually accountable".* Others stress the importance of member interdependence on a team, noting that team members must rely on each other and feel accountable to one another in the accomplishment of their goals to be considered a team. A group might consist of a large number of individuals, all of whom perform the same general job task but do not count on other members in the accomplishment of individual tasks.

### Characteristics of Successful Teams:

Commonly held **characteristics** of teams include the following:

- Members participate in decision-making and setting goals.
- Members communicate frequently with one another in the accomplishment of team tasks.
- The team has a defined and recognised identity by others in the organisation, outside the team.
- Members have defined roles and they recognise how these roles interrelate.

**Effective Teams**

Much work has been done by researchers to identify the characteristics that distinguish high-performing, effective teams. In an extensive survey of different types of teams in different types of organisation environments and circumstances, **Larson** and **LaFasto** conducted detailed interviews of members of high-performing executive teams, project teams, sports teams, government and military teams. They concluded that eight characteristics set the successful teams apart :

1.  **A clear, evaluating goal:** That is, the goal is understood and seen as challenging to team members**.**

2.  **A result driven structure:** Team members must have clear roles, effective communication processes, and an ability to use available data to evaluate progress and take corrective action when necessary. Members must also understand how their roles interrelate.

3.  **Competent members:** The team must comprise of members with the right technical knowledge and interpersonal skills to contribute to the team's goal.

4.  **Unified commitment:** Team members must be willing to dedicate efforts and energy to the team.

5.  **A collaborative climate:** The team must develop a climate of trust in one another in order to collaborate.

6.  **Standards of excellence:** High-performing teams have high standards for individual performance and members feel pressure to achieve.

7.  **External support and recognition:** Teams need external rewards but also support in the form of resources necessary for the team to accomplish its work.

8.  **Principled leadership:** Leaders provide the necessary motivation and alignment to complete the team's work.

Glenn Parker also looked at the characteristics of effective teams and developed a similar list as under:

**Characteristics of Effective Teams:**

1.  **Clear purpose:** Defined and accepted vision, mission, goal or task and an action plan.

2.  **Informality:** Informal, comfortable and relaxed.

3.  **Participation:** Much discussion with everyone encouraged to participate.

4.  **Listening:** Use of effective listing techniques such as questioning, paraphrasing and summarising.

5.  **Civilised disagreement:** Team is comfortable with disagreement, does not avoid, smooth over, or suppress conflict.

6.  **Consensus decision making:** Substantial agreement through thorough discussion, avoidance of voting.

7.  **Open communication:** Feelings seen as legitimate, few hidden agendas.

8.  **Clear roles and work assignments:** Clear expectations and work evenly divided.

9.  **Shared leadership:** In addition to a formal leader, everyone shares in effective leadership behaviours.

10. **External relations:** The team pays attention to developing outside relationships, resources, credibility.

11. **Style diversity:** Team has broad spectrum of group process and task skills.

12. **Self-assessment:** Periodic examination of how well the team is functioning.

High-performance teams have the same characteristics but to a higher degree. Strong personal commitment to each other, commitment to the others growth and success, distinguishes high-performance teams from effective teams.

## Stages of Team Development

Team development programmes proactively encourage teams to develop as healthier groups. These programmes "employ a training approach to team building that relies heavily on the use of team exercise and simulations". A team development intervention might help a new team with start-up needs. For existing teams, it might help them to move from stage one to stage two of the model discussed below. Team development programmes often work with groups throughout the group process so that the team develops in a healthy way. There are often opportunities to allow healthy groups to develop even more effective patterns.

1.  **Forming:** Team members explore initial interactions with one another in an orientation period as they begin to build relationships. There is generally a low level of trust and high anxiety and confusion about the group's purpose and objectives. There are likely to be conversations about expectations, group rules and structures. Communication may be guarded, exploratory and cautious. Disagreement is rarely expressed. The group is highly dependent on the team leader, who is usually unchallenged and members generally consent to what the leader says.

2.  **Storming:** Members begin to express disagreements with one another and with the leader as members feel more comfortable and safe with the team. Emotions may rise high as members have conflicts over goals, roles or group values. Group cohesion may give way to subgroups or coalitions. Previously agreed-to group norms or rules may be broken. Members may try to negotiate the conflicts, work through them and move on to the next stage, or they may become held up in unhealthy conflict.

3.  **Norming:** The groups attempt to manage some of its conflicts by coming to agreement on group norms, roles, goals and more. There is increased cohesion and a return

to the harmonious climate of the first stage, but with increased trust, cooperation and commitment. The team generally begins to focus again on task achievement with less dependency on the leader. Conflict management techniques are now used effectively, and individuals feel free to express their opinions.

4.    **Performing:** team members find synergy and begin to find repeated and successful ways of interacting to achieve group goals. Team members have clarity and agreement on goals, roles and working processes. The team begins to see a period of high productivity and accomplishment of their objectives as energy is devoted to work tasks. The team monitors its own results and evaluates its own effectiveness, discussing problems and identifying opportunities for improvement. Team leaders more frequently delegate or leave routine decisions to the groups.

5.    **Adjourning:** As the team's work is completed, the team may disband or members may leave.

---

**Case 4.1 :** Dyer lists 12 signs that a team intervention is necessary :

- Loss of production or unit productivity.
- Increase of grievances or complaints from the staff.
- Evidence of conflicts or hostility among staff members.
- Confusion about assignments, missed signals and unclear relationships.
- Decisions misunderstood or not carried through properly.
- Apathy and general lack of interest or involvement of staff members.
- Lack of initiation, imagination, innovative action taken for solving complex problems.
- Ineffective staff meetings, low participation, minimal effective decisions.
- Slow start-up of a new group that needs to develop quickly into a working team.
- High dependency on or negative response to the manager or team leader.
- Complaints from users or customers about quality of service.
- Continued unaccounted increase of costs.

---

**Techniques and Exercises Used in Team Building**

A number of techniques and exercises are used in team building to facilitate team performance and to address specific problematic issues. They are useful and powerful ways to structure the team's activities and energies in order to achieve understanding of the issues and to take corrective actions. Before using these techniques, a careful diagnosis should be made to ensure that the technique is appropriate. Team-building sessions often include many of these techniques and exercises.

### 1. Role Analysis

The Role Analysis Technique intervention is designed to clarify role expectations and obligations of team members to improve team effectiveness. Ishwar Dayal and John M. Thomas developed a technique for clarifying the roles of the top management of a new organisation in India. This technique is particularly applicable for new teams, but it may also be helpful in established teams where role ambiguity or confusion exists.

In a structured series of steps, role incumbents, in conjunction with team members define and delineate role requirements. The role being defined is called the 'focal role'. In a new organisation it may be desirable to conduct a role analysis for each of the major roles.

**Step 1:** The **first step** consists of an analysis of the focal role initiated by the focal role individual. The role, its place in the organisation, the rationale for its existence and its place in achieving overall organisation goals are examined along with the specific duties of the office. The specific duties and behaviours are listed on a chalkboard and are discussed by the entire team. Behaviours are added and deleted until the group and the role incumbent are satisfied that they have defined the role completely.

Team members are interdependent with interrelating work activities, they can often find themselves in a frustrating position of not knowing how the various pieces of work fit together to achieve the overall team objectives. Whether team members have worked together at length or are just starting, member roles are the frequent areas of confusion. Consider the following common situations:

- Members may not be clear about one another's assignments, so they do not know whom to approach with a question or problem.
- There may be overlapping work, with multiple team members performing the same activities.
- There may be work necessary to accomplish that no team member is performing.
- There may be confusion about how the work contributes to the team's goals.
- The team may have evolved the new vision, purpose or strategy but old roles still remain.
- The team may have no process for assigning the work to a new team member.
- There may be frustrations about the equitable distribution of work like who gets the good assignments, who gets too many or too few assignments.
- The team leader may assign multiple people to similar activities, leading team members to wonder who is truly responsible for the task, or whether the tasks relate to all.

The result can be team members who fight for the same work while other work gets lost and inevitable last-minute crises that come about because of the confusion. These roles related challenges can be categorised into several types of role problems that often occur in teams.

**Step 2:** Next, the completed flip charts are placed around a room and every team members reads each flip chart.

**Step 3:** Each team member writes a list on a separate piece of notebook paper with what he or she wants any other team member to do (a) more of, (b) less of, or (c) keep doing the same. Every team member comments on each other team member's role.

**Step 4:** The lists are sorted so that each team member has a list completed for his or her role by every other member. These may be written on flip charts posted publicly for all to read or they may simply be handed out to each person. Team members can then meet in pairs or as a whole team to discuss their lists and negotiate what they would like each other to keep doing or to do differently. It is in this step where the value of the exercise becomes more meaningful, with members usually needing to compromise and be willing to change in at least some small degree. As Harrison puts it "quid pro quo can be offered in return for a desired behaviour change, there is little point in having a discussion about it". Members will thus learn how to express their own needs from one another and negotiate how or whether those needs can be fulfilled. Harrison also suggests that following a role negotiations exercise, team members try to keep to the negotiated agreements they have made for at least a short time, but that if they do not work, they should try to renegotiate them. Over time, he believes, the team will learn how to do this negotiation as part of its ongoing work activity.

Collaborative role analysis and definition by the entire work group not only clarifies who is to do what but ensures commitment to the role once it has been clarified.

## 2. Role Negotiations

When the causes of team ineffectiveness are based on people's behaviours that they are unwilling to change because it would mean a loss of power or influence to the individual, a technique developed by Roger Harrison called "role negotiation" can often be used to great advantage.

"Role negotiation intervenes directly in the relationships of power, authority and influence within the group. The change effort is directed at the work relationships among members. It avoids probing into the likes and dislikes of members for one another and their personal feelings about one another."

Harrison states that the techniques rests on one basic assumption : "Most people prefer a fair negotiated settlement to a state of unresolved conflict and they are willing to invest some time and make some concessions in order to achieve a solution."

Role negotiations require an environment of openness and safety, comfort in expressing disagreement and getting beyond disagreement, the ability to express one's wants and needs and mutual commitment to each other and to the group. Lest it sound too simple: The analysis, charting and negotiation of member roles on a team is not simply a matter of documenting who will do what, as this process intervention may appear. Complex identity matters and political struggles are at play when members negotiate responsibilities. If Mr. Rakesh used to be responsible for reviewing all mechanical engineering designs for the company's products and the team decides that everyone will share that action and he now will begin to work more closely with suppliers only on designs he reviewed, he may feel that he has lost a part of professional identity. He may feel like he has been demoted or that he is no longer as significant a contributor as he once was. Consequently, change agents who implement role analysis and clarification interventions will be more successful if they are aware of and sensitive to the complexities of managing personal impacts and transitions.

The role negotiation technique usually takes at least one day to conduct. The steps of the technique are outlined by Harrison.

**Step 1: Contract Setting:** Here the consultant sets the climate and establishes the ground rules: we are looking at work behaviours, not feeling about people. Be specific in stating what an individual wants others to do more of or do better or to do less of or stop doing or remain unchanged. All expectations and demands must be written. No one is to agree to change any behaviour unless there is a quid pro quo in which the other must agree to a change also. The session will consist of individuals negotiating with each other to arrive at a written contract of what behaviours each will change.

**Step 2: Issue Diagnosis:** Individuals think about how their own effectiveness can be improved if others change their work behaviours. Then each person fills out an Issue Diagnosis Form for every other person in the group. On this form the individual states what he or she would like the other to do more of, do less of, or maintain unchanged. These messages are then exchanged among all members and the messages received by each person are written on a chalkboard or newsprint for all to see.

**Step 3: Influence Trade or Negotiation Period:** In which two individuals also discuss the most important behaviour changes they want from the other and the changes they are willing to make themselves. A quid pro quo is required in the step : each person must give something in order to get something. Often this step is demonstrated by two individuals with the rest of the group watching. Then the group breaks into negotiating pairs. The negotiation process consists of parties making contingent offers to one another such as "If you do X, I will do Y." The negotiation ends when all parties are satisfied that they will receive a reasonable return for whatever they are agreeing to give. All agreements are written, with each party having a copy. The influence trade step is concluded when all the negotiated agreements have been made and written down.

Harrison's role negotiation technique is an effective way of bringing about positive improvement in a situation where power and influence issues are working to maintain an unsatisfactory status quo.

### 3. Appreciation and Concerns Exercise

The appreciation and concern exercise may be appropriate if interview data suggest that one of the deficiencies in the interactions of members of a group is lack of expression of appreciation and that another deficiency is the avoidance of confronting concerns and irritations. Various versions of the appreciations and concerns exercise can be used, it is conducted as follows:

(a) The facilitator asks each member of the group to jot down one or two appreciations for each member of the group.

(b) Each member is also asked to jot down one or two minor irritations or concerns relative to each person that may be interfering with communications, getting the work done effectively and so on.

(c) Along with the assignment, the facilitator may make some suggestions such as: "you are the judge of which concerns to raise – will it be helpful to the relationship? Can the person do anything about it? Would it be better to talk privately with the person? On the positive side, sometimes raising concerns in a team setting can provide an opportunity for others to validate what is being perceived or to provide another perspective. By the way, there will be plenty of time to work things through if there are any misunderstandings."

(d) Someone is asked to volunteer to be the first person to listen to members of the group. Each group member mentions both the appreciations and concerns about the volunteer who hears from all of the group members before responding, with the exception that questions of clarification are encouraged after each person mentions his or her items.

(e) Each group member listens in turn, either through volunteering to the next or through the simple procedure of rotating clockwise or counter clockwise from the first person.

Each member of the group puts his or her name on the top of the sheet of flip-chart paper and makes two column headings: Appreciations and Concerns. Sheets are taped to the walls and with a marking pen each member writes appreciation and concerns on each sheet. Once the writing is finished a volunteer is asked to display his or her sheet and read the items aloud to the group. This version is usually productive since it permits more face-to-face interaction.

When lack of appreciation is a much more serious deficiency than concerns, focusing solely on appreciations can be a powerful and positive intervention in the life of the group. When the concerns segment is used, a mini-lecture from the facilitator on the nature of constructive feedback is desirable. Whenever a substantial conflict exists within the group a more structured exercise such as the role negotiation techniques is likely to be more appropriate.

### 4. Interdependency

An interdependency exercise is a useful intervention if team members have expressed a desire to improve cooperation among themselves and among their units. This exercise is also useful for assisting people in getting better acquainted in surfacing problems that may be latent and not previously examined and in providing useful information about current challenges being faced in others areas of responsibility.

The interdependency exercise can be structured as follows – it works well with approximately ten people, but can become too cumbersome and time consuming if more than that number is involved. For instance, if top ten people of an organisation or a division of the organisation are present:

(a) Two straight lines of five persons each are formed with each line facing each other. Each person is seated facing the other person, but with pairs of people seated far enough apart to minimise distractions. Thus, persons 1, 2, 3, 4 and 5 will be seated facing persons 6, 7, 8, 9 and 10. Person 1 faces person 6; person 2 faces person 7 and so on.

(b) Using the assignment sheets for taking notes persons facing each other are instructed to interview each other about the important interdependence between their two jobs and/or units. Furthermore, they are instructed to interview each other about what seems to be going particularly well in the interdependencies and what present or potential snags are perceived. They are also instructed to make mutual action plans at the end of the interview or to meet further, if desired.

(c) At the end of ten minutes, people in one row are asked to shift positions one chair within their row. That is, person 1 moves to where 2 had been sitting, 2 moves to where 3 had been sitting and so on and 5 moves from the end of the row to where 1 has been sitting. Only one row moves, persons 6 to 10 sit on their same seats

(d) Once the first round of five interviews is completed the group takes a break. After the break, the persons in each row pair up and interview each other. This requires a series of five more interview periods with one person sitting out each period.

Since there are ten persons involved, each person must interview nine others, for a total of 90 minutes of interviewing. Approximately two hours is required to do the total exercise. In some of the cases, participants report that this procedure is tiring, but in many ways exhilarating and extremely productive.

The exercise requires the participants' cooperation and assumes no serious conflict situations. Serious, intense conflict situations require a different structure and more time.

After the five paired interviews are completed, all of the 'experts' about one question are now asked to meet together. Thus, ten new groups are formed by asking all six people who had the same question to meet and share what they found out. That is, persons 1 from each of the six clusters meet together; persons 2 meet together and so on. These new groups share the data, extract themes, and report the themes to the total group. This procedure is a rapid way to gather a great deal of data for diagnostic purpose.

## 5. Visioning

Visioning is a term used for an intervention in which group members in one or more organisation groups develop and/or describe their vision of what they want the organisation to be like in the future. The time frame may be anywhere from, say, six months to five years in the future.

The concept of visioning is credited to Ronald Lippitt. Lippitt began to tape-record planning meetings and found that "people's voices grew softer, more stressed, depressed, as problems were listed and prioritised. One can hear the energy drain away as the lists grew longer."

Various visioning techniques are used in team building. However, simple steps as given can be used in most of them:

**Step 1:** On a note paper, write down the characteristics an individual would like to see this organisation have one and then two years from now. Using the following categories: the categories might include products, customer and supplier relationships, human resources practices, leadership style, organisation structure and so on. The individuals have 90 minutes.

**Step 2:** Using a marking pen, make the characteristics visible on flipchart paper and display on the wall.

**Step 3:** Report to the group and be prepared to answer questions pertaining to clarification. However, no debate is permitted at this point.

**Step 4:** During a half-hour break a subgroup of three people extracts the themes from the individual reports and prepares to report them to the total group for discussion.

For example, each person takes a marking pen (and/or yarn, glue, magazines from which to cut pictures, scissors and so on) and makes a collage of what you would like this organisation to be two years from now. After an hour, be prepared to describe your collage to the group. Each person displays and describes his or her collage and the group discusses and extracts the common themes.

Various forms of visioning or the use of mental imaginary or the development of cognitive maps are extensively used in strategic planning and in future search conferences.

## 4.4 Organisation Process Approaches

Human process interventions that typically focus on the total organisation or an entire department as well as on relations between groups include the following programmes:

1. Organisation Confrontation Meeting
2. Intergroup Relations
3. Large Group Interventions

### 4.4.1 Organisation Confrontation Meeting

This change method mobilises organisation members to identify problems, set action targets and begin working on problems. It is usually applied when organisations are experiencing stress and when management needs to organise resources for immediate problem solving. The intervention generally includes various groupings of employees in identifying and solving problems.

It is designed to mobilise the resources of the entire organisation to identify the problems, set proprieties and action targets and work on identified problems. This intervention is particularly useful when the organisation is in stress and a gap exists between the top level manager and the rest of the organisational members.

It typically involves the following steps:

- A group meeting, of all the concerned people is scheduled and held to identify the actual problem.
- Groups are appointed representing all the departments of the organisation. People belonging to the same hierarchy form a group,
- Openness, trust and honesty are expected from the groups.
- The groups are given an hour or two to identify the problems. During this process, the OD consultant acts as a catalyst to facilitate all the groups to achieve their target.
- All the groups meet in a central meeting place, report their identified problem(s) and offer solutions. Because each group hears the reports of the other groups, maximum amount of information is shared.
- Then the master list of problems is broken down into categories. Now depending on their own expertise, members join problem-solving groups, which are often different from their earlier group.
- Each group ranks the problems, develops a tactical action plan and determines an appropriate timetable for completing this phase of the process.
- Each group periodically reports its list of priorities and tactical plans of action to management.
- Follow-up meetings are scheduled at regular intervals.

### 4.4.2 Intergroup Relations

These interventions are designed to improve interactions among different groups or departments in organisations. The microcosm group intervention involves a small group of people whose backgrounds closely match the organisation problems being addressed. This group addresses the problem and develops means to solve it. The intergroup conflict model typically involves a consultant helping two groups understand the causes of their conflict and choose appropriate solutions.

This type of intervention can be broadly categorised into two types:

- Microcosm groups
- Inter-group conflict resolution

A microcosm group consists of a small number of individuals that reflect the issues being addressed. For example, it can be composed of members representing a range of ethnic backgrounds, cultures and races to address the diversity issues in the organisation. This intervention involves the following steps:

- Identification of an issue from an organisational diagnosis.
- Convening the group consisting of appropriate mix of stakeholders related to the issue.
- Providing group training for effective problem-solving and decision-making.
- Addressing the actual issue.
- Dissolving the group.

The inter-group conflict resolution intervention is specifically designed to help two groups or departments within an organisation to resolve dysfunctional conflict. Following steps are involved in this type of intervention:

- A consultant, external to the two groups, obtains the groups' agreement to work directly on improving inter-group relationship.
- A time is set for the two groups to meet, preferably away from their normal work situations.
- The consultants describes the purpose and objectives of the meetings to the groups. The groups are asked to identify their own group attributes and those of others, and identify how the other group would describe them.
- The groups are encouraged to discuss their own perception on the above and rethink.
- The groups try to form common agreements and reduce the identified discrepancies.
- The groups are then asked to develop specific plans of action for solving specific problems and for improving their relationships.
- Follow-up meeting is scheduled to monitor the progress.

## 4.4.3 Large Group Interventions

Large scale interventions typically involve a full-size group of stakeholders, working towards the definition of a future state. These interventions start from top levels of the organisation, to analyse, plan, and define the intervention's outcomes, then, people are involved in the solution, creating with this a shared commitment, and effort, which will support the implementation of defined actions in the long term. Some examples include the following: appreciative inquiry summit, future search, open space and real time strategic change. Large scale interventions are highly structured; each activity is carefully planned beforehand – this is particularly important since the whole system participates simultaneously, in the same room, at the same time. Cummings and Worley describe the three step process involved in any large scale intervention as follows:

(i)   The preparation of the large group meeting,

(ii)  Conducting the meeting, and

(iii) Following on meeting outcomes.

Large-scale interventions are quicker, build organisation confidence, give immediate and broad based information, promote a total organisation mindset, inspire action, and sustained commitment.

These interventions focus on issues that affect the whole organisation or large segments of it such as budget cuts, introduction of new technology and changes in the senior leadership. This type can vary on several dimensions including purpose, size, length, structure and number. Conducting this intervention involves the following steps:

- **Preparing for the large group meeting:** The team consists of OD consultant and key organisational members. The key ingredients for successful large group meetings are: a compelling meeting theme, appropriate members to participate and relevant task to address the theme.

- **Conducting meetings** in which the flow of events vary depending on its purpose. However, the following activities can be observed in most of the cases: developing common grounds among participants, discussing the issues and creating an agenda for change.

- Follow-up on the meeting outcomes.

Following is a checklist for observing group processes (Ramnarayan and Sendil Kumar 1998: 155):

How did the group define or approach its task?

- Was there clarity in terms of the goals that the group was trying to achieve in the meeting?

- Were the goals broken down into specific tasks?

- Were the group goals or tasks shared by different individuals or subgroups?

- How did the group, decide on the way to proceed or tackle the problem?

- How was information sought, clarified, synthesised, tested and shared?

- What seemed to be the role expectation from different members?

## Points to Remember

- Human process- based interventions are directed at improving interpersonal, intragroup and intergroup relation.
- **Types of human process interventions involve**:
  1. Interpersonal and group process approaches
  2. Organisation process approaches
- Interpersonal relationships and group dynamics, involve four types of interventions:
  1. T-group.
  2. Process consultation.
  3. Third-party intervention.
  4. Team building.
- **T-Group training** emphasises learning by means of an unstructured group experience. It attempts to apply behavioural science concepts in the design and conduct of the experiences which the members of the group undergo.
- **Process Consultation** intervention focuses on interpersonal relationships and social dynamics occurring in work groups. A process consultant helps group members diagnose group functioning and devise appropriate solutions to process problems, such as dysfunctional conflicts, poor communication and effective norms.
- **Third-party** intervention focuses on conflicts arising between two or more people within the same organisation.
- **Team development** and group processes interventions aim at improving different aspects of a group performance, such as goal setting, development of interpersonal relations among team members, role clarification and analysis, decision making, problem solving, and communities of practice, among other.
- **Stages of Team Development**
  1. Forming
  2. Storming
  3. Norming
  4. Performing
  5. Adjourning
- **Organisation Process Approaches**
  1. Organisation Confrontation Meeting
  2. Intergroup Relations
  3. Large Group Interventions

- **Organisation Confrontation Meeting** method mobilises organisation members to identify problems, set action targets and begin working on problems.
- **Intergroup Relations interventions** are designed to improve interactions among different groups or departments in organisations.
- Large scale interventions typically involve a full-size group of stakeholders, working towards the definition of a future state.

## Questions for Discussion

1. What do you understand by the concept of human process intervention?
2. Discuss the interpersonal and group process approaches of human process intervention.
3. Explain the organisation process approaches of human process intervention.

$\mathcal{C}hapter$ **5**...

# Techno-Structural Interventions

## Contents ...

**Learning Objectives ...**

- To study the aspects of techno-structural interventions involving restructuring organisations, employee involvement and work design
- To understand the human resource management intervention aspects including performance management, developing talent and managing workforce diversity and wellness

## 5.1 Techno-Structural Interventions

These interventions focus on an organisation's technology (for example, task methods and job design) and structure (for example, division of labour and hierarchy). These change techniques are receiving increasing attention in OD, especially in light of contemporary concerns about productivity and organisational effectiveness.

It involves approaches to employee involvement, as well as methods for designing organisations, groups, and jobs. Techno-structural interventions are embedded in the disciplines of engineering, sociology, and psychology and in the applied fields of socio-technical systems and organisation design, practitioners generally stress both productivity and human fulfillment and expect that organisation effectiveness will result from appropriate work designs and organisation structures.

## 5.1.1 Restructuring Organisations

These new forms of organising are highly adaptive and innovative, but require more sophisticated managerial capabilities to function successfully. They often result in fewer managers and employees and in streamlined work flows that break down functional barriers.

Interventions intended at structural design involve moving from more traditional ways of dividing the organisation's overall work, such as functional, divisional, and matrix structures, to more integrative and flexible forms, such as process, customer-centric, and network structures. Diagnostic guidelines facilitate in determining which structure is appropriate for particular organisational environments, technologies, and conditions.

Downsizing seeks to reduce costs and bureaucracy by decreasing the size of the organisation. This reduction in personnel can be achieved through layoffs, organisation redesign, and outsourcing. Successful downsizing is closely associated with the organisation's strategy.

Reengineering fundamentally redesigns the organisation's core work processes to give tighter linkage and coordination among the different tasks. This work-flow integration results in faster, more responsive task performance. Reengineering often is accomplished with new information technology that permits employees to control and coordinate work processes more effectively.

### 5.1.1.1 Structural Design

Organisation structure describes how the overall work of the organisation is divided into subunits and how these subunits are synchronised for task completion. Based on a contingency perspective shown in Figure 5.1, organisation structures should be designed to fit with at least four factors: the environment, organisation size, technology, and organisation strategy. Organisation effectiveness depends on the extent to which its structures are responsive to these contingencies.

Organisations traditionally have structured themselves into one of three forms: functional departments that are task specialised; self-contained divisional units that are oriented to specific products, customers, or regions; or matrix structures that combine both functional specialisation and self containment.

Faced with speed up changes in competitive environments and technologies, however, organisations increasingly have redesigned their structures into more integrative and flexible forms. These more recent innovations include process structures that design subunits around the organisation's core work processes, customer-centric structures that focus attention and resources on specific customers or customer segments, and network-based structures that link the organisation to other, interdependent organisations. The advantages and disadvantages, of the different structures are described below.

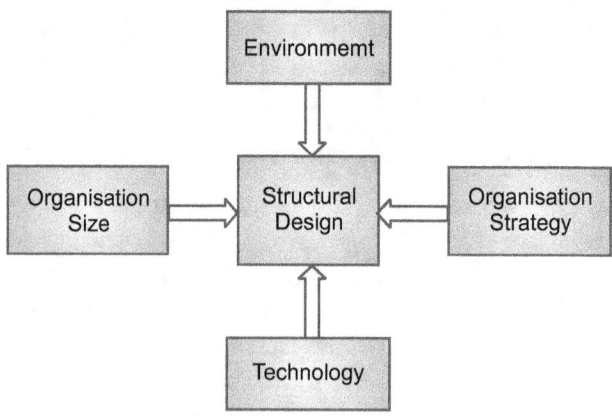

**Fig. 5.1: Contingencies Influencing Structural Design**

## 1.   The Functional Structure

The most widely used organisational structure is the basic *functional structure*, shown in Figure 5.2. The organisation is generally divided into functional units, such as marketing, operations, research and development, human resources, and finance. This structure is based on early management theories regarding specialisation, line and staff relations, span of control, authority, and responsibility. The key functional units are staffed by specialists from such disciplines as engineering and accounting. It is considered easier to manage specialists if they are grouped together under the same head and if the head of the department has been trained and has experience in that particular discipline.

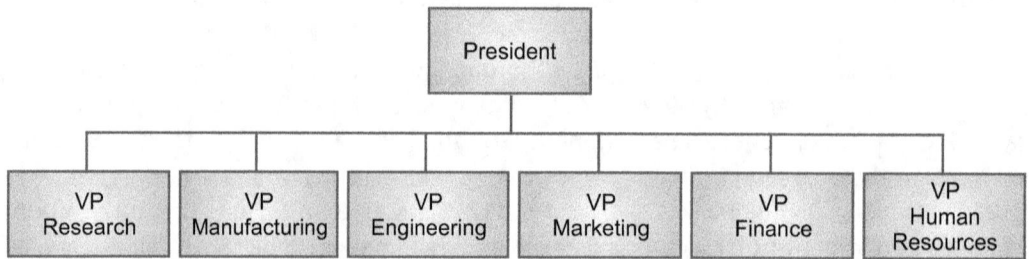

**Fig. 5.2: The Functional Organisation**

**Advantages**

   (a)  Promotes skill specialisation.

   (b)  Reduces duplication of scarce resources and uses resources full time.

   (c)  Enhances career development for specialists within large departments.

   (d)  Facilitates communication and performance because superiors share expertise with their subordinates.

   (e)  Exposes specialists to others within the same specialty.

**Disadvantages**

    (a) Emphasises routine tasks, which encourages short time horizons.

    (b) Fosters provincial perspectives by managers, which limit their potential for top management positions.

    (c) Reduces communication and cooperation between departments.

    (d) Multiplies the interdepartmental dependencies, which can make coordination and scheduling difficult.

    (e) Vague accountability for overall outcomes.

## 2. The Divisional Structure

The *divisional structure* represents a fundamentally different means of organising. Also known as a product or self-contained-unit structure, it was developed by General Motors, Sears, Standard Oil of New Jersey (now ExxonMobil), and DuPont. It groups organisational activities on the basis of products, services, customers, or geography. All or most of the resources and functions necessary to achieve a specific objective are set up as a division headed by a product or division manager.

A typical division structure is shown in Figure 5.3. It is interesting to note that the formal structure within a self- contained unit is functional in nature.

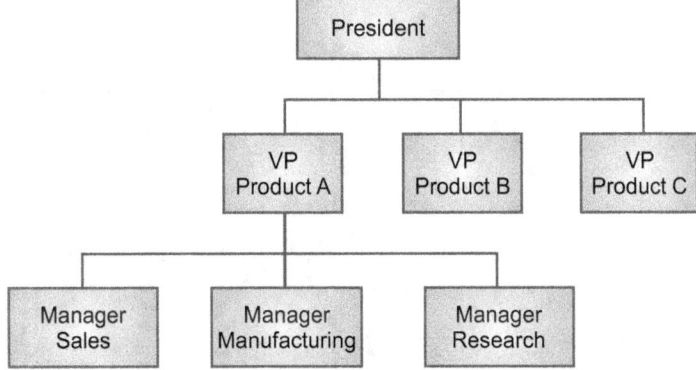

**Fig. 5.3: The Divisional Organisation**

**Advantages**

    (a) Recognises sources of interdepartmental dependencies.

    (b) Fosters a direction toward overall outcomes and clients.

    (c) Allows diversification and expansion of skills and training.

    (d) Ensures accountability by departmental managers and so promotes delegation of authority and responsibility.

    (e) Heightens departmental cohesion and involvement in work.

**Disadvantages**

    (a) May use skills and resources incompetently.

    (b) Limits career advancement by specialists to movements out of their departments.

    (c) Hampers specialists' exposure to others within the same specialties.

    (d) Puts multiple-role demands on people and so creates stress.

    (e) May promote departmental objectives, as opposed to overall organisational objectives.

## 3. The Matrix Structure

Some OD practitioners have focused on maximising the strengths and minimising the weaknesses of both the functional and the divisional structures, and this effort has resulted in the *matrix structure*. It superimposes a lateral structure that focuses on product or project coordination on a vertical functional structure, as shown in Figure 5.4.

Matrix organisation designs originally evolved in the aerospace industry where changing customer demands and technological conditions caused managers to focus on lateral relationships between functions to develop a flexible and adaptable system of resources and procedures, and to accomplish a series of project objectives. Matrix structures now are used widely in manufacturing, service, non-profit, governmental, and professional organisations.

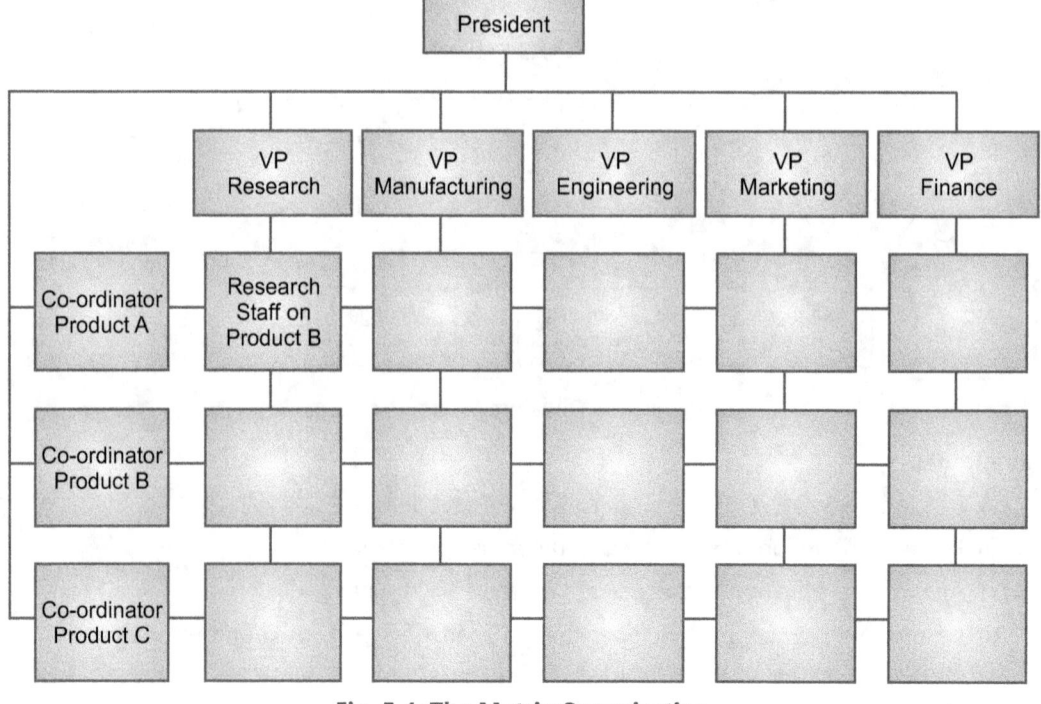

**Fig. 5.4: The Matrix Organisation**

**Advantages**

    (a)    Makes specialised, functional knowledge available to all projects.

    (b)    Uses people flexibly, as departments maintain reservoirs of specialists.

    (c)    Maintains consistency between different departments and projects by forcing communication between managers.

    (d)    Recognises and provides mechanisms for dealing with legitimate, multiple sources of power in the organisation.

    (e)    Can adapt to environmental changes by shifting emphasis between project and functional aspects.

**Disadvantages**

    (a)    Can be very difficult to introduce without a prevailing supportive management climate.

    (b)    Increases role ambiguity, stress, and anxiety by assigning people to more than one department.

    (c)    Without power balancing between product and functional forms, lowers overall performance.

    (d)    Makes inconsistent demands, which may result in unproductive conflicts and short-term crisis management.

    (e)    May reward political skills as opposed to technical skills.

## 4.   The Process Structure

A fundamentally new logic for structuring organisations is to form multidisciplinary teams around core processes, such as product development, order fulfillment, sales generation, and customer support. As shown in Figure 5.5, *process-based structures* emphasise lateral rather than vertical relationships. All tasks crucial to produce a product or service are placed in a common unit usually managed by a role labelled a "process owner." There are certain hierarchical levels, and the senior executive team is comparatively small, typically consisting of the chair, the chief operating officer, and the heads of a few key support services such as strategic planning, human resources, and finance. Process structures lessen many of the hierarchical and departmental boundaries that can hinder task coordination and slow decision making and task performance. They reduce the massive costs of managing across departments and up and down the hierarchy. Process-based structures facilitate organisations to focus most of their resources on serving customers, both inside and outside the firm. The use of process-based structures is growing rapidly in a array of manufacturing and service companies.

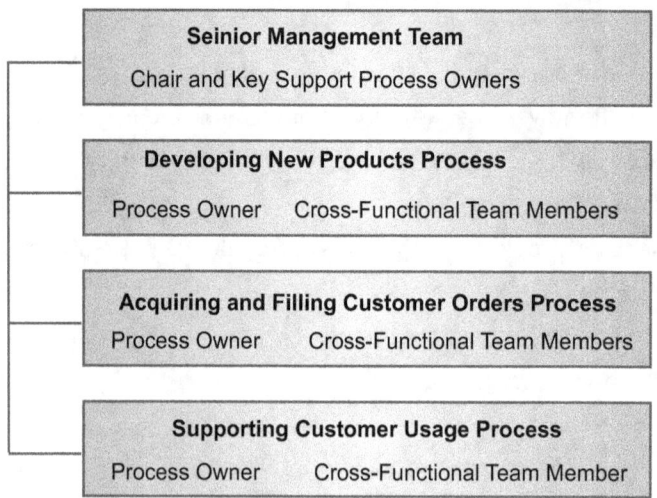

**Fig. 5.5: The Process-Based Structure**

**Advantages**

(a)    Focuses resources on customer satisfaction.

(b)    Improves speed and efficiency, often dramatically.

(c)    Adapts to environmental change rapidly.

(d)    Reduces boundaries between departments.

(e)    Increases ability to see total work flow.

(f)    Enhances employee involvement.

(g)    Lowers costs because of less overhead structure.

**Disadvantages**

(a)    Can threaten middle managers and staff specialists.

(b)    Requires changes in command-and-control mindsets.

(c)    Duplicates scarce resources.

(d)    Requires new skills and knowledge to manage lateral relationships and teams.

(e)    May take longer to make decisions in teams.

(f)    Can be ineffective if wrong processes are identified.

**5.    The Customer-Centric Structure**

Closely related to the process-based structure, the *customer-centric structure* focuses subunits on the creation of solutions and the satisfaction of key customers or customer groups. As shown in Figure 5.6, these customer or market-facing units are supported by other units that develop new products, manufacture components and products, and manage the supply chain. A range of organisations, including the Lord Corporation, DOW, IBM, and Citibank, have implemented these complex structures. Also known as front–back organisations, these structures excel at putting customer needs at the top of an organisation's agenda.

Galbraith notes that globalisation, e-commerce, and the desire for solutions has greatly improved the power of the customer to demand organisational structures that service their needs. These new structures highlight the fundamental differences between product focused organisations, like the function or divisional structure, and customer-centric organisations.

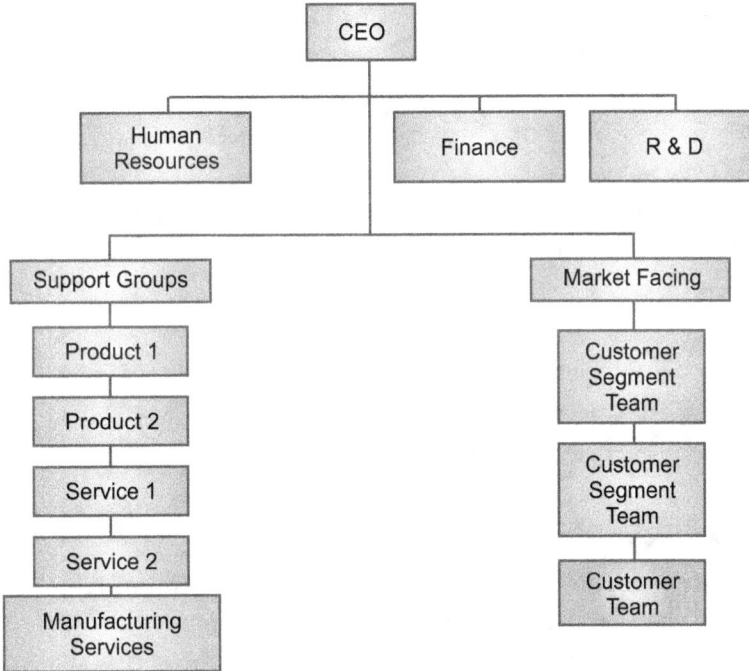

**Fig. 5.6: The Customer Centric Organisation**

**Advantages**
  (a)    Presents one integrated face to the customer.
  (b)    Generates a deep understanding of customer requirements.
  (c)    Enables organisation to customise and tailor solutions for customers.
  (d)    Builds a robust customer response capability.

**Disadvantages**
  (a)    Customer teams can be too inwardly focused.
  (b)    Sharing learning and developing functional skills is difficult.

(c)   Managing lateral relations between customer-facing and back office units is difficult.

(d)   Developing common processes in the front and back is problematic.

(e)   Clarifying the marketing function is problematic.

## 6.   The Network Structure

A *network structure* manages the diverse, complex, and dynamic relationships among multiple organisations or units, each specialising in a particular business function or task. Organisations that employ network structures include shamrock organisations and virtual, modular, or cellular corporations. Less formally, they have been described as "pizza" structures, spiderwebs, starbursts, and cluster organisations.

**Advantages**

(a)   Enables highly flexible and adaptive response to dynamic environments.

(b)   Creates a "best-of-the-best" organisation to focus resources on customer and market needs.

(c)   Enables each organisation to leverage a distinctive competency.

(d)   Permits rapid global expansion.

(e)   Can produce synergistic results.

**Disadvantages**

(a)   Managing lateral relations across autonomous organisations is difficult.

(b)   Motivating members to relinquish autonomy to join the network is troublesome.

(c)   Sustaining membership and benefits can be problematic.

(d)   May give partners access to proprietary knowledge/technology.

## 5.1.1.2 Downsizing

*Downsizing* refers to interventions aimed at reducing the size of the organisation. This typically is accomplished by decreasing the number of employees through layoffs, attrition, redeployment, or early retirement or by reducing the number of organisational units or managerial levels through divestiture, outsourcing, reorganisation, or delayering. In practice, downsizing generally involves layoffs where a certain number or class of organisation members is no longer employed by the organisation. Although traditionally associated with lower-level workers, downsizing increasingly has claimed the jobs of staff specialists, middle managers, and senior executives. An important consequence of downsizing has been the rise of the contingent workforce. In companies like Cisco or Motorola, less expensive temporary or permanent part-time workers often are hired by the same organisations that just laid off thousands of employees.

Organisations may downsize for their own sake and not think about future growth. They may lose key employees who are necessary for future success, cutting into the organisation's core competencies and leaving a legacy of mistrust among members. In such situations, it is questionable whether downsizing is developmental as defined in OD.

**Application Stages**

Successful downsizing interventions tend to proceed by the following steps:

1.  **Clarify the Organisation's Strategy:** As a first step, organisation leaders specify corporate and business strategy and communicate clearly how downsizing relates to it. They seek to inform members that downsizing is not a goal in itself, but a restructuring process for achieving strategic objectives. Leaders need to provide visible and consistent support throughout the process. They can provide opportunities for members to voice their concerns, ask questions, and obtain counselling if necessary.

2.  **Assess Downsizing Options and Make Relevant Choices:** Once the strategy is clear, the full range of downsizing options can be identified and assessed. Three primary downsizing methods are: workforce reduction, organisation redesign, and systemic change. A specific downsizing strategy may use elements of all three approaches. Workforce reduction is aimed at reducing the number of employees, usually in a relatively short timeframe. It can include attrition, retirement incentives, outplacement services, and layoffs. Organisation redesign attempts to restructure the firm to prepare it for the next stage of growth. This is a medium-term approach that can be accomplished by merging organisational units, eliminating management layers, and redesigning tasks. Systemic change is a longer-term option aimed at changing the culture and strategic orientation of the organisation. It can involve interventions that alter the responsibilities and work behaviours of everyone in the organisation and that promote continual improvement as a way of life in the firm.

3.  **Implement the Changes:** This stage involves implementing methods for reducing the size of the organisation. Several practices characterise successful implementation. First, downsizing is best controlled from the top down. Many difficult decisions are required, and a broad perspective helps to overcome people's natural instincts to protect their enterprise or function. Second, specific areas of inefficiency and high cost need to be identified and targeted. The morale of the organisation can be hurt if areas commonly known to be redundant are left untouched. Third, specific actions should be linked to the organisation's strategy. Organisation members need to be reminded consistently that restructuring activities are part of a plan to improve the organisation's performance. Finally, communicate frequently using a variety of media. This keeps people informed, lowers their anxiety over the process, and makes it easier for them to focus on their work.

4.  **Address the Needs of Survivors and those who Leave:** Most downsizing eventually involves reduction in the size of the workforce, and it is important to support not only employees who remain with the organisation but also those who leave. When layoffs occur, employees are generally asked to take on additional responsibilities and to learn new jobs, often with little or no increase in compensation. This added workload can be stressful, and when combined with anxiety over past layoffs and possible future ones, it can lead to what researchers have labelled the "survivor syndrome." This syndrome involves a narrow set of self-absorbed and risk-averse behaviours that can threaten the organisation's survival. Rather than working to ensure the organisation's success, survivors often are preoccupied with whether additional layoffs will occur, with guilt over receiving pay and benefits while coworkers are struggling with termination, and with the uncertainty of career advancement.

5.  **Follow Through with Growth Plans:** This final stage of downsizing involves implementing an organisation renewal and growth process. Failure to move quickly to implement growth plans is a key determinant of ineffective downsizing.

## 5.1.1.3 Reengineering

The final restructuring intervention is *reengineering*—the fundamental rethinking and radical redesign of business processes to achieve dramatic improvements in performance.

Reengineering transforms how organisations traditionally produce and deliver goods and services. Beginning with the Industrial Revolution, organisations have increasingly fragmented work into specialised units, each focusing on a limited part of the overall production process. Although this division of labour has enabled organisations to mass-produce standardised products and services efficiently, it can be overly complicated, difficult to manage, and slow to respond to the rapid and unpredictable changes experienced by many organisations today.

Reengineering addresses these problems by breaking down specialised work units into more integrated, cross functional work processes. This streamlines work processes and makes them faster and more flexible; consequently, they are more responsive to changes in competitive conditions, customer demands, product life cycles, and technologies. As might be expected, successful reengineering requires an almost revolutionary change in how organisations design their structures and their work. It identifies and questions the often-unexamined assumptions underlying how organisations perform work and why do they do it in a particular way. This effort typically results in radical changes in thinking and work methods—a shift from specialised jobs, tasks, and structures to integrated processes that deliver value to customers. Such revolutionary change differs considerably from incremental approaches to performance improvement, such as continuous improvement and total quality management, which emphasise incremental changes in existing work processes. Because reengineering radically alters the status quo, it seeks to produce dramatic increases in organisation performance.

**Application Stages**

Early reengineering efforts emphasised identifying which business processes to reengineer and technically assessing the work flow. More recent efforts have extended reengineering practice to address issues of managing change, such as how to deal with resistance to change and how to manage the transition to new work processes. The following application steps are included in most reengineering efforts, although the order may change slightly from one situation to another:

1.   **Prepare the Organisation:** Reengineering begins with clarification and assessment of the organisation's context, including its competitive environment, strategy, and objectives. This effort establishes and communicates the need for reengineering and the strategic direction that the process should follow.

2.   **Fundamentally Rethink the Way Work Gets Done:** This step lies at the heart of reengineering and involves these activities: identifying and analysing core business processes, defining their key performance objectives, and designing new processes. These tasks are the real work of reengineering and typically are performed by a cross-functional design team who is given considerable time and resources to accomplish them.

(a)   **Identify and analyse core business processes:** Core processes are considered essential for strategic success. They include activities that transform inputs into valued outputs. Core processes typically are assessed through development of a process map that identifies the three to five activities required to deliver an organisation's products or services. For a health care system, the core processes include the intake of patients through the primary care physician, inpatient and outpatient services, and medical records and billing.

(b)   **Define performance objectives:** Challenging performance goals are set in this step. The highest possible level of performance for any particular process is identified, and dramatic goals are set for speed, quality, cost, or other measures of performance. These standards can derive from customer requirements or from benchmarks of the best practices of industry leaders.

(c)   **Design new processes:** This task involves designing new business processes to achieve breakthrough goals. It often starts with a clean sheet of paper and addresses the question "If we were starting this company today, what is the most effective and efficient way to deliver this product or service?"

3.   **Restructure the Organisation Around the New Business Processes:** This last step in reengineering involves changing the organisation's structure to support the new business

processes. This endeavour typically results in the kinds of process-based structures that were described earlier in this chapter. Reengineered organisations typically have the following characteristics:

(a)    Work units change from functional departments to process teams.

(b)    Jobs change from simple tasks to multidimensional work.

(c)    People's roles change from controlled to empowered.

(d)    The focus of performance measures and compensation shifts from activities to results.

(e)    Organisation structures change from hierarchical to flat.

(f)    Managers change from supervisors to coaches; executives change from scorekeepers to leaders.

## 5.1.2 Employee Involvement

Faced with competitive demands for lower costs, higher performance, and greater flexibility, organisations are increasingly turning to employee involvement (EI) to enhance the participation, commitment, and productivity of their members. Increased employee involvement can lead to quicker, more responsive decisions, continuous performance improvements, and greater employee flexibility, commitment, and satisfaction.

Employee involvement is a broad term that has been variously referred to as "empowerment," "participative management," "engagement," "work design," "high involvement," "industrial democracy," and "quality of work life." It covers diverse approaches to gain greater participation in relevant workplace decisions.

### 5.1.2.1 Meaning of Employee Involvement

Employee involvement is the current label used to describe a set of practices and philosophies that started with the quality-of-work-life movement in the late 1950s. The phrase "quality of work life" (QWL) was used to stress the prevailing poor quality of life at the workplace. Both the term "QWL" and the meaning attributed to it have undergone considerable change and development. More recently, the term "engagement" has been popular, and a great deal of effort has been invested in differentiating the term. "Engagement" refers to an organisation member's work experience. Engaged employees are motivated, committed, and interested in their work. Engagement, then, is the outcome of EI interventions.

### 5.1.2.2 Elements of Employee Involvement

*Employee involvement* seeks to increase members' input into decisions that affect organisation performance and employee well-being. It can be described in terms of four key elements that promote worker involvement:

1. **Power:** This element of EI includes providing people with enough authority to make work-related decisions covering various issues such as work methods, task assignments, performance outcomes, customer service, and employee selection. The amount of power afforded employees can vary enormously, from simply asking them for input into decisions that managers subsequently make, to managers and workers jointly making decisions, to employees making decisions themselves.

2. **Information:** Timely access to relevant information is vital in making effective decisions. Organisations can promote EI by ensuring that the necessary information flows freely to those with decision authority. This can include data about operating results, business plans, competitive conditions, new technologies and work methods, and ideas for organisational improvement.

3. **Knowledge and skills:** Employee involvement contributes to organisational effectiveness only to the extent that employees have the requisite skills and knowledge to make good decisions. Organisations can facilitate EI by providing training and development programmes for improving members' knowledge and skills. Such learning can cover an array of expertise having to do with performing tasks, making decisions, solving problems, and understanding how the business operates.

4. **Rewards:** People generally do those things for which they are recognised, rewards can have a powerful effect on getting people involved in the organisation. Meaningful opportunities for involvement can provide employees with internal rewards, such as feelings of self-worth and accomplishment. External rewards, such as pay and promotions, can reinforce EI when they are linked directly to performance outcomes that result from participation in decision-making.

### 5.1.2.3 Employee Involvement Applications

This section describes three major EI applications that vary in the amounts of power, information, knowledge and skills, and rewards that are moved downward through the organisation (from least to most involvement): parallel structures, including cooperative union–management projects and quality circles; total quality management; and high-involvement organisations.

### (A) Parallel Structures

*Parallel structures* involve members in resolving ill-defined, complex problems and build adaptability into bureaucratic organisations. Also known as "collateral structures," "dualistic structures," or "shadow structures," parallel structures operate in conjunction with the formal organisation. They provide members with an alternative setting in which to address problems and to propose innovative solutions free from the existing, formal organisation structure and culture.

**Application Stages:** Cooperative union–management projects and quality circle interventions fall at the lower end of the EI scale. Member participation and influence typically are restricted to making proposals and to offering suggestions for change because subsequent decisions about implementing the proposals are reserved for management. Membership in parallel structures also tends to be limited, primarily to volunteers and to numbers of employees for which there are adequate resources. Management heavily influences the conditions under which parallel structures operate. It controls the amount of authority that members have in making recommendations, the amount of information that is shared with them, the amount of training they receive to increase their knowledge and skills, and the amount of monetary rewards for participation. Because parallel structures offer limited amounts of EI, they are most appropriate for organisations with little or no history of employee participation, top-down management styles, and bureaucratic cultures. Cooperative union–management and quality circle programmes typically are implemented in the following steps:

1.  **Define the Purpose and Scope:** This first step involves defining the purpose for the parallel structure and initial expectations about how it will function. Organisational diagnosis can help clarify which specific problems and issues to address, such as productivity, absenteeism, or service quality. In addition, management training in the use of parallel structures can include discussions about the commitment and resources necessary to implement them; the openness needed to examine organisational practices, operations, and policies; and the willingness to experiment and learn.

2.  **Form a Steering Committee:** Parallel structures typically use a steering committee composed of acknowledged leaders of the various functions and constituencies within the formal organisation. For example, in cooperative union–management projects, the steering committee would include key representatives from management, such as a president or chief operating officer, and each of the unions and employee groups involved in the project, such as local union presidents.

3.  **Communicate with Organisation Members:** The effectiveness of a parallel structure depends on a high level of involvement from organisation members. Communicating the purpose, procedures, and rewards of participation can promote that involvement. Moreover, employee participation in developing a structure's vision and purpose can increase ownership and visibly demonstrate the "new way" of working. Continued communication concerning parallel structure activities can ensure member awareness.

4.  **Create Forums for Employee Problem Solving:** These forums are the primary means of accomplishing the purpose of the parallel learning structure. The most

common forum is the employee problem-solving group. Their formation involves selecting and training group members, identifying problems for the groups to work on, and providing appropriate facilitation. Selecting group members is important because success often is a function of group membership. Members need to represent the appropriate hierarchical levels, expertise, functions, and constituencies that are relevant to the problems at hand. This allows the parallel structure to identify and communicate with the formal structure. It also provides the necessary resources to solve the problems.

5. **Address the Problems and Issues:** Parallel structures solve problems by using an action research process. They diagnose specific problems, plan appropriate solutions, and implement and evaluate them. Problem solving can be facilitated when the groups and the steering committee relate effectively to each other. This permits the steering committee to direct problem-solving efforts in an appropriate manner, to acquire the necessary resources and support, and to approve action plans. It also helps ensure that the solutions and changes are linked appropriately to the formal organisation. In this manner, early attempts at change will have a better chance of succeeding.

6. **Implement and Evaluate the Changes:** This step involves implementing appropriate organisational changes and assessing the results. Change proposals need the support of the steering committee and the formal authority structure. As changes are implemented, the organisation needs information about their effects. This lets members know how successful the changes have been and if they need to be modified. In addition, feedback on changes helps the organisation learn to adapt and innovate.

## (B) Total Quality Management

Total Quality Management (TQM) is a more comprehensive approach to employee involvement. Also known as "continuous process improvement," "continuous quality," "lean," and "six-sigma," TQM grew out of a manufacturing emphasis on quality control and represents a long-term effort to orient all of an organisation's activities around the concept of quality. Quality is achieved when organisational processes reliably produce products and services that meet or exceed customer expectations. Although it is possible to implement TQM without employee involvement, member participation in the change process increases the likelihood of sustaining the results. Quality improvement processes were popular in the 1990s, and many organisations, including Morton Salt, Weyerhaeuser, Xerox, Boeing's Airlift and Tanker Programs, Motorola, and Analog Devices, incorporated TQM interventions. Today, a continuous quality improvement capability is essential for global competitiveness.

TQM increases workers' knowledge and skills through extensive training, provides relevant information to employees, pushes decision-making power downward in the organisation, and ties rewards to performance. When implemented successfully, TQM also is aligned closely with a firm's overall business strategy and attempts to direct the entire organisation toward continuous quality improvement.

**Application Stages:** TQM typically is implemented in five major steps. With the exception of gaining senior management commitment, most of the steps can occur somewhat concomitantly.

1.  **Gain Long-Term Senior Management Commitment:** This stage involves helping senior executives understand the importance of long-term commitment to TQM. Without a solid understanding of TQM and the key success factors for implementation, managers often believe that workers are solely responsible for quality. Yet only senior executives have the authority and larger perspective to address the organisationwide, cross-functional issues that hold the greatest promise for TQM's success.

    Senior managers' role in TQM implementation includes giving direction and support throughout the change process. For example, establishing organisationwide TQM generally takes three or more years, although technical improvements to the workflow can be as quick as six to eight months. Senior managers need to clarify and communicate throughout the organisation a totally new orientation to producing and delivering products and services.

2.  **Train Members in Quality Methods:** TQM implementation requires extensive training in the principles and tools of quality improvement. Depending on the organisation's size and complexity, such training can be conducted in a few weeks to more than two years. Members typically learn problem-solving skills and simple statistical process control (SPC) techniques, usually referred to as the seven tools of quality brainstorming, histograms, flowcharts, scatter diagrams, Pareto charts, cause-and-effect diagrams, control charts, and other problem-solving procedures.

3.  **Start Quality Improvement Projects:** In this phase of TQM implementation, individuals and work groups apply the quality methods to identify the few projects that hold promise for the largest improvements in organisational processes. They identify output variations, intervene to minimise deviations from quality standards, monitor improvements, and repeat this quality improvement cycle indefinitely. Identifying output variations is a key aspect of TQM. Such deviations from quality standards typically are measured by the percentage of defective products or, in the case of customer satisfaction, by on-time delivery percentages or customer survey ratings.

4.  **Measure Progress:** This stage of TQM implementation involves measuring organisational processes against quality standards. Knowing and analysing the competition's performance are essential for any TQM effort because it sets

minimum standards of quality, cost, and service and ensures the organisation's position in the industry over the short run. For the longer term, such analytical efforts concentrate on identifying world-class performance, regardless of industry, and creating stretch targets, also known as *benchmarks*. Benchmarks represent the best in organisational achievements and practices for different processes and generally are accepted as "world class."

5. **Rewarding Accomplishment:** In this final stage of TQM implementation, the organisation links rewards to improvements in quality. TQM does not monitor and reward outcomes that are normally tracked by traditional reward systems, such as the number of units produced. Such measures do not necessarily reflect product quality and can be difficult to replace because they are ingrained in the organisation's traditional way of doing business. Rather, TQM rewards members for "process-oriented" improvements, such as increased        on-time delivery, gains in customers' perceived satisfaction with product performance, and reductions in cycle time—the time it takes a product or service to be conceived, developed, produced, and sold. Rewards usually are designed initially to promote finding solutions to the organisation's key problems. The linkage between rewards and process oriented improvements reinforces the belief that continuous improvements, even small ones, are an important part of the new organisational culture associated with TQM.

## (C) High-Involvement Organisations

Over the past two decades, an increasing number of employee involvement projects have been aimed at using high-involvement work practices to create high-involvement organisations (HIOs). These interventions create organisational conditions that support high levels of employee participation. What makes HIOs unique is the comprehensive nature of their design process. Unlike parallel structures that do not alter the formal organisation or TQM interventions that tend to focus on particular processes, HIOs address almost all organisation features. Structure, work design, information and control systems, physical layout, personnel policies, and reward systems are designed jointly by management and workers to promote high levels of involvement and performance.

## Features of High-Involvement Organisations

1. **Flat, lean organisation structures** contribute to involvement by pushing the scheduling, planning, and controlling functions typically performed by management and staff groups toward the shop floor. Similarly, mini-enterprise, team-based structures that are oriented to a common purpose or outcome help focus employee participation on a shared objective. Participative structures, such as work councils and union–management committees, create conditions in which workers can influence the direction and policies of the organisation.

2. **Job designs** that provide employees with high levels of discretion, task variety, and meaningful feedback can enhance involvement. They enable workers to influence

day-to-day workplace decisions and to receive intrinsic satisfaction by performing work under enriched conditions. Self-managed teams encourage employee responsibility by providing cross-training and job rotation, which give people a chance to learn about the different functions contributing to organisational performance.

3.  **Open information systems** that are tied to jobs or work teams provide the necessary information for employees to participate meaningfully in decision making. Goals and standards of performance that are set participatively can provide employees with a sense of commitment and motivation for achieving those objectives.

4.  **Career systems** that provide different tracks for advancement and counselling to help people choose appropriate paths can help employees plan and prepare for long-term development in the organisation. Open job posting, for example, makes employees aware of jobs that can further their development.

5.  **Selection** of employees for HIOs can be improved through a realistic job preview providing information about what it will be like to work in such situations. Team member involvement in a selection process oriented to potential and process skills of recruits can facilitate a participative climate.

6.  **Training** employees for the necessary knowledge and skills to participate effectively in decision making is a heavy commitment in HIOs. This effort includes education on the economic side of the enterprise, as well as interpersonal skill development. Peer training is emphasised as a valuable adjunct to formal, expert training.

7.  **Reward systems** can contribute to EI when information about them is open and the rewards are based on acquiring new skills, as well as on sharing gains from improved performance. Similarly, participation is enhanced when people can choose among different fringe benefits and when reward distinctions among people from different hierarchical levels are minimised.

8.  **Personnel policies** that are participatively set and encourage stability of employment provide employees with a strong sense of commitment to the organisation. People feel that the policies are reasonable and that the firm is committed to their long-term development.

9.  **Physical layouts** of organisations also can enhance EI. Physical designs that support team structures and reduce status differences among employees can reinforce the egalitarian climate needed for employee participation. Safe and pleasant working conditions provide a physical environment conducive to participation.

**Application Factors**

At present, there is no universally accepted approach to implementing the high-involvement features described here. The actual implementation process often is specific to the situation, and little systematic research has been devoted to understanding the change process itself. Nevertheless, at least two distinct factors seem to characterise how HIOs are implemented. First, implementation generally is guided by an explicit statement of values that members want the new organisation to support. Typically, such values as teamwork, equity, quality, and empowerment guide the choice of specific design features. Values that are strongly held and widely shared by organisation members can provide the energy, commitment, and direction needed to create HIOs. A second feature of the implementation process is its participative nature. Managers and employees take active roles in choosing and implementing the design features. They may be helped by OD practitioners, but the locus of control for the change process resides clearly within the organisation. This participative change process is congruent with the high-involvement design being created. In essence, high involvement design processes promote high-involvement organisations.

## 5.1.3 Work Design

Work design refers to creating jobs and work groups that generate high levels of employee fulfillment and productivity. This technostructural intervention can be part of a larger employee involvement application, or it can be an independent change programme. Work design has been researched and applied extensively in organisations. Recently, organisations have tended to combine work design with formal structure and supporting changes in goal setting, reward systems, work environment, and other performance management practices. These organisational factors can help structure and reinforce the kinds of work behaviours associated with specific work designs.

There are three approaches to work design. First, the engineering approach focuses on efficiency and simplification, and results in traditional job and work-group designs. A second approach to work design rests on motivational theories and attempts to enrich the work experience. Job enrichment involves designing jobs with high levels of meaning, discretion, and knowledge of results. The third and most recent approach to work design derives from sociotechnical systems methods, and seeks to optimise both the social and the technical aspects of work systems.

### 5.1.3.1 The Engineering Approach

The oldest and most prevalent approach to designing work is based on engineering concepts and methods. It proposes that the most efficient work designs can be determined by clearly specifying the tasks to be performed, the work methods to be used, and the work flow among individuals. The engineering approach is based on the pioneering work of

Frederick Taylor, the father of scientific management. He developed methods for analysing and designing work and laid the foundation for the professional field of industrial engineering.

The engineering approach scientifically analyses workers' tasks to discover those procedures that produce the maximum output with the minimum input of energies and resources. This generally results in work designs with high levels of specialisation and specification. Such designs have several benefits: They allow workers to learn tasks rapidly; they permit short work cycles so performance can take place with little or no mental effort; and they reduce costs because lower-skilled people can be hired and trained easily and paid relatively low wages.

### 5.1.3.2 The Motivational Approach

The motivational approach to work design views the effectiveness of organisational activities primarily as a function of member needs and satisfaction, and seeks to improve employee performance and satisfaction by enriching jobs. The motivational method provides people with opportunities for autonomy, responsibility, closure (that is, doing a complete job), and performance feedback.

The motivational approach usually is associated with the research of Herzberg and of Hackman and Oldham. Herzberg's two-factor theory of motivation proposed that certain attributes of work, such as opportunities for advancement and recognition, which he called motivators, help increase job satisfaction. Other attributes, which Herzberg called hygiene factors, such as company policies, working conditions, pay, and supervision, do not produce satisfaction but rather prevent dissatisfaction—important contributors because only satisfied workers are motivated to produce.

### 5.1.3.3 The Sociotechnical Systems Approach

The Sociotechnical Systems (STS) approach is currently the most extensive body of scientific and applied work underlying employee involvement and innovative work designs. Its techniques and design principles derive from extensive action research in both public and private organisations across diverse national cultures. This section reviews the conceptual foundations of the STS approach and then describes its most popular application: self-managed work teams.

STS theory is based on two fundamental premises: that an organisation or work unit is a combined, social-plus-technical system (sociotechnical), and that this system is open in relation to its environment.

1.  **Sociotechnical System:** The first assumption suggests that whenever human beings are organised to perform tasks, a joint system is operating—a sociotechnical system. This system consists of two independent but related parts: a social part, including the people performing the tasks and the relationships among them; and a

technical part, including the tools, techniques, and methods for task performance. These two parts are independent of each other because each follows a different set of behavioural laws.

The social part operates according to biological and psychosocial laws, whereas the technical part functions according to mechanical and physical laws. Nevertheless, the two parts are related because they must act together to accomplish tasks. Hence, the term "sociotechnical" signifies the joint relationship that must occur between the social and the technical parts, and the word "system" communicates that this connection results in a unified whole. Because a sociotechnical system is composed of social and technical parts, it follows that it will produce two kinds of outcomes: products, such as goods and services; and social and psychological consequences, such as job satisfaction and commitment.

The key issue is how to design the relationship between the two parts so that both outcomes are positive (referred to as joint optimisation). Sociotechnical practitioners design work and organisations so that the social and technical parts work well together, producing high levels of product and human satisfaction. This effort contrasts with the engineering approach to designing work, which focuses on the technical component, worries about fitting in people later, and often leads to mediocre performance at high social costs. The STS approach also contrasts with the motivational approach, which views work design in terms of human fulfillment and that can lead to satisfied employees but inefficient work processes.

2.  **Environmental Relationship:** The second major premise underlying STS theory is that such systems are open to their environments. Open systems must interact with their environments to survive and develop. The environment provides the STS with necessary inputs of energy, raw materials, and information, and the STS provides the environment with products and services.

    The key issue here is how to design the interface between the STS and its environment so that the system has sufficient freedom to function while exchanging effectively with the environment. In what is typically called boundary management, STS practitioners structure environmental relationships both to protect the system from external disruptions and to facilitate the exchange of necessary resources and information. This enables the STS to adapt to changing conditions and to influence the environment in favourable directions.

## 5.2 Human Resources Management Interventions

These interventions would focus on personnel practices used to integrate people into organisations. These practices include career planning, reward systems, goal setting, and performance appraisal - change methods that traditionally have been associated with the personnel function in organisations.

In recent years, interest has grown in integrating human resources management with OD. Human resources management interventions are rooted in the disciplines of economics and labour relations and in the applied personnel practices of wages and compensation employee selection and placements performance appraisal, and career development. Practitioners in this area typically focus on the people in organisations believing that organisational effectiveness results from improved practices for integrating employees into organisations

## 5.2.1 Performance Management

Human resources management interventions are concerned with managing individual and group performance. Performance management involves goal setting, performance appraisal, and reward systems that align member work behaviour with business strategy, employee involvement, and workplace technology. Goal setting describes the interaction between managers and employees in jointly defining member work behaviours and outcomes.

Performance appraisal involves collecting and disseminating performance data to improve work outcomes. It is the primary human resources management intervention for providing performance feedback to individuals and work groups.

Reward systems are concerned with eliciting and reinforcing desired behaviours and work outcomes through compensation and other forms of recognition. They can support goal setting and feedback systems by acknowledging the kinds of behaviours required to implement a particular work design or support a business strategy.

Performance management interventions traditionally are implemented by the human resources department within organisations, whose managers have special training in these areas. Because of the breadth and depth of knowledge required to carry out these kinds of change programmes successfully, practitioners tend to specialise in one part of the human resources function, such as performance appraisal or compensation.

The interest in integrating human resources management with organisation development continues unabated.

## 5.2.1.1 A Model of Performance Management

Performance management is an integrated process of defining, assessing, and reinforcing employee work behaviours and outcomes. Organisations with a well-developed performance management process often outperform those without this element of organisation design. As shown in Fig. 5.7, performance management includes practices and methods for goal setting, performance appraisal, and reward systems. These practices jointly influence the performance of individuals and work groups.

**Fig. 5.7: A Performance Management Model**

Goal setting specifies the kinds of performances that are desired; performance appraisal assesses those outcomes; reward systems provide the reinforcers to ensure that desired outcomes are repeated. Because performance management occurs in a larger organisational context, at least three contextual factors determine how these practices affect work performance: business strategy, workplace technology, and employee involvement. High levels of work performance tend to occur when goal setting, performance appraisal, and reward systems are aligned jointly with these contextual factors.

Business strategy defines the goals and objectives, policies, and intended relationships between the organisation and its environment to compete successfully, and performance management focuses, assesses, and reinforces member work behaviours toward those objectives and intentions. This ensures that work behaviours are strategically driven.

Workplace technology affects whether performance management practices should be based on the individual or the group. When technology is low in interdependence and work is designed for individual jobs, goal setting, performance appraisal, and reward systems should be aimed at individual work behaviours. Conversely, when technology is highly interdependent and work is designed for groups, performance management should be aimed at group behaviours.

Finally, the level of employee involvement in an organisation should determine the nature of performance management practices. When organisations are highly bureaucratic, with low levels of participation, then goal setting, performance appraisal, and reward systems should be formalised and administered by management and staff personnel.

In high-involvement situations, on the other hand, performance management should be heavily participative, with both managers and employees setting goals and appraising and rewarding performance. In high-involvement organisations, for example, employees participate in all stages of performance management, and are heavily involved in both designing and administering its practices.

## 5.2.1.2 Goal Setting

*Goal setting* involves managers and subordinates in jointly establishing and clarifying employee goals. In some cases, such as management by objectives, it also can facilitate employee counselling and support. In other cases, such as the *balanced scorecard*, it generates goals in several defined categories, at different organisational levels, to establish clear linkages with business strategy. The process of establishing challenging goals involves managing the level of participation and goal difficulty. Once goals have been established, the way they are measured is an important determinant of member performance.

Goal setting can affect performance in several ways. It influences what people think and do by focusing their behaviour in the direction of the goals, rather than elsewhere. Goals energise behaviour, motivating people to put forth the effort to reach difficult goals that are accepted, and when goals are difficult but achievable, goal setting prompts persistence over time.

### Characteristics of Goal Setting

An impressive amount of research underlies goal-setting interventions and practices; it has revealed that goal setting works equally well in both individual and group settings. This research has identified two major processes that affect positive outcomes: establishment of challenging goals and clarification of goal measurement.

### 1. Establishing Challenging Goals

The first element of goal setting concerns establishing goals that are perceived as challenging but realistic and to which there is a high level of commitment. This can be accomplished by varying the goal difficulty and the level of employee participation in the goal-setting process. Increasing the difficulty of employee goals, also known as stretch goals, can increase their perceived challenge and enhance the amount of effort expended to achieve them. Thus, more difficult goals tend to lead to increased effort and performance, as long as they are seen as feasible.

If goals are set too high, however, they may lose their motivating potential and employees will give up when they fail to achieve them. An important method for increasing the acceptance of a challenging goal is to collect benchmarks or best-practice referents. When employees see that other people, groups, or organisations have achieved a specified level of performance, they are more motivated to achieve that level themselves.

### 2.  Clarifying Goal Measurement

The second element in the goal-setting process involves specifying and clarifying the goals. When given specific goals, workers perform higher than when they are simply told to "do their best" or when they receive no guidance at all. Specific goals reduce ambiguity about expectations and focus the search for appropriate behaviours. To clarify goal measurement, objectives should be operationally defined.

### Application Stages

Based on these features of the goal-setting process, OD practitioners have developed specific approaches to goal setting. The following steps characterise those applications:

(a) **Diagnosis:** The first step is a thorough diagnosis of the job or work group, of employee needs, and of the three context factors, business strategy, workplace technology, and level of employee involvement. This provides information about the nature and difficulty of specific goals, the appropriate types and levels of participation, and the necessary support systems.

(b) **Preparation for Goal Setting:** This step prepares managers and employees to engage in goal setting, typically by increasing interaction and communication between managers and employees, and offering formal training in goal-setting methods. Specific action plans for implementing the programme also are made at this time.

(c) **Setting of Goals:** In this step challenging goals are established and methods for goal measurement are clarified. Employees participate in the process to the extent that contextual factors support such involvement and to the extent that they are likely to set higher goals than those assigned by management.

(d) **Review:** At this final step the goal-setting process is assessed so that modifications can be made, if necessary. The goal attributes are evaluated to see whether the goals are energising and challenging and whether they support the business strategy and can be influenced by the employees.

### Management by Objectives

A common form of goal setting used in organisations is *management by objectives* (MBO). This method is chiefly an attempt to align personal goals with business strategy by increasing communications and shared perceptions between the manager and subordinates, either individually or as a group, and by reconciling conflict where it exists. All organisations have goals and objectives; all managers have goals and objectives. In many instances, however, those goals are not stated clearly, and managers and subordinates have misunderstandings about what those objectives are. MBO is an approach to resolving these differences in perceptions and goals. MBO is characterised by systematic and periodic manager–subordinate meetings designed to accomplish organisational goals by joint planning of the work, periodic reviewing of accomplishments, and mutual solving of problems that arise in the course of getting the job done.

MBO has its origin in two different backgrounds: organisational and developmental. The organisational root of MBO was developed by Drucker, who emphasised that organisations need to establish objectives in eight key areas: "market standing; innovation; productivity; physical and financial resources; profitability; manager performance and development; worker performance and attitude; and public responsibility." Drucker's work was expanded by Odiorne, whose first book on MBO stressed the need for quantitative measurement.

According to Levinson, MBO's second root is found in the work of McGregor, who stressed the qualitative nature of MBO and its use for development and growth on the job. McGregor attempted to shift emphasis from identifying weaknesses to analysing performance in order to define strengths and potentials. He believed that this shift could be accomplished by having subordinates reach agreement with their bosses on major job responsibilities; then, individuals could develop short-term performance goals and action plans for achieving those goals, thus allowing them to appraise their own performance. Subordinates then would discuss the results of this self-appraisal with their supervisors and develop a new set of performance goals and plans. This emphasis on mutual understanding and performance rather than personality would shift the supervisor's role from judge to helper, thereby reducing both role conflict and ambiguity. The second root of MBO reduces role ambiguity by making goal setting more participative and transactional, by increasing communication between role incumbents, and by ensuring that both individual and organisational goals are identified and achieved.

An MBO programme often goes beyond the one-on-one, manager–subordinate relationship to focus on problem-solving discussions involving work teams as well. Setting goals and reviewing individual performance are considered within the larger context of the job. In addition to organisational goals, the MBO process gives attention to individuals' personal and career goals and tries to make those and the organisational goals more complementary. The target-setting procedure allows real (rather than simulated) subordinate participation in goal setting, with open, problem-centered discussions among team members, supervisors, and subordinates.

There are six basic steps in implementing an MBO process.

1.  **Work-group involvement:** In the first step of MBO, the members of the primary work group define overall group and individual goals and establish action plans for achieving them. If this step is omitted or if organisational goals and strategies are unclear, the effectiveness of an MBO approach may be greatly reduced over time.

2.  **Joint manager–subordinate goal setting:** Once the work group's overall goals and responsibilities have been determined, attention is given to the job duties and

responsibilities of the individual role incumbents. Roles are carefully examined in light of their interdependence with the roles of others outside the work group.

3.  **Establishment of action plans for goals:** The subordinate develops action plans for goal accomplishment, either in a group meeting or in a meeting with the immediate manager. The action plans reflect the individual style of the subordinate, not that of the supervisor.

4.  **Establishment of criteria, or yardsticks, of success:** At this point, the manager and the subordinate agree on the success criteria for the goals that have been established—criteria that are not limited to easily measurable or quantifiable data. A more important reason for jointly developing the success criteria is to ensure that the manager and the subordinate have a common understanding of the task and what is expected of the subordinate. Frequently, the parties involved discover that they have not reached a mutual understanding. The subordinate and the manager may have agreed on a certain task, but in discussing how to measure its success, they find that they have not been communicating clearly. Arriving at a joint understanding and agreement on success criteria is the most important step in the entire MBO process.

5.  **Review and recycle:** Periodically, the manager reviews work progress, either in the larger group or with the subordinate. There are three stages in this review process. First, the subordinate takes the lead, reviewing progress and discussing achievements and the obstacles faced. Next, the manager discusses work plans and objectives for the future. Last, after the action plans have been made, a more general discussion covers the subordinate's future ambitions and other factors of concern. In this final phase, a great deal of coaching and counselling usually takes place.

6.  **Maintenance of records:** In many MBO programmes, the working documents of the goals, criteria, yardsticks, priorities, and due dates are forwarded to a third party. Although the evidence is indirect, it is likely that the MBO programme, as an OD effort, suffers when the working papers are reviewed regularly by a third party, such as higher management or the personnel department. Experience shows that when the working papers routinely are passed on, they are less likely to reflect open, honest communication within the supervisor–subordinate pair or the work group. Often they represent instead an effort to impress the third party or to comply with institutionalised rules and procedures.

### 5.2.1.3 Performance Appraisal

*Performance appraisal* is a feedback system that involves the direct evaluation of individual or work-group performance by a supervisor, manager, or peers. Most organisations have some kind of evaluation system that is used for performance feedback, pay administration, and, in some cases, counselling and developing employees. Thus, performance appraisal represents an important link between goal-setting processes and reward systems.

### The Performance Appraisal Process

Table 5.1 summarises several common elements of performance appraisal systems. For each element, two contrasting features are presented, representing traditional bureaucratic approaches and newer, high-involvement approaches. Performance appraisals are conducted for a variety of purposes, including affirmative action, pay and promotion decisions, and human resources planning and development. Because each purpose defines what performances are relevant and how they should be measured, separate appraisal systems are often used. For example, appraisal methods for pay purposes are often different from systems that assess employee development or promotability.

Employees also have a variety of reasons for wanting appraisal, such as receiving feedback for career decisions, getting a raise, and being promoted. Rather than trying to meet these multiple purposes with a few standard appraisal systems, the new appraisal approaches are more tailored to balance the multiple organisational and employee needs. This is accomplished by actively involving the appraisee, coworkers, and managers in assessing the purposes of the appraisal at the time it takes place and adjusting the process to fit that purpose. Thus, at one time the appraisal process might focus on pay decisions, another time on employee development, and still another time on employee promotability. Actively involving all relevant participants can increase the chances that the purpose of the appraisal will be correctly identified and understood and that the appropriate appraisal methods will be applied.

#### Table 5.1: Performance Appraisal Elements

| Elements | Traditional Approaches | High-Involvement Approaches |
|---|---|---|
| **Purpose:** | Organisational, legal fragmented | Developmental integrative |
| **Appraiser:** | Supervisor, managers | Appraisee, co-workers and others |
| **Role of appraisee:** | Passive recipient | Active participant |
| **Measurement:** | Subjective concerned with validity | Objective and subjective |
| **Timing:** | Periodic, fixed, administratively driven | Dynamic, timely, employee or work-driven |

The new methods tend to expand the appraiser role beyond managers to include multiple raters, such as the appraisee, peers or coworkers, and direct reports and others having direct exposure to the manager's or employee's performance. Also known as *360-degree feedback*, this broader approach is used more for member development than for compensation purposes. This wider involvement provides a number of different views of the appraisee's performance. It can lead to a more comprehensive assessment of the employee's performance and can increase the likelihood that both organisational and personal needs will be taken into account.

The key task is to form an overarching view of the employee's performance that incorporates all of the different appraisals. Thus, the process of working out differences and arriving at an overall assessment is an important aspect of the appraisal process. This improves the appraisal's acceptance, the accuracy of the information, and its focus on activities that are critical to the business strategy.

The newer methods also expand the role of the appraisee. Traditionally, the employee is simply a receiver of feedback. The supervisor unilaterally completes a form concerning performance on predetermined dimensions, usually personality traits, such as initiative or concern for quality, and presents its contents to the appraisee. The newer approaches actively involve appraisees in all phases of the appraisal process. The appraisee joins with superiors and staff personnel in gathering data on performance and identifying training needs. This active involvement increases the likelihood that the content of the performance appraisal will include the employee's views, needs, and criteria, along with those of the organisation. This newer role for employees increases their acceptance and understanding of the feedback process.

Performance measurement is typically the source of many problems in appraisal because it is seen as subjective. Traditionally, performance evaluation focused on the consistent use of prespecified traits or behaviours. To improve consistency and validity of measurement, considerable training is used to help raters (supervisors) make valid assessments. This concern for validity stems largely from legal tests of performance appraisal systems and leads organisations to develop measurement approaches, such as the *behaviourally anchored rating scale* (BARS) and its variants. In newer approaches, validity is not only a legal or methodological issue but a social issue as well; all appropriate participants are involved in negotiating acceptable ways of measuring and assessing performance. Increased participation in goal setting is a part of this new approach. All participants are trained in methods of measuring and assessing performance. Because it focuses on both objective and subjective measures of performance, the appraisal process is more understood, accepted, and accurate.

### Application Stages

The process of designing and implementing a performance appraisal system has received increasing attention. OD practitioners have recommended the following six steps:

1. **Select the Right People:** For political and legal reasons, the design process needs to include human resources staff, legal representatives, senior management, and system users. Failure to recognise performance appraisal as part of a complex performance management system is the single most important reason for design problems. Members representing a variety of functions need to be involved in the design process so that the essential strategic and organisational issues are addressed.

2. **Diagnose the Current Situation:** A clear picture of the current appraisal process is essential to design a new one. Diagnosis involves assessing the contextual factors (business strategy, workplace technology, and employee involvement), current appraisal practices and satisfaction with them, work design, and the current goal-setting and reward system practices. This information is used to define the current system's strengths and weaknesses.

3. **Establish the System's Purposes and Objectives:** The ultimate purpose of an appraisal system is to help the organisation achieve better performance. Managers, staff, and employees can have more specific views about how the appraisal process can be used. Potential purposes can include serving as a basis for rewards, career planning, human resources planning, and performance improvement or simply giving performance feedback.

4. **Design the Performance Appraisal System:** Given the agreed-upon purposes of the system and the contextual factors, the appropriate elements of an appraisal system can be established. These should include choices about who performs the appraisal, who is involved in determining performance, how performance is measured, and how often feedback is given. Criteria for designing an effective performance appraisal system include timeliness, accuracy, acceptance, understanding, focus on critical control points, and economic feasibility.

   - First, the timeliness criterion recognises the time value of information. Individuals and work groups need to get performance information before evaluation or review. When the information precedes performance evaluation, it can be used to engage in problem-solving behaviour that improves performance and satisfaction.

   - Second, the information contained in performance feedback needs to be accurate. Inaccurate data prevent employees from determining whether their performance is above or below the goal targets and discourage problem-solving behaviour.

   - Third, the performance feedback must be accepted and owned by the people who use it. Participation in the goal-setting process can help to ensure this commitment to the performance appraisal system.

- Fourth, information contained in the appraisal system needs to be understood if it is to have problem-solving value. Many organisations use training to help employees understand the operating, financial, and human resources data that will be fed back to them.

- Fifth, appraisal information should focus on critical control points. The information received by employees must be aligned with important elements of the business strategy, employee performance, and reward system. For example, if the business strategy requires cost reduction but workers are measured and rewarded on the basis of quality, the performance management system may produce the wrong kinds of behaviour.

- Finally, the economic feasibility criterion suggests that an appraisal system should meet a simple cost–benefit test. If the costs associated with collecting and feeding back performance information exceed the benefits derived from using the information, then a simpler system should be installed.

5. **Experiment with Implementation:** The complexity and potential problems associated with performance appraisal processes strongly suggest using a pilot test of the new process to spot, gauge, and correct any flaws in the design before it is implemented systemwide.

6. **Evaluate and Monitor the System:** Although the experimentation step may have uncovered many initial design flaws, ongoing evaluation of the system once it is implemented is important. User satisfaction from human resources staff, manager, and employee viewpoints is an essential input. In addition, the legal defensibility of the system should be tracked by noting the distribution of appraisal scores against age, sex, and ethnic categories.

## 5.2.1.4 Reward Systems

Organisational rewards are powerful incentives for improving employee and work-group performance. Rewards also can produce high levels of employee satisfaction. OD traditionally has relied on intrinsic rewards, such as enriched jobs and opportunities for decision-making, to motivate employee performance. Early quality-of-work-life interventions were based mainly on the intrinsic satisfaction derived from performing challenging, meaningful types of work. More recently, OD practitioners have expanded their focus to include extrinsic rewards: pay; various incentives, such as stock options, bonuses, and gain sharing; promotions; and benefits. They have discovered that both intrinsic and extrinsic rewards can enhance performance and satisfaction.

OD practitioners increasingly are attending to the design and implementation of reward systems. This recent attention to rewards has derived partly from research in organisation design and employee involvement. These perspectives treat rewards as an integral part of an organisation. They hold that rewards should be congruent with other organisational systems and practices, such as the organisation's structure, top management's human relations philosophy, and work designs. Many reward system features contribute to both employee fulfillment and organisational effectiveness. In this section, we describe the structural features of a reward system and how rewards affect individual and group performance; discuss four specific rewards, including skillbased pay, performance-based pay, gain sharing, and promotions; and the process issues involved in establishing and administrating reward systems.

**Structural and Motivational Features of Reward Systems**

A reward system is an important part of an organisation's design and must be aligned with the strategy, structure, employee involvement, and work. The design features of a reward system are summarised in Table 5.2.

1.  **Person/Job Based Vs. Performance Based:** One of the first and most important design choices is the focus or basis of the reward system. The most prevalent system is the job-based system. Here, job descriptions are created for each position in the organisation and a value is attached to the work performed. Pay is based on that valuation process. More recently, reward systems have been crafted around the person in the job and the value brought by their skills and knowledge. Skill-based pay and knowledge-based pay are important examples of this system. The other major alternative is to base rewards on the performance achieved by a job or person. In this system, pay is contingent on the outcomes produced.

**Table 5.2: Reward System Design Features**

| Design Feature | Definition |
| --- | --- |
| **Person/Job based Vs. Performance based:** | The extent to which rewards and incentives are based on the person in a job, the job itself, or the outcomes of the work. |
| **Market position (External equity):** | The relationship between what an organisation pays and what other organisation pays. |
| **Internal equity:** | The extent to which people doing similar work in an organisation are rewarded the same. |
| **Hierarchy:** | The extent to which people in higher positions get more and varied types of rewards than people lower in the organisation. |
| **Centralisation:** | The extent to which reward system design features, decisions and administration are standardised across an organisation. |
| **Rewards mix:** | The extent to which different types of rewards are available and offered to people. |
| **Security:** | The extent to which work is guaranteed. |
| **Seniority:** | The extent to which rewards are based on length of service. |

2. **Individual Vs. Group Rewards:** The interdependency among work tasks is another important reward system contingency. When work is complex and the performance of one task depends on prior tasks, the appropriate work design is team based because successfully adding value requires tight coordination. This tight coordination is reinforced by reward systems that recognise group-level outputs. When work tasks are independent, individual reward systems incent individual behaviour.

3. **Internal and External Equity:** Member satisfaction and motivation can be influenced by design features that ensure that the organisation's pay policies are equitable or fair. Internal equity involves whether similar rewards are given to people holding similar jobs or performing similarly in the organisation. Internal inequities typically occur when employees are paid a similar salary or hourly wage regardless of their position or level of performance. Many organisations work hard to establish practices to ensure that people who are doing similar kinds of activities have similar levels of compensation. External equity involves comparing the organisation's rewards with those of other organisations in the same labour market. Most human resources policies commit to a reward and compensation system relative to the market. Organisations can decide to pay below, at, or above market rates. In their quest for attracting and retaining scarce human resource talent, many organisations have had to commit to above-market pay schemes. When an organisation's reward level does not compare favourably with the level of other organisations, employees are likely to feel inequitably rewarded and may leave.

4. **Hierarchy:** Although not often a formal policy, many organisations offer different types of rewards based on a position's level in the organisation structure. The recent concerns over CEO pay reflect the increasing prevalence of hierarchical reward systems. In hierarchical systems, senior managers have access to a variety of perquisites, such as reserved parking, corporate transportation, financial aid, or health benefits that others do not.

5. **Rewards Mix:** This design feature involves specifying the extent to which different types of rewards are included in the overall reward strategy. These rewards can include pay in various forms, including base salary, bonuses, commissions, and stock; benefits, such as health care, insurance, child care, leaves, and education; and perquisites, including preferred office space, cell phones, cars, or health club memberships. Recent changes in the laws governing the expensing of stock options are changing the way stock is viewed as part of the rewards mix. In addition, although pay receives most of the attention in reward systems, the contribution of other rewards, such as benefit programmes and status incentives, should not be underestimated. For example, rising health care costs and increasing interest in

retaining important skills and competencies have resulted in a variety of benefit innovations to increase the value of this reward.

6.  **Security:** Organisations, such as IBM and AT&T, once offered organisation members lifetime employment as a formal policy. Today, the rapid expansion and contraction of markets and the realities of downsizing have dramatically altered the psychological employment contract. Instead of job security, a more instrumental relationship has emerged. However, organisations can and do make commitments to people and job security and this remains an important feature of reward systems.

7.  **Seniority:** Many reward systems include an implicit or explicit policy concerning the value of longevity. Organisations, especially unionised companies covered by a collective bargaining agreement, often have built-in rewards for increasing lengths of service. The structural features of a reward system represent important design choices available to human resources and other senior managers. These features interact with work design and employee involvement practices to produce goal-directed behaviour and task performance.

Considerable research has been done on how different rewards and reward system features affect individual and group performance. The most popular model describing this relationship is value expectancy theory. In addition to explaining how performance and rewards are related, it suggests requirements for designing and evaluating reward systems. The *value expectancy model* posits that employees will expend effort to achieve performance goals that they believe will lead to outcomes that they value. This effort will result in the desired performance goals if the goals are realistic, if employees fully understand what is expected of them, and if they have the necessary skills and resources. Ongoing motivation depends on the extent to which attaining the desired performance goals actually results in valued outcomes. Consequently, key objectives of reward systems interventions are to identify the intrinsic and extrinsic outcomes (rewards) that are highly valued and to link them to the achievement of desired performance goals. Based on value expectancy theory, the ability of rewards to motivate desired behaviour depends on these five factors:

(i)  **Availability:** For rewards to reinforce desired performance, they must be not only desired but also available. Too little of a desired reward is no reward at all. For example, pay increases are often highly desired but unavailable. Moreover, pay increases that are below minimally accepted standards may actually produce negative consequences.

(ii) **Timeliness:** Like effective performance feedback, rewards should be given in a timely manner. A reward's motivating potential is reduced to the extent that it is separated in time from the performance it is intended to reinforce.

(iii) **Performance contingency:** Rewards should be closely linked with particular performances. If the goal is met, the reward is given; if the target is missed, the reward is reduced or not given. The clearer the linkage between performance and rewards, the better able rewards are to motivate desired behaviour. Unfortunately, this criterion often is neglected in practice. Many, if not most, employees nationwide believe that there is no linkage between pay and performance. If salary increases are concentrated at certain levels, almost everyone, regardless of performance level, will get about the same raise.

(iv) **Durability:** Some rewards last longer than others. Intrinsic rewards, such as increased autonomy and pride in workmanship, tend to last longer than extrinsic rewards. Most people who have received a salary increase realise that it gets spent rather quickly.

(v) **Visibility:** To leverage a reward system, it must be visible. Organisation members must be able to see who is getting the rewards. Visible rewards, such as placement on a high-status project, promotion to a new job, and increased authority, send signals to employees that rewards are available, timely, and performance contingent. Reward systems interventions are used to elicit and maintain desired levels of performance.

**Types of Reward System**

1. **Skill and Knowledge-Based Pay Systems**

The most traditional reward system is individual and job based. The characteristics of a particular job are determined, and pay is made comparable to what other organisations pay for jobs with similar characteristics. Pay increases are primarily a function of cost-of-living adjustments (COLA) or small merit pools that are awarded with little relationship to performance. This job evaluation and reward method tends to result in pay systems with high external and internal equity. However, it fails to reward employees for all of the skills that they have, discourages people from learning new skills, and results in a view of pay as an entitlement.

Skill-based pay systems must first establish the skills needed for effective operations, identify the optimal skill profile and number of employees needed with each skill, price each skill and skill set, develop rules to sequence and acquire skills, and develop methods to measure member skill acquisition. Typically, employees are paid according to the number of different jobs that they can perform. Skill-based pay systems have a number of benefits. They contribute to organisational effectiveness by providing a more flexible workforce and by giving employees a broad perspective on how the entire plant operates. This flexibility can result in leaner staffing and fewer problems with absenteeism, turnover, and work disruptions. Skill-based pay can lead to durable employee satisfaction by reinforcing individual development and by producing an equitable wage rate.

The three major drawbacks of skill-based pay schemes are the tendency to "top out," the expense, and the lack of performance contingency. Top-out occurs when employees learn all the skills there are to learn and then run up against the top end of the pay scale, with no higher levels to attain. Some organisations have resolved this topping-out effect by installing a gain-sharing plan after most employees have learned all relevant jobs. *Gain sharing*, discussed later in this section, ties pay to organisational effectiveness, allowing employees to push beyond previous pay ceilings. Other organisations have resolved this effect by making base skills obsolete and adding new ones, thus raising the standards of employee competence. Skill-based pay systems also require a heavy investment in training, as well as a measurement system capable of indicating when employees have learned the new jobs. These systems typically increase direct labour costs, as employees are paid highly for learning multiple tasks. In addition, because pay is based on skill and not performance, the workforce could be highly paid and flexible but not productive.

## 2.    Performance-Based Pay Systems

In addition to person- or job-based reward systems, organisations have introduced many ways of linking pay to performance, making it the fastest-growing and most popular segment of pay-based reward systems. Studies suggest that 60–70% of businesses have some form of performance-based or variable pay system. They are used in such organisations as American Express, Frito-Lay, and DOW. Pay-for-performance plans tend to compromise three dimensions: (1) the organisational unit by which performance is measured for reward purposes—an individual, group, or organisation basis; (2) the way performance is measured—the subjective measures used in supervisors' ratings or objective measures of productivity, costs, or profits; and (3) what rewards are given for good performance—salary increases, stock, or cash bonuses.

While linking pay to performance, individual pay plans are rated highest, followed by group plans and then organisation plans. The last two plans score lower on this factor because pay is not a direct function of individual behaviour. At the group and organisation levels, an individual's pay is determined by the behaviour of others and by external market conditions. Generally, stock and bonus plans link pay to performance better than do salary plans. The amount of awarded stock may vary sharply from year to year, whereas salary increases tend to be more stable because organisations seldom reduce employees' salaries. Finally, objective measures of performance score higher than subjective measures. Objective measures, such as profit or costs, are more credible, and people are more likely to see the link between pay and objective measures.

As might be expected, group- and organisation-based pay plans encourage cooperation among workers more than do individual plans. Under the former, it is generally to everyone's advantage to work well together because all share in the financial rewards of higher performance. The organisation plans also tend to promote cooperation among functional departments. Because members from different departments feel that they can benefit from each other's performance, they encourage and help each other make positive contributions.

The least acceptable pay plans are individual bonus programmes. Employees tend to dislike such plans because they encourage competition among individuals and because they are difficult to administer fairly. Such plans may be inappropriate in some technical contexts. For example, technical innovations typically lead engineers to adjust piece-rate quotas upward because employees should be able to produce more with the same effort. Workers, on the other hand, often feel that the performance worth of such innovations does not equal the incremental change in quotas, thus resulting in feelings of pay inequity. Employees tend to favour salary increases to bonuses. This follows from the simple fact that a salary increase becomes a permanent part of a person's pay, but a bonus does not.

### 3. Gain-Sharing Systems

As the name suggests, *gain-sharing* involves paying employees a bonus based on improvements in the operating results of an organisation. Although not traditionally associated with employee involvement, gain sharing increasingly has been included in comprehensive employee involvement projects. Many organisations, such as Nucor, Weyerhaeuser, and 3M, are discovering that when designed correctly, gain-sharing plans can contribute to employee motivation, involvement, and performance.

Developing a gain-sharing plan requires making choices about the following design elements:

(a) **Process of Design:** The success of a gain-sharing system depends on employee acceptance and cooperation. Recommended is a participative approach that involves a cross section of employees to design the plan and be trained in gain-sharing concepts and practice. The task force should include people who are credible and represent both management and non-management interests.

(b) **Organisational Unit Covered:** The size of the unit included in the plan can vary widely, from departments or plants with less than 50 employees to companies with several thousand people. A plan covering the entire plant would be ideal in situations where there is a freestanding plant with good performance measures and an employee size of less than 500. When the number of employees exceeds 500, multiple plans may be installed, each covering a relatively discrete part of the company.

(c) **Bonus Formula:** Gain-sharing plans are based on a formula that generates a bonus pool, which is divided among those covered by the plan. Although most plans are custom-designed, there are two general considerations about the nature of the bonus formula. First, a standard of performance must be developed that can be used as a baseline for calculating improvements or losses. Some plans use past performance to form a historical standard, whereas others use engineered or estimated standards. When available, historical data provide a relatively fair standard of performance; engineer-determined data can work, however, if there is a high level of trust in the standard and how it is set. Second, the costs included in arriving at the bonus must be chosen. The key is to focus on those costs that are most controllable by employees. Some plans use labour costs as a proportion of total sales; others include a wider range of controllable costs, such as those for materials and utilities.

(d) **Sharing Process:** Once the bonus formula is ascertained, it is necessary to decide how to share gains when they are obtained. This decision includes choices about what percentage of the bonus pool should go to the company and what percentage to employees. In general, the company should take a percentage low enough to ensure that the plan generates a realistic bonus for employees. Other decisions about dividing the bonus pool include who will share in the bonus and how the money will be divided among employees. Typically, all employees included in the organisational unit covered by the plan share in the bonus. Most plans divide the money on the basis of a straight percentage of total salary payments.

(e) **Frequency of Bonus:** Most plans calculate a bonus monthly. This typically fits with organisational recording needs and is frequent enough to spur employee motivation. Longer payout periods generally are used in seasonal businesses or where there is a long production or billing cycle for a product or service.

(f) **Change Management:** Organisational changes, such as new technology and product mixes, can disrupt the bonus formula. Many plans include a committee to review the plan and to make necessary adjustments, especially in light of significant organisational changes.

(g) **The Participative System:** Many gain-sharing plans include a participative system that helps to gather, assess, and implement employee suggestions and improvements. These systems generally include a procedure for formalising suggestions and different levels of committees for assessing and implementing them.

Although gain-sharing plans are tailored to each situation, three major plans are used most often: the Scanlon plan, the Rucker plan, and Improshare. The most popular programme is the Scanlon plan, and was pioneered in such firms as Donnelly Corporation, De Soto, Midland-Ross, and Dana Corporation.

The incentive part of the Scanlon plan generally includes a bonus formula based on a ratio measure comparing total sales volume to total payroll expenses. This measure of labour cost efficiency is relatively responsive to employee behaviours and is used to construct a historical base rate at the beginning of the plan.

Savings resulting from improvements over this base make up the bonus pool. The bonus is often split equally between the company and the employees, with all members of the organisation receiving bonuses of a percentage of their salaries. The Rucker plan and Improshare use different bonus formulas and place less emphasis on worker participation than does the Scanlon plan.More recently, *goal-sharing* plans have also emerged. Like gain sharing, goal-sharing plans pay bonuses when performance exceeds a standard, but differ in that goalsharing plans are not based on historical and well-understood performance measures.

Rather, goal-sharing plans use changing strategic objectives as the primary standard of performance. Thus, goal sharing is a more flexible reward system than gain sharing.

Gain-sharing plans link the goals of workers to the organisation's goals. It is to the financial advantage of employees to work harder, to cooperate with each other, to make suggestions, and to implement improvements. Reviews of the empirical literature and individual studies suggest that when such plans are implemented properly, organisations can expect specific improvements.

## 4.   Promotion Systems

Like decisions about pay increases, many decisions about promotions and job movements in organisations are made in a closed manner: Higher-level managers decide whether lower-level employees will be promoted. This process can be secretive, with people often not knowing that a position is open, that they are being considered for promotion, or the reasons why some people are promoted but others are not. Without such information, capable people who might be interested in a new job may be overlooked. Furthermore, because employees may fail to see the connection between good performance and promotions, the motivational potential of promotions is reduced. Finally, emphasizing promotions as a reward focuses attention on advancement instead of developing new skills and knowledge and can lead to reduced flexibility in the workforce.

Fortunately, this is changing. Most organisations today have tried to reduce the secrecy surrounding promotions and job changes by openly posting the availability of new jobs and inviting people to nominate themselves. Although open job posting attracts extra administrative costs, it can lead to better promotion decisions. Open posting increases the pool of available personnel by ensuring that interested people will be considered for new jobs and that capable people will be identified. Open posting also can increase employee motivation by showing that a valued reward is available and contingent on performance.

Some organisations have increased the accuracy and equity of job-change decisions by including peers and subordinates in the decision-making process. Peer and subordinate judgements about a person's performance and promotability help bring all relevant data to bear on promotion decisions. Such participation can increase the accuracy of these decisions and can make people feel that the basis for promotions is equitable. In many self-regulating work teams, for example, the group interviews and helps select new members and supervisors. This ensures that new people will fit in and that the group is committed to making that happen. Evidence from high-involvement plants suggests that participation in selecting new members can lead to greater group cohesiveness and task effectiveness.

## 5.2.2 Developing Talent

It consists of three interventions concerned with managing talent in organisations. First, coaching interventions attempt to improve an individual's ability to set and meet goals, lead change, improve interpersonal relations, handle conflict, or address style issues. These resource-intense interventions focus on the skills, knowledge, and capabilities of an organisation member, usually a manager or executive but in the case of mentoring can also apply to individual contributors. Second, career planning and development interventions address different professional needs and concerns as members progress through their work lives. Third, management and leadership development processes are human resource interventions that attempt to transfer knowledge and skills to many individuals. They can include in-house training programmes, external educational opportunities, action-learning projects, and other activities. In the following chapter, we present interventions that address workforce diversity, stress, and employee wellness.

### 5.2.2.1 Coaching and Mentoring

Coaching involves working with organisational members, typically managers and executives, on a regular basis to help them clarify their goals, deal with potential stumbling blocks, and improve their performance. This intervention is highly personal and generally involves a one-on-one relationship between the OD practitioner and the client. Almost every OD intervention involves some coaching.

However, the intervention described here helps managers to gain perspective on their problems and transfer their learning into organisational results; it increases their leadership skill and effectiveness.

Similar to coaching, mentoring involves establishing a relationship between a manager or someone more experienced and another organisation member who is less experienced. Unlike coaching, mentoring is often more directive, with the mentor intentionally transferring specific knowledge and skill and guiding the client's activities, perhaps as part of a career development process (see career planning and development processes in the next section).

Coaching can be seen as a specialised form of OD, one that is focused on using the principles of applied behavioural science to increase the capacity and effectiveness of individuals as opposed to groups or organisations. It is one of the fastest-growing areas of OD practice.

## The Goals of Coaching

Coaching typically addresses one or more of the following goals: assisting an executive to more effectively execute some transition, such as a merger integration or downsizing; addressing a performance problem; or developing new behavioural skills as part of a leadership development programme. In any case, coaching is often confused with therapy. Most coaching approaches acknowledge that coaching is not therapy. While both coaching and therapy focus on personal development, coaching assumes that the client is healthy rather than suffering from some pathology. Coaching is also primarily futuristic and action-oriented rather than focused on the past, as are many therapeutic models. Coaching involves helping clients understand how their behaviours are contributing to the current situation. Such understanding is often difficult to achieve and often deeply personal. Therefore, the limits of a coach's skills and abilities must be acknowledged. Many coaching failures have been attributed to working too far from the practical application of behavioural principles, or too close to the boundaries of therapy, and to the failure of the coach to understand the difference.

## Application Stages

The coaching process closely follows the process of planned change, including entry and contracting, assessment, feedback, action planning, intervention, and assessment. The mentoring process is similar except that the assessment is generally presumed and the process moves straight to action planning interventions.

1.  **Establish the Principles of the Relationship:** The initial phases of a coaching intervention involve establishing the goals of the engagement; the parameters of the relationship, such as schedules, resources, and compensation; and ethical considerations, such as confidentiality and boundary issues.

2.  **Conduct an Assessment:** This process can be personal or systemic. In a personal assessment, the client is guided through an assessment framework. It can involve a set of interview questions that bring forth development opportunities or a more formal personal-style instrument, such as the Myers–Briggs Type Indicator, the FIRO-B, or DISC profile. Other instruments, including the Hogan's battery of tests, the Minnesota Multiphasic Personality Inventory (MMPI), or the "Big 5" instrument, can also be used, but they require extensive training and certification. OD practitioners should carefully consider the ethics of using different instruments and their qualifications for administering and interpreting the results. In a systemic assessment, the client's team, peers, and relevant others are engaged in the

process. The most common form of systemic assessment involves a 360-degree feedback process.

**3.   Debrief the Results:** The coach and client review the assessment data and agree on a diagnosis. The purpose of the feedback session is to get the client to move to action. In light of the assessment data, intervention goals can be further refined and revised if necessary.

**4.   Develop an Action Plan:** The specific activities the client and coach will engage in are outlined. These can include new actions that will lead to goal achievement, learning opportunities that build knowledge and skill, or projects to demonstrate competence. Developing an action plan can be the most difficult part of the process because the client must own the results of the assessment and begin to see new possibilities for action. The action plan should also include methods and milestones to monitor progress and to evaluate the effectiveness of the coaching process.

**5.   Implement the Action Plan:** In addition to the elements of the action plan listed above, much of the coaching process involves one-on-one meetings between the coach and the client. In these sessions, the coach supports and encourages the client to act on her/his intentions. A considerable amount of skill is required to confront, challenge, and facilitate learning.

**6.   Assess the Results:** At periodic intervals, the coach and client review and evaluate the results of implementation. Based on this information, the goals or action plans can be changed, or the process can be terminated.

## `5.2.2.2` Career Planning and Development Interventions

Organisations are relying more and more on their "intellectual capital." The war for talent, the changing nature of the workforce, shifting social expectations about work and family, and increasingly knowledge-based strategies have pressured organisations to rethink their role in managing careers and developing their human capital. Providing career planning and development opportunities as well as management and leadership development programmes help to recruit and retain skilled and knowledgeable workers. Many talented job candidates, especially minorities and women, are showing interest and more loyalty for employers who offer career and leadership development opportunities.

Career planning and development interventions are an important tool in developing and retaining an effective workforce. Many managers and professional staff are seeking more control over their work lives. Organisation members, especially women, minorities, mid-career workers, and new college recruits, are not willing to have their careers "just happen" and are taking an active role in planning and managing them.

## The Goals of Career Planning

Career planning and development interventions provide the appropriate resources, tools, and processes necessary to help organisation members plan and attain their career objectives. A career consists of a sequence of work-related positions occupied by a person during the course of a lifetime. *Career planning* is concerned with individuals choosing jobs, occupations, and organisations at each stage of their careers. *Career development* involves helping employees attain career objectives. Although both of these interventions generally are aimed at managerial and professional employees, a growing number of programmes are including lower-level employees, particularly those in white-collar jobs.

Research suggests that employees progress through at least four distinct career stages as they mature and gain experience. Each stage has unique concerns, needs, and challenges.

1.  **The Establishment Stage (ages 21–26):** This phase is at the beginning of a career when people are generally uncertain and may be stressed about their competence and potential. They are dependent on others, especially bosses and more experienced employees, for guidance, support, and feedback. At this stage, people are making initial choices about committing themselves to a specific career, organisation, and job. They are exploring possibilities while learning about their own capabilities.

2.  **The Advancement Stage (ages 26–40):** During this phase, employees become independent contributors who are concerned with achieving and advancing in their chosen careers. They have learned to perform autonomously and need less guidance from bosses and closer ties with colleagues. This settling-down period also encourages attempts to clarify the range of long-term career options.

3.  **The Maintenance Stage (ages 40–60):** This phase involves holding on to career successes. Many people at this stage have achieved their greatest advancements and are now concerned with helping less-experienced subordinates. For those who are dissatisfied with their career progress, this period can be confusing and depressing, as suggested by the term "midlife crisis." People often reassess their circumstances, search for alternatives, and redirect their career efforts. Success in these endeavours can lead to continuing growth, whereas failure can lead to early decline.

4.  **The Withdrawal Stage (age 60 and above):** This final stage is concerned with leaving a career. It involves letting go of organisational attachments and getting ready for greater leisure time and retirement. The employee's major contributions are imparting knowledge and experience to others. For those people who are generally satisfied with their careers, this period can result in feelings of fulfilment and a willingness to leave the career behind. The different career stages represent a broad developmental perspective on people's jobs. They provide insight into the personal and career issues that people are likely to face at different career phases. These issues can be potential sources of stress because employees

are likely to go through the phases at different rates, and to experience personal and career issues differently at each stage. For example, one person may experience the maintenance stage as a positive opportunity to develop less-experienced employees; another person may experience the maintenance stage as a stressful levelling off of career success.

**Application Stages**

The two primary application steps are establishing a system for career planning and assembling an appropriate set of career development processes.

**1.    Establish a Career Planning system:** Career planning involves setting individual career objectives. It is highly personalised and generally includes determining one's interests, capabilities, values, and goals; exploring alternative careers; taking decisions that may affect the current job; and planning how to progress in the desired direction. This process results in people choosing jobs, occupations, and organisations. It determines, for example, whether individuals will accept or decline promotions and transfers and whether they will stay with or leave the company for another job or for retirement. Individual responsibility for careers and career planning has increased significantly, and recent estimates project that an individual career beginning now will involve an average of eight major job and/or organisation changes.

Further, as organisations downsize and restructure, there is less trust in the organisation to provide job security. In the past, when employees more frequently spent their entire career in one organisation, careers were judged in terms of advancement and promotion upward in the organisational structure. Today, they are defined in more appropriate ways to include a person's attitudes, experiences, and ability to perform. For example, individuals may make numerous job changes to acquire additional responsibilities, skills, and knowledge within or across organisations, or they can remain in the same job, acquiring and developing new skills, and have a successful career. Similarly, people may move horizontally through a series of jobs in different functional areas of the firm. Although they may not be promoted upward in the organisational structure, their broadened job experiences constitute a successful career.

The four career stages can be used to make career planning more effective. Table 5.3 shows the different career stages and the career planning issues relevant at each phase. Applying the table to a particular employee involves first diagnosing the person's existing career stage—establishment, advancement, maintenance, or withdrawal. Next, available career planning resources are used to help the employee address important issues. Career planning programmes include some or all of the following resources.

### Table 5.3: Career Stages and Career Planning Issues

| Career Stage | Career Planning Issues |
|---|---|
| Establishment: | What are alternative occupations, organisations, and jobs?<br>What are my interests and capabilities?<br>How do I get the work accomplished?<br>Am I performing as expected?<br>Am I developing the necessary skills for advancement? |
| Advancement: | Am I advancing as expected?<br>How can I advance more effectively?<br>What long-term options are available?<br>How do I get more exposure and visibility?<br>How do I develop more effective peer relationships?<br>How do I better integrate career choices with my personal life? |
| Maintenance: | How do I help others become established and advance?<br>Should I reassess myself and my career?<br>Should I redirect my actions? |
| Withdrawal: | What are my interests outside of work?<br>What post-retirement work options are available to me?<br>How can I be financially secure?<br>How can I continue to help others? |

Communication about career opportunities and resources available to employees within the organisation.

Workshops to encourage employees to assess their interests, abilities, and job situations and to formulate career development plans.

Career counselling by managers or human resources personnel.

Self-development materials, such as books, videotapes, and other media, directed toward identifying life and career issues.

Assessment programmes that provide various tests of vocational interests, aptitudes, and abilities relevant to setting career goals.

(a)  According to Table 5.3, the company should provide members in the establishment stage with considerable communication and counselling about available career paths and the skills and abilities needed to progress in them. Workshops, self-development materials, and assessment techniques should be undertaken in helping employees assess their interests, aptitudes, and capabilities and at linking that information to possible careers and jobs.

Considerable attention should be given to employees' continual feedback about job performance and counselling them on how to improve it. The supervisor–subordinate relationship is especially important for these feedback and development activities.

(b) In the advancement stage, organisations should provide members with communication and counselling about challenging assignments and possibilities for more exposure and demonstration of skills. This communication and counselling should help clarify the range of possible long-term career options and provide members with some idea about where they stand in achieving them. Workshops, developmental materials, and assessment methods should be aimed at helping employees develop wider collegial relationships, join with effective mentors and sponsors, and develop more creativity and innovation. These activities also should help people assess both career and personal life spheres and integrate them more successfully.

(c) At the maintenance stage, the firm should provide individuals with communications about the broader organisation and how their desires and roles might fit into it. Workshops, developmental materials, counselling, and assessment techniques should be aimed at helping employees to assess and develop skills to train and coach others.

(d) Organisations should provide members in the withdrawal stage with communications and counselling about options for post-retirement work and financial security, and it should convey the message that the employee's experience in the organisation is still valued. Retirement planning workshops and materials can help employees gain the skills and information necessary to make a successful transition from work to nonwork life. They can prepare people to shift their attention away from the organisation to other interests and activities.

Effective career planning and development requires a comprehensive programme integrating both corporate business objectives and employee career needs. As shown in Figure 18.1, this is accomplished through human resources planning aimed at developing and maintaining a workforce to meet business objectives. It includes recruiting new talent, matching people to jobs, helping them develop careers and perform effectively, and preparing them for satisfactory retirement. Career planning activities also support career development and human resources planning activities.

**2. Assemble an Appropriate Set of Career Development Processes:** Career development processes help individuals achieve their career objectives. Career development follows closely from career planning and includes organisational practices that help employees implement those plans. Career development can be integrated with people's career needs by linking it to different career stages. Employees progress through distinct career stages, each with unique issues relevant to career planning: establishment, advancement, maintenance, and withdrawal. Career development interventions help members implement these plans.

Table 5.4 identifies career development processes, lists the career stages to which they are most relevant, and defines their key purposes and intended outcomes. It shows that career development practices may apply to one or more career stages and that many processes double as both career development processes and interventions in their own right. Performance management, for example, is relevant to all stages, but especially in establishment and advancement stages, and is an important independent intervention.

Career development processes also can contribute to different organisational outcomes such as lowering turnover and costs and enhancing member satisfaction. Career development processes traditionally have been applied to younger employees who have a longer time period to contribute to the firm than do older members. Managers often stereotype older employees as being less creative, alert, and productive than younger workers and consequently provide them with less career development support. However, the aging of the workforce has focused new attention on older workers, including a focus on the pace and organisation of work, physical and psychological factors, and ergonomic factors.

To sustain a highly committed and motivated workforce, organisations increasingly will have to address the career needs of older employees. They will have to recognise and reward the contributions that older workers make to the company. Workforce diversity interventions, discussed in the next chapter, are a positive step in that direction. We present eight interventions that can be mixed and matched to meet the needs of a diverse workforce, including realistic job previews, assessment centres, job rotation and challenging assignments, consultative roles and mentoring, performance management, developmental training, work–life balance, and phased retirement.

**(a) Realistic Job Preview:** This intervention provides applicants with credible expectations about the job during the recruitment process. It provides recruits with information about whether the job is likely to be consistent with their needs and career plans. Knowledge resulting from realistic job previews can be especially useful during the establishment stage, when people are most in need of full and balanced information about organisations and jobs. It also can help employees during the advancement stage, when job changes are likely to occur because of promotion.

Research suggests that people may develop unrealistic expectations about the organisation and job. They can suffer from "reality shock" when those expectations are not fulfilled and may leave the organisation or stay and become disgruntled and unmotivated. To overcome these problems, organisations such as Texas Instruments, Prudential Insurance, and Johnson & Johnson provide new recruits with information about both the positive and the negative aspects of the company and the job. They furnish recruits with booklets, talks, and site visits showing what organisational life is really like. Such information reduces the chances that employees will develop unrealistic job expectations, become disgruntled, and leave the company, especially when their tenure is viewed over the long term.

**Table 5.4**

| Intervention | Career Stage | Purpose | Intended Outcome |
| --- | --- | --- | --- |
| Realistic job: | Establishment Maintenance Advancement | To provide members with an accurate expectation of work requirements | Reduce turnover Reduce training costs Increase commitment |
| Assessment centres: | Establishment Maintenance Advancement | To select and develop members for managerial and technical jobs | Increase person-job fit Identify high-potential candidates |
| Job rotation and challenging assignments: | Establishment Maintenance Advancement | To provide members with interesting work assignments leading to career objects | Reduce turnover Build organisational knowledge increase job satisfaction Maintain member motivation |
| Consultative roles: | Maintenance Withdrawal | To help members fill productive roles later in their careers and provide less experienced members with exposure to key knowledge and skill | Increase problem-solving capacity Increase job satisfaction Increase member motivation |
| Developmental training: | Establishment Maintenance Advancement Withdrawal | To provide education and training opportunities that help members achieve career goals | Increase organisational capacity |
| Performance management: | Establishment Maintenance Advancement Withdrawal | To provide education and training opportunities that help members achieve career progress and work effectiveness | Increase productivity Increase job satisfaction Monitor human resources development |
| Work-life balance: | Establishment Maintenance Advancement Withdrawal | To help members balance work and personal goals | Improve quality of life Increase productivity and morale Increase organisational commitment Decrease absenteeism Decrease turnover |

**(b) Assessment Centres:** This intervention was traditionally designed to help organisations select and develop employees with high potential for managerial jobs. More recently, assessment centres have been extended to career development and to selection of people to fit new work designs, such as self-managing teams. Assessment centres can be designed and operated "in house," but are often contracted out to consulting firms that specialise in selection and assessment psychology.

When used to evaluate managerial capability, assessment centres typically process 12–15 people at a time and require them to spend two to three days on site. Participants are given a comprehensive interview, take several tests of mental ability and knowledge, and participate in individual and group exercises intended to resemble managerial work. An assessment team consisting of experienced managers and human resources specialists observes the behaviours and performance of each candidate. This team arrives at an overall assessment of each participant's managerial potential, including a rating on several items believed to be relevant to managerial success in the organisation, and pass the results to management for use in making promotion decisions.

Assessment centres have been applied to career development as well, where the emphasis is on feedback of results to participants. Trained staff help participants hear and understand feedback about their strong and weak points. They help participants become clearer about career advancement and identify training experiences and job assignments to promote that progress. When used for developmental purposes, assessment centres can provide employees with the support and direction needed for career development. They can demonstrate that the company is a partner rather than an adversary in that process. Although assessment centres can help people's careers at all stages of development, they seem particularly useful at the advancement stage, when employees need to assess their talents and capabilities in light of long-term career commitments.

**(c) Job Rotation and Challenging Assignments:** The purpose of these interventions is to provide employees with the experience and visibility needed for career advancement or with the challenge needed to refresh a stagnant career at the maintenance stage. A more formalised approach to job rotation is called *job pathing* or *career ladders*, which specify a sequence of jobs to reach a career objective, although the notion of a job path in the new economy is being challenged. Job rotation and challenging assignments are less planned and may not be as oriented to promotion opportunities. Job rotation during the establishment and advancement stages help members develop new skills, knowledge, and competencies in new jobs. Organisation members in the advancement stage may be moved into new job areas after they have demonstrated competence in a particular work specialty.

Research suggests that employees who receive challenging job assignments early in their careers do better in later jobs. Companies such as Corning, Hewlett-Packard, American

Crystal Sugar Company, and Fidelity Investments identify "comers" (managers under 40 with potential for assuming top management positions) and "hipos" (high-potential candidates) and provide them with crossdivisional job experiences during the advancement stage. These job transfers provide managers with a broader range of skills and knowledge as well as opportunities to display their managerial talent to a wider audience of corporate executives.

Such exposure helps the organisation identify members who are capable of handling senior executive responsibilities; it helps the members decide whether to seek promotion to higher positions or to particular departments. Retaining "hipos" is seen as critical to success in today's highly competitive labour market. To reduce the risk of transferring employees across divisions or functions, some firms create "fallback positions." These jobs are identified before the transfer, and employees are guaranteed that they can return to them without negative consequences if the transfers or promotions do not work out. Fallback positions reduce the risk that employees in the advancement stage will become trapped in a new job assignment that is neither challenging nor highly visible in the company.

In the maintenance stage, challenging assignments or job pathing can help revitalise veteran employees by providing them with new challenges and opportunities for learning and contribution. Research on enriched jobs suggests that people are most responsive to them during the first one to three years on a job, when enriched jobs are likely to be seen as challenging and motivating. People who remain on enriched jobs for three years or more tend to become unresponsive to them, and may no longer be motivated and satisfied by enriched jobs. One way to prevent this loss of job motivation—especially among mid-career employees who are likely to remain on jobs for longer periods of time than are people in the establishment and advancement phases—is to rotate workers to new, more challenging jobs at about three-year intervals, or to redesign their jobs at those times. Such job changes would keep employees responsive to challenging jobs and sustain motivation and satisfaction during the maintenance phase.

**(d) Consultative Roles:** This role involves opportunities to apply wisdom and knowledge to help others develop in their careers and solve organisational problems, and is most frequently offered to employees in the maintenance and withdrawal stages. Such roles, which can be structured around specific projects or problems, involve offering advice and expertise to those responsible for resolving the issues, thus increasing the organisation's problem-solving abilities.

For example, a large aluminium-forging manufacturer was having problems developing accurate estimates of the cost of producing new products. The sales and estimating departments lacked the production experience to make accurate bids for potential new business, thus either losing customers or losing money on products. The company temporarily assigned an old-line production manager who was nearing retirement to consult with the salespeople and estimators about bidding on new business. The consultant applied his years of forging experience to help the sales and estimating people make more accurate estimates. In about a year, the sales staff and estimators gained the skills and invaluable knowledge necessary to make more accurate bids. Perhaps equally important, the pre-retirement production manager felt that he had made a significant contribution to the company—something he had not experienced for years.

In contrast to coaching and mentoring, consultative roles are directed at helping others deal with complex problems or projects. Similarly, in contrast to managerial positions, consultative roles do not include the performance evaluation and control inherent in being a manager. They are based more on wisdom and experience than on authority. Consequently, consultative roles provide an effective transition for moving pre-retirement managers into more support-staff positions. They free up managerial positions for younger employees while allowing older managers to apply their experience and skills in a more supportive and less threatening way than might be possible from a strictly managerial role.

**(e) Developmental Training:** Training and development interventions are among the oldest strategies for organisational change. They provide new or existing organisation members with the skills and knowledge they need to perform work. The focus of training interventions has broadened from classroom methods aimed at hourly workers to varied methods, including simulations, action learning, computer-based or online training, and case studies, intended for all levels and types of organisation members. Training and development is a large practice area with growing importance in organisations.

This intervention is applicable to all career stages and helps employees gain the skills and knowledge for successfully fulfilling current job responsibilities. It may include workshops and training materials oriented to communications or supervising others as well as technical aspects of work. It can also involve substantial investments in education, such as tuition reimbursement programmes that assist members in achieving advanced degrees. Developmental training interventions generally are aimed at increasing the organisation's reservoir of skills and knowledge, and can be related to increased retention and performance. This enhances its capability to implement personal and organisational strategies.

**(f) Performance Management:** One of the most effective interventions during the establishment and advancement phases is the integration of performance management systems with career development conversations. Employees need continual feedback about goal achievement as well as the necessary support to improve their performances. Feedback and support, in the form of coaching, developmental training, or management development, are particularly relevant when employees are establishing careers. They will have concerns about how to perform the work, whether they are performing up to expectations, and whether they are gaining the necessary skills for advancement.

A manager can facilitate career establishment by providing feedback on performance and on-the-job training. These activities can help employees get the job done while meeting their career development needs. Companies such as Intel and Monsanto, for example, are effective at integrating performance management processes with employee career development. They separate the career development aspect of performance appraisal from the salary review component, thus ensuring that employees' career needs receive as much attention as salary issues. Feedback and support interventions can increase employee performance, satisfaction, and morale, and provide a systematic way to monitor the development of human resources in the firm, at little or no cost.

**(g) Work–Life Balance Interventions:** This OD intervention helps employees better integrate and balance work and home life. Restructuring, downsizing, and increased global competition have contributed to longer work hours and more stress.

Early work–life balance programmes started with a focus on women with young children in the workforce, but now these programmes serve men and women, all ages, and all family and life situations. Work–life programmes continue to not only focus on dependent care of both children and elders, but also focus on job scheduling and flexibility, paid and unpaid leaves, employee wellness, concierge services, and others.

Work–life balance planning helps members better manage the interface between work or paid employment and all the work and responsibilities associated with a person's life. Although these interventions can apply to all career stages, they are especially relevant during advancement. This is because of the increased number of dual-career households. Transfer to another location—a common occurrence during the advancement stage—usually means that the working partner must also relocate. In many cases, the company employing the partner must either lose the employee or arrange a transfer to the same location. Dual careers also affect expatriate assignments, and being able to facilitate or accommodate a spouse or partner's wish to work may make the difference in terms of an employee accepting such an assignment. Similar problems can occur in recruiting employees. A recruit may not join an organisation if its location does not provide career opportunities for the partner.

**(h) Phased Retirement:** This provides older employees with an effective way of withdrawing from the organisation and establishing a productive leisure life, by gradually reducing work hours and moving to full retirement. A recent study of women over 35 indicates a strong interest for phased retirement plans, which may put new demands on related human resource management programmes. Employees gradually devote less of their time to the organisation and more time to leisure pursuits (which to some might include developing a new career). For example, people may use the extra time off work to take courses, to gain new skills and knowledge, and to create opportunities for productive leisure.

Equally important, phased retirement lessens the reality shock often experienced by those who retire all at once. It helps employees grow accustomed to leisure life and withdraw emotionally from the organisation. A growing number of companies have some form of phased retirement. Pepperdine University and the University of Southern California, for example, implemented a phased retirement programme for professors that allows them some choice about part-time employment starting at age 55. The programme is intended to provide more promotional positions for younger academics and to give older professors greater opportunities to establish a leisure life and still enjoy many benefits of the university.

### 5.2.2.3 Management and Leadership Development

**Interventions**

Management and leadership development programmes are one of the most popular OD interventions aimed at developing talent and increasing employee retention. These programmes build an individual's skills, socialise leaders in corporate values, and prepare executives for strategic leadership roles. A large number of organisations offer leadership development programmes, including Procter & Gamble, Federal Express, PepsiCo, Cisco Systems, IBM, Microsoft, and Hewlett-Packard.

Management and leadership development interventions can be differentiated from career development. In management and leadership development, the focus is on developing the skills and knowledge the organisation believes will be necessary to implement future strategies and manage the business. In career development, the focus is on building the skills and knowledge the individual believes will best equip them for the career they prefer. Ideally, there is considerable overlap between the two.

**The Goals of Training and Management Development**

The term *training* is typically used when the goal is development of the workforce, while the terms *management development* and *leadership development* are normally applied when the goal is development of the organisation's management and executive talent. There is a wide range of training and development interventions, and not all involve OD. For leadership development to be considered an OD intervention, it must focus on changing the skills and knowledge of a group of organisation members to improve their effectiveness or to build the capabilities of an organisation system. For example, a leadership development programme that provides information about the organisation's strategy would not qualify as an OD intervention.

**Application Stages**

Management and leadership development interventions generally follow a process of needs assessment, setting instructional objectives and design, delivery, and evaluation.

1.   **Perform a needs assessment:** Similar to the diagnostic process in the general model of planned change, a needs assessment typically determines the competencies believed to characterise effective leaders in the organisation. This can be done by interviewing well-respected executives or reviewing lists of published leadership

competencies. The logic assumes that if the right leadership skills and knowledge can be identified, a programme can be developed to educate and equip participants with these competencies. McCall has challenged this approach and suggested that good leaders develop competencies from experience, not training. As a result, a needs assessment must gather data on the strategy, the organisation, and the individuals who might attend the leadership programme.

(a) The ***strategy assessment*** involves understanding the knowledge and experiences future leaders will need to execute the business strategy. It includes tasks, activities, and decisions that participants should perform better after training as well as the conceptual frameworks that guide these activities. This can be done by identifying the top three to five external and internal leadership challenges facing the business and the experiences that might help build the competence to deal with them.

(b) The **organisation** *assessment* focuses on the systems that may affect the ability to transfer learning and developmental experiences back to the organisation. For transfer to occur, participants must be provided with the opportunity and appropriate conditions to apply their new skills, knowledge, and abilities to the work situation. The organisation assessment determines whether the necessary support exists in the organisation to make leadership development worthwhile.

For example, if executives are generally unwilling to send their managers to the programme for fear of losing them to promotion, then the organisation assessment would suggest addressing management's readiness for change before implementing the programme.

(c) The final element, ***individual assessment***, aims to understand the existing pool of people who should be candidates for the programme. Such an assessment would include their current level and ranges of skills, knowledge, and abilities. Recently, leadership development programmes have begun to focus on the personal growth of the participants, and so an important part of the assessment would be to understand individuals' attitudes toward personal reflection and its role in leadership effectiveness.

**2.  Develop the objectives and design of the training:** This step first establishes outcome objectives for development intervention. These objectives should describe both the results expected from a competent leader and how those results were achieved. For a leadership development programme, an appropriate objective might be "the ability to produce an acceptable strategic plan for a strategic business unit" or "to increase participants' commitment to the strategic direction of the corporation." The design of the training involves making choices from among a wide variety of techniques. The more traditional methods of classroom lectures, 360-degree feedback, simulations, case studies, or experiential exercises have been augmented by more recent emphases on rotational assignments, on-the-job training, coaching, or action-learning projects.

3.   **Deliver the training:** This stage implements the development programme. Participants apply, or are invited, to attend the programme, complete the activities included in its design, and return to their normal work routines.

4.   **Evaluate the training:** This final step assesses the training to determine whether it met its objectives. The four criteria most commonly used to evaluate training effectiveness are reaction, learning, behaviour, and results. *Reaction* is the most commonly used evaluation criterion and refers simply to the participants' initial judgment about the training's usefulness. It is often assessed via questionnaires completed immediately following the training activity. The *learning* criterion refers to whether or not participants acquired the knowledge that should have been transferred during the training; it stops short of assessing performance or behaviour on the job. This can be assessed via interview or questionnaire. The *behaviour* criterion assesses whether new skills and abilities gained in the training are actually applied to job activities. These data can be collected through observation or through interviews with the participant's manager. The final criterion, *results*, determines whether or not the training can be credited with improvements in the participant's or the system's effectiveness.

## 5.2.3 Managing Workforce Diversity and Wellness

Increasing workforce diversity provides an especially challenging environment for human resources management, and an attractive opportunity for line managers looking for a source of innovation. The mix of age, gender, race, sexual orientation, disabilities, and culture and value orientations in the modern workforce is increasingly varied. Management's perspectives, strategic responses, and implementation approaches can help address pressures posed by this diversity and leverage this resource for organisation effectiveness. In addition, wellness interventions, such as stress management programmes and employee assistance programmes (EAPs), are addressing several important social trends, such as the relationship and interaction between professional and personal roles and lives, fitness and health consciousness, and drug and alcohol abuse.

### 5.2.3.1 Workforce Diversity Interventions

Several profound trends are shaping the labour markets of modern organisations. Researchers suggest and managers confirm that contemporary workforce characteristics are radically different from what they were just 20 years ago. Employees represent every ethnic background and colour; range from highly educated to illiterate; vary in age from 18 to 80; may appear perfectly healthy or may have a terminal illness; may be single parents or part of dual-income, divorced, same-sex, or traditional families; and may be physically or mentally challenged.

Workforce diversity is more than a euphemism for cultural or racial differences. Such a definition is too narrow and focuses attention away from the broad range of issues that a diverse workforce poses. Diversity results from people who bring different resources and perspectives to the workplace and who have distinctive needs, preferences, expectations, and lifestyles. Organisations must design human resources systems that account for these differences if they are to attract and retain a productive workforce and if they want to turn diversity into a competitive advantage.

## The Goals of Workforce Diversity and Wellness

Social norms and globalisation support the belief that organisation performance is enhanced when the workforce's diversity is embraced as an opportunity. But diversity is often discouraged by those who fear that too many perspectives, beliefs, values, and attitudes dilute organisation performance.

Second, management's *perspective and priorities* with respect to diversity can range from resistance to active learning and from marginal to strategic. For example, organisations can resist diversity by implementing only legally mandated policies such as affirmative action, or equal employment opportunity.

On the other hand, a learning and strategic perspective can lead management to view diversity as a source of competitive advantage. For example, a health care organisation with a diverse customer base can not only improve perceptions of service quality by having a more diverse physician base, it can embrace diversity by tailoring the range of services to that market and building systems and processes that are flexible.

Third, within management's priorities, the organisation's *strategic responses* can range from reactive to proactive. Diversity efforts at Texaco and Denny's had little momentum until a series of embarrassing race-based events forced a response. Fourth, the organisation's *implementation style* can range from episodic to systemic. A diversity approach will be most effective when the strategic responses and implementation style fit with management's intent and internal and external pressures. Unfortunately, organisations have tended to address workforce diversity pressures in a piecemeal fashion; only five percent of more than 1,400 companies surveyed in the mid-1990s thought they were doing a "very good job" of managing diversity. As each trend makes itself felt, the organisation reacts with appropriate but narrow responses.

## Application Stages

Many of the OD interventions described in this book can be applied to the strategic responses and implementation of workforce diversity, as shown in Table 5.5. It summarizes several of the internal and external pressures facing organisations, including age, gender, race, disability, culture and values, and sexual orientation. For example, the median age of the workforce is increasing, women make up a larger percentage of the workforce, and globalisation is increasing the number of different cultural values present in the workplace. The table also reports the major trends characterising those dimensions, organisational implications and workforce needs, and specific OD interventions that can address those implications.

**1. Age:** To address age diversity, organisation development interventions, such as work design, wellness programmes (discussed below), career planning and development, and reward systems must be adapted to these different age groups and demographic cohorts. For the older employee, work designs can reduce the physical components or increase the knowledge and experience components of a job. At Builder's Emporium, a chain of home improvement centres, the store clerk job was redesigned to eliminate heavy lifting by assigning night crews to replenish shelves and emphasizing sales ability instead of strength. Generation-X workers will likely require more challenge and autonomy. Wellness programmes can be used to address the physical and mental health of both generations. Career planning and development programmes will have to recognise the different career stages of each generation and offer resources tailored to that stage.

Finally, reward system interventions may offer increased health benefits, time off, and other perks for the older workforce while using promotion, ownership, and pay to attract and motivate the younger workforce.

### Table 5.5: Work Diversity Dimensions and Interventions

| Workforce Differences | Trends | Implications and Needs | Interventions |
|---|---|---|---|
| Age: | Median age up<br>Distribution of ages changing | Health care<br>Mobility<br>Security | Wellness programme<br>Job design<br>Career planning and development<br>Reward system |
| Gender: | Percentage of women increasing<br>Dual-income families | Child care<br>Maternity/Paternity leave<br>Single parents | Job design<br>Fringe benefit rewards |
| Disability: | The number of people with disabilities entering the workforce is increasing | Job challenge<br>Job skills<br>Physical space<br>Respect and dignity | Performance management<br>Job design<br>Career planning and development |
| Culture and values: | Rising proportion of immigrant and minority-group workers<br>Shift in rewards | Flexible organisational policies<br>Autonomy<br>Affirmation respect | Career planning and development<br>Employee involvement<br>Reward systems |
| Sexual orientation: | Number of single-sex households up<br>Morale liberal attitudes toward sexual orientation | Discrimination | Equal employment opportunities<br>Fringe benefits<br>Education and training |

**2.** **Gender:** Work design, reward systems, and career development are among the more important interventions for addressing issues arising out of the gender trend. For example, jobs can be modified to accommodate the special demands of working mothers. A number of organisations, such as AstraZeneca, Volkswagen of America, and Hewlett-Packard, have instituted job sharing, by which two people perform the tasks associated with one job. The firms have done this to allow their female employees to pursue both family and work careers. Reward system interventions, especially fringe benefits, can be tailored to offer special leaves to mothers and fathers, child-care options, flexible working hours, and health and wellness benefits.

The Container Store offers a family-friendly shift from 9 a.m. to 2 p.m. so that working mothers can easily drop off and pick up kids from school. Career development interventions help maintain, develop, and retain a competent and diverse workforce. Recent research on career development programmes suggests that organisations consider the assumptions embedded in their career development programmes to ensure programmes are not biased toward masculine experiences and worldviews, especially those related to careers.

Unfortunately, many programmes over the last several years have tended to focus more on the symptoms, as opposed to sources of gender inequity. Recent research suggests that once an organisation recognises the problem, diagnosis through interviews with employees is critical to addressing the sources of gender inequity. The research further suggests that using a strategy of small interventions, "small wins," or small initiatives that combine behaviour and understanding and that target the organisation's specific issues are more effective. For example, one European retail company discovered upon interviewing its employees that a key issue in turnover among female employees was the company's lack of discipline regarding time. Last-minute scheduling, meeting overruns, and tardiness wreaked havoc on female employees trying to manage work and home responsibilities. Company leadership began a more disciplined approach to time, resulting in greater efficiency and effectiveness. Resolving such issues requires careful and organisation-specific diagnosis and intervention.

**3.** **Race/Ethnicity:** Race continues to be an important issue in diversity interventions, especially as organisations work to increase diversity among top leadership and board members. Training can increase the likelihood that effective diversity management programmes rely on data (not impressions or perceptions) and are responsive, move beyond eliminating obvious racism to eradicating more subtle forms as well, eliminate vague selection and promotion criteria which can let discrimination persist, link diversity management to individual performance appraisals, and develop and enforce appropriate rules.

**4.** **Sexual Orientation:** Diversity in sexual and affectional orientation, including gay, lesbian, and bisexual individuals and couples, increasingly is affecting the way that organisations think about human resources. The primary organisational implication of sexual orientation diversity is discrimination. Gay men and lesbians often are reticent to discuss how organisational policies can be less discriminatory because they fear their openness will lead to unfair treatment. People can have strong emotional reactions to sexual orientation. When these feelings interact with the gender, culture, and value trends described in this section, the likelihood of both overt and unconscious discrimination is high, especially around the often-misperceived relationship between sexual orientation and AIDS/HIV.

Interventions aimed at this dimension of workforce diversity are relatively new in OD and are being developed as organisations encounter sexual orientation issues in the workplace. The most frequent response is education and training. This intervention increases members' awareness of the facts and decreases the likelihood of overt discrimination. While sexual orientation is not protected under federal equal employment opportunity (EEO) laws, many cities and states have passed legislation protecting sexual orientation. Human resources practices having to do with EEO and fringe benefits also can help to address sexual orientation parity issues.

**5.   Disability:** The organisational implications of the disability trend represent both opportunity and adjustment. The productivity of physically and mentally disabled workers often surprises managers. Training is required to increase managers' awareness of this opportunity and to create a climate where accommodation requests can be made without fear. Employing disabled workers, however, also means a need for more comprehensive health care, new physical workplace layouts, new attitudes toward working with the disabled, and challenging jobs that use a variety of skills.

OD interventions, including work design, career planning and development, and performance management, can be used to integrate the disabled into the workforce. For example, traditional approaches to job design can simplify work to permit physically handicapped workers to complete an assembly task. Career planning and development programmes need to focus on making disabled workers aware of career opportunities. Too often these employees do not know that advancement is possible, and they are left feeling frustrated. Career paths need to be developed for these workers.

Performance management interventions, including goal setting, monitoring, and coaching performance, aligned with the workforce's characteristics are important. At Blue Cross and Blue Shield of Florida, for example, a supervisor learned sign language to communicate with a deaf employee whose productivity was low but whose quality of work was high. Two other deaf employees were transferred to that supervisor's department, and over a two-year period, the performance of the deaf workers improved 1,000% with no loss in quality.

**6. Culture and Values:** Cultural diversity has broad organisational implications. Different cultures represent a variety of values, work ethics, and norms of correct behaviour. Not all cultures want the same things from work, and simple, piecemeal changes in specific organisational practices will be inadequate if the workforce is culturally diverse. Management practices will have to be aligned with cultural values and support both career and family orientations. English is a second language for many people. This implies that jobs of all types (processing, customer contact, production, and so on) may need to be adjusted for English-speaking customers, but it also represents opportunity. If there are large non-English-speaking markets, the organisation has an important resource for reaching those markets. Finally, the organisation will be expected to satisfy both monetary needs, as well as personal growth needs.

Several planned change interventions, including employee involvement, reward systems, and career planning and development, can be used to adapt to cultural diversity. Employee involvement practices can be adapted to the needs for participation in decision making.

Participation in an organisation can take many forms, from suggestion systems and attitude surveys to high-involvement work designs and performance management systems. Organisations can maximise worker productivity by basing the amount of power and information workers have on cultural and value orientations. Reward systems can focus on increasing flexibility. For example, flexible working hours enable employees to meet personal obligations without sacrificing organisational objectives. Many organisations have implemented this innovation, and most report that the positive benefits outweigh the costs. Work locations also can be varied.

Finally, career planning and development programmes can help workers identify advancement opportunities that are in line with their cultural values. Some cultures value technical skills over hierarchical advancement; others see promotion as a prime indicator of self-worth and accomplishment. By matching programmes with people, job satisfaction, productivity, and employee retention can be improved.

### 5.2.3.2 Employee Stress and Wellness Interventions

In the past two decades, organisations have become increasingly aware of the relationship between employee wellness and productivity.

**The Goals of Wellness Programmes**

Individual well-being or wellness comprises "the various life/non-work satisfactions enjoyed by individuals, work/job-related satisfactions, and general health." Health is a subcomponent of well-being and includes both mental/psychological and physical/ physiological factors. In addition, a person's work setting, personality traits, and stress-coping skills affect overall well-being. In turn, well-being impacts personal and organisational outcomes, including absenteeism, productivity, and health insurance costs.

Concern has been growing in organisations about managing the dysfunction caused by stress. The price most workers and managers have paid to get more interesting and enriched jobs is an increased amount of stress. Stress has been linked to hypertension, heart attacks, diabetes, asthma, chronic pain, allergies, headache, backache, various skin disorders, cancer, immune system weakness, and a decrease in the number of white blood cells and changes in their function. It can also lead to alcoholism and drug abuse, two problems that are reaching epidemic proportions in organisations and society. For organisations, these personal effects can result in costly health benefits, absenteeism, turnover, and low performance.

## Applications Stages

Stress and wellness interventions involve: (1) diagnosing stress and being aware of its causes and (2) alleviating and coping with stress to improve wellness.

1. **Diagnosing stress and becoming aware of its causes:** Stress refers to the reaction of people to their environments. It involves both physiological and psychological responses to environmental conditions, causing people to change or adjust their behaviours. Stress is generally viewed in terms of the fit of people's needs, abilities, and expectations with environmental demands, changes, and opportunities. A good person–environment fit results in positive reactions to stress; a poor fit leads to the negative consequences already described. Stress is generally positive when it occurs at moderate levels and contributes to effective motivation, innovation, and learning.

For example, a promotion is a stressful event that is experienced positively by most employees. On the other hand, stress can be dysfunctional when it is excessively high (or low) or persists over a long period of time. It can overpower a person's coping abilities and cause physical and emotional exhaustion. For example, a boss who is excessively demanding and unsupportive can cause subordinates undue tension, anxiety, and dissatisfaction. Those factors, in turn, can lead to withdrawal behaviours, such as absenteeism and turnover; to ailments, such as headaches and high blood pressure; and to lowered performance. Situations in which there is a poor fit between employees and the organisation produce negative stress consequences.

A tremendous amount of research has been conducted on the causes and consequences of work stress. Figure 5.8 identifies specific occupational stressors, potential dysfunctional consequences, and interventions to address stress. People's individual differences determine the extent to which the stressors are perceived negatively. For example, people with strong social support perceive the stressors as less stressful than those who do not have such support. This greater perceived stress can lead to such negative consequences as anxiety, poor decision making, increased blood pressure, and low productivity.

The stress model shows that almost any dimension of the organisation, including the physical environment, structure, roles, or relationships, can cause negative stress. This suggests that much of the material covered so far in this book provides knowledge about work-related stressors, and implies that virtually all of the OD interventions included in the book can play a role in stress management. Team building, employee involvement, reward systems, and career planning and development all can help alleviate stressful working conditions. Thus, to some degree stress management has been under discussion throughout this book. Here, the focus is on those occupational stressors and stress management techniques that are unique to the stress field and that have received the most systematic attention from stress researchers.

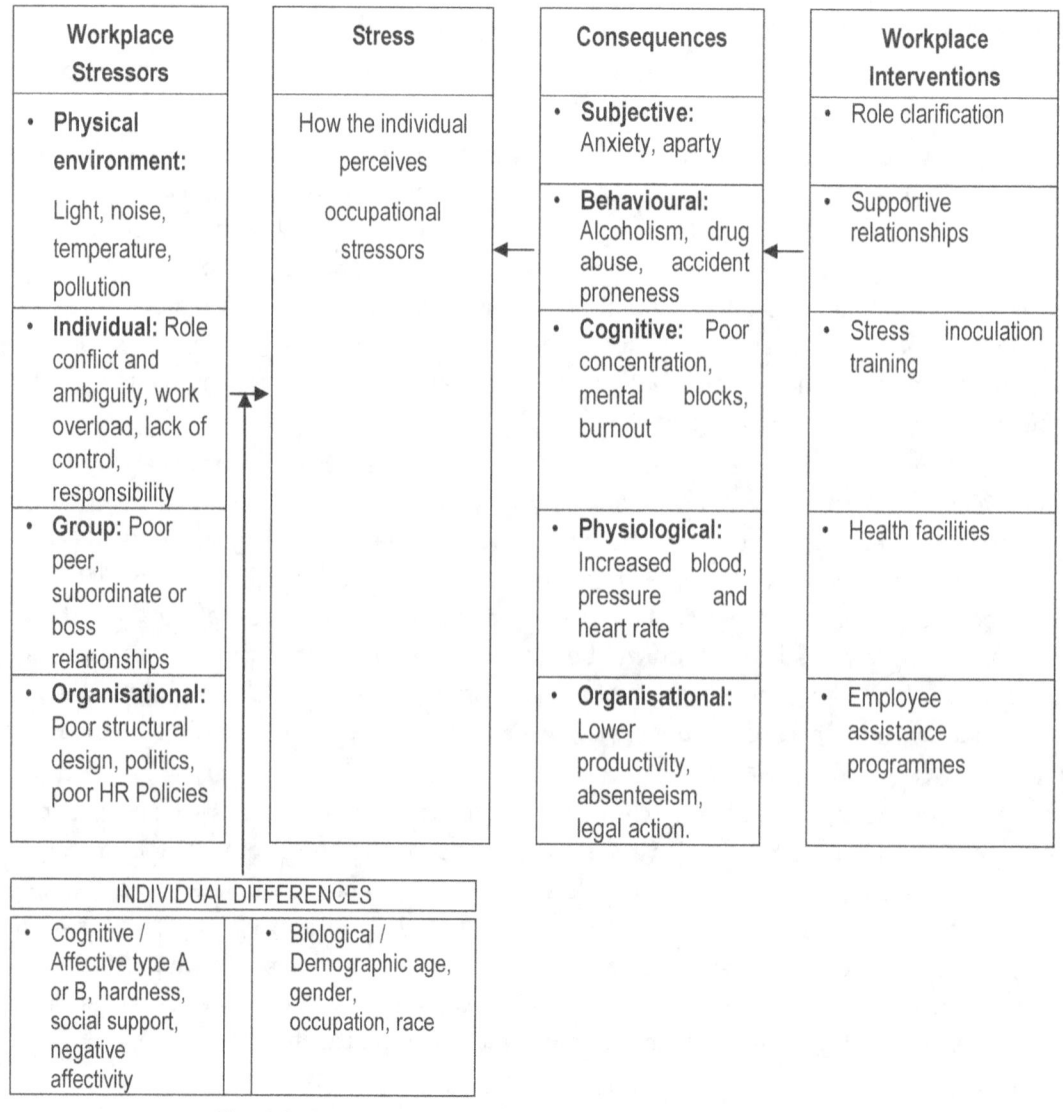

**Fig. 5.8: Stress Management: Diagnosis and Intervention**

**2.    Workplace Stressors:** Figure 5.8 identifies several organisational sources of stress, including the physical environment, individual situations, group pressures, and organisational conditions. Extensive research has been done on three key individual sources of stress: the individual items related to work overload, role conflict, and role ambiguity.

Research relating workload to stress outcomes reveals that both too much or too little work can have negative consequences. Apparently, when the amount of work is in balance with people's abilities and knowledge, stress has a positive impact on performance and satisfaction, but when workload either exceeds employees' abilities (overload) or fails to challenge them (underload), people experience stress negatively. This negative experience can lead to lowered self-esteem and job dissatisfaction, nervous symptoms, increased absenteeism, and reduced participation in organisational activities.

People's roles at work also can be a source of stress. A role can be defined as the sum total of expectations that the individual and significant others have about how the person should perform a specific job. Problems arise when there is role ambiguity and the person does not clearly understand what others expect of him or her, or when there is role conflict and the employee receives contradictory expectations that cannot be satisfied at the same time. Extensive studies of role ambiguity and conflict suggest that both conditions are prevalent in organisations, especially among managerial jobs where clarity often is lacking and job demands often are contradictory.

For example, managerial job descriptions typically are so general that it is difficult to know precisely what is expected on the job. Similarly, managers spend most of their time interacting with people from other departments, and opportunities for conflicting demands abound in these lateral relationships. Role ambiguity and conflict can cause severe stress, resulting in increased tension, dissatisfaction, and withdrawal, and reduced commitment and trust in others.

**3.    Individual Differences:** The two classes of individual differences that can affect how people respond to workplace stressors: cognitive/affective characteristics and biological/demographic characteristics. Much research has been devoted to the cognitive/affective category, especially the Type A behaviour pattern, which is characterised by impatience, competitiveness, and hostility. Type A personalities (in contrast to Type Bs) invest long hours working under tight deadlines, and put themselves under extreme time pressure by trying to do more and more work in less and less time. Type A people are especially prone to stress. For example, a longitudinal study of 3,500 men found that Type A personalities had twice as many heart diseases, five times as many second heart attacks, and twice as many fatal heart attacks as did Type B personalities.

Stress management is directed at preventing negative stress outcomes either by changing the organisational conditions causing the stress or by enhancing employees' abilities to cope with them. This preventive approach starts from a diagnosis of the current situation, including employees' self-awareness of their own stress and its sources. This diagnosis provides the information needed to develop an appropriate stress management programme. There are two methods for diagnosing stress.

*(a)* **Charting stressors** involves identifying organisational and personal stressors operating in a particular situation. For example, researchers at the University of Michigan's Institute for Social Research have developed standardised instruments for measuring most of the stressors. Similarly, there are specific instruments for measuring the individual differences, such as hardiness, social support, and Type A or B behaviour pattern. In addition to perceptions of stressors, it is necessary to measure stress consequences, such as subjective moods, performance, job satisfaction, absenteeism, blood pressure, and cholesterol level. Various instruments and checklists have been developed for obtaining people's perceptions of negative consequences, and these can be supplemented with hard measures taken from company records, medical reports, and physical examinations.

Once measures of the stressors and consequences are obtained, the two sets of data must be related to reveal which stressors contribute most to negative stress in the situation under study. For example, a relational analysis might show that qualitative overload and role ambiguity are highly related to employee fatigue, absenteeism, and poor performance, especially for Type A employees. This kind of information points to specific organisational conditions that must be improved to reduce stress. Moreover, it identifies the kinds of employees who may need special counselling and training in stress management.

*(b)* **Health profiling** is aimed at identifying stress symptoms so that corrective action can be taken. Many firms contract with local health care facilities to provide the service. It starts with a questionnaire asking people for their medical history; personal habits; current health; and vital signs, such as blood pressure, cholesterol level, and triglyceride levels. It also may include a physical examination if some of the information is not readily available. Information from the questionnaire and physical examination is then analysed, usually by a computer that outlines the individual's health profile. This profile compares the individual's characteristics with those of an average person of the same gender, age, and race. The profile identifies the person's future health prospects, typically by placing him or her in a health-risk category with a known probability of fatal disease, such as cardiovascular risk. The health profile also indicates how the health risks can be reduced by making personal and environmental changes such as dieting, exercising, or travelling.

**4.    Alleviating and Coping with Stress to Improve Wellness:** After diagnosing the presence and causes of stress, the next step in stress management is to do something about it. OD interventions for reducing negative stress tend to fall into two groups: those aimed at changing the organisational conditions causing stress and those directed at helping people to cope better with stress. Because stress results from the interaction between people and the environment, both strategies are needed for effective stress management. Five such interventions are described as follows.

**5.   Role Clarification:** This involves helping employees better understand the demands of their work roles. A manager's role is embedded in a network of relationships with other managers, each of whom has specific expectations about how the manager should perform the role. Role clarification is a systematic process for revealing others' expectations and arriving at a consensus about the activities constituting a particular role. There are several role clarification methods that follow a similar strategy. First, the people relevant to defining a particular role are identified (e.g., members of a managerial team, a boss and subordinate, and members of other departments relating to the role holder) and brought together at a meeting, usually in a location away from the organisation.

Second, the role holder discusses his or her perceived job duties and responsibilities and the other participants are encouraged to comment on and to agree or disagree with the role holder's perceptions. An OD practitioner may act as a process consultant to facilitate interaction and reduce defensiveness. Third, when everyone has reached consensus on defining the role, the role holder is responsible for writing a description of the activities that are seen now as constituting the role. A copy of the role description is distributed to all participants to ensure that they fully understand and agree with the role definition. Fourth, the participants periodically check to see whether the role is being performed as intended and make modifications if necessary.

**6.   Supportive Relationships:** Building supportive relationships is aimed at helping employees cope with stress rather than at changing the stressors themselves. It involves establishing trusting and genuinely positive relationships among employees, including bosses, subordinates, and peers. Supportive relations have been a hallmark of organisation development and are a major part of such interventions as team building, intergroup relations, employee involvement, work design, goal setting, and career planning and development. Considerable research shows that supportive relationships can buffer people against stress. When people feel that relevant others really care about what happens to them and are willing to help, they can cope with stressful conditions.

**7.   Work Leaves:** While some differences can be explained by cultural values or government policies, the potential to affect wellness through work leaves should not be ignored. As organisations struggle to minimise the effects of work stress, paid and unpaid work leaves are receiving increasing attention. Paid leaves include vacation, holidays, personal days, as well as maternity and paternity leaves. The comparative statistics suggest that globalisation may place increasing pressure on vacation allowances.

Unpaid leaves, or leaves of absence, also offer employees a chance to renew and to bring new experiences to the organisation, while guaranteeing a job for them upon their return. For example, personal growth leaves or social service leaves may allow an employee to explore an individual interest or cause. Such a leave is an exchange, offering the employee a chance for time off, renewal, and pursuit of a given interest, while retaining a valued employee for the organisation.

**8.    Health Facilities:** A growing number of organisations are providing facilities for helping employees cope with stress. Elaborate exercise facilities are maintained by such firms as Qualcomm, Xerox, Weyerhaeuser, Google, and PepsiCo, and a majority of the Fortune 500 operate corporate cardiovascular fitness programmes. Employees at Aetna can earn a financial incentive for their involvement in weight management and fitness programmes.

Before starting such programmes, employees must take an exercise tolerance test and have the approval of either a private or a company doctor. Each participant is then assigned a safe level of heart response to the various parts of the fitness programme. In addition to exercise facilities, some companies, such as McDonald's and Equitable Life Assurance Society, provide biofeedback facilities in which managers take relaxation breaks using biofeedback devices to monitor respiration and heart rate. Feedback of such data helps managers lower their respiration and heart rates. Some companies provide time for employees to meditate, and other firms have stay-well programmes that encourage healthy diets and lifestyles.

**9.    Employee Assistance Programs:** This final stress and wellness intervention is an organisational intervention and a method for helping individuals directly. EAPs help identify, refer, and treat workers whose personal problems affect their performance. Other factors, too, have contributed to increased problems: altered family structures, the growth of single parent households, the increase in divorce, greater mobility, and changing modes of child rearing are all fairly recent phenomena that have added to the stress experienced by employees. These trends indicate that an increasing number of employees need assistance with personal problems, and the research suggests that EAP use increases during downsizing and restructuring.

When other stress management interventions are not effective or when employees have particular types of wellness and/or health issues, employee assistance programmes provide a means of responding to employee wellness problems, including extreme or chronic stress, drug and alcohol abuse, problems with child and/or elder care, grief, and financial problems. Central to the philosophy underlying EAPs is the belief that although the organisation has no right to interfere in the private lives of its employees, it does have a right to impose certain standards of work performance and to establish sanctions when these are not met. Anyone whose work performance is impaired because of a personal problem is eligible for admission into an EAP programme. Successful EAPs have been implemented at General Motors, Johnson & Johnson, Motorola, Burlington Northern Railroad, and Dominion Foundries and Steel Company.

Numerous websites, including the Employee Assistance Professionals Association, share or provide at minimal cost detailed guidelines on establishing an EAP. These steps include developing an appropriate EAP policy, deciding to insource or outsource the programme, communicating the programme to organisation members, and providing training on EAP use.

## Points to Remember

- **Techno-structural Interventions** focus on an organisation's technology (for example, task methods and job design) and structure (for example, division of labour and hierarchy).

- Interventions intended at structural design involve moving from more traditional ways of dividing the organisation's overall work, such as functional, divisional, and matrix structures, to more integrative and flexible forms, such as process, customer-centric, and network structures.

- **Organisation structure** describes how the overall work of the organisation is divided into subunits and how these subunits are synchronized for task completion.

- *Downsizing* refers to interventions aimed at reducing the size of the organisation.

- **Reengineering** transforms how organisations traditionally produce and deliver goods and services.

- **Increased employee involvement** can lead to quicker, more responsive decisions, continuous performance improvements, and greater employee flexibility, commitment, and satisfaction.

- **Work design** refers to creating jobs and work groups that generate high levels of employee fulfillment and productivity.

- **Human Resources Management** Interventions would focus on personnel practices used to integrate people into organisations.

- **Performance management** involves goal setting, performance appraisal, and reward systems that align member work behaviour with business strategy, employee involvement, and workplace technology.

- *Goal setting* involves managers and subordinates in jointly establishing and clarifying employee goals.

- *Performance appraisal* is a feedback system that involves the direct evaluation of individual or work-group performance by a supervisor, manager, or peers.

- **Organisational rewards** are powerful incentives for improving employee and work-group performance.

## Questions for Discussion

1. Discuss in detail the techno-structural interventions in organisational development.

2. What are the human resource management interventions in organisational development?

# CASELETS AND CASES ON OD

## CASE 1 : A WHOLE SYSTEM EVENT FOR REAL-TIME STRATEGIC CHANGE; USE OF AFRICAN-INFLUENCED FACILITATION THROUGH *LEKGOTLA*

**Goals**

- Post-merger transformation and integration of two large, listed IT service provider organisations.
- Integration of two companies and cultures.
- Aligning employees to the purpose, values, goals and new customer-centric strategy of the merged organisation.

**Critical Actions**

Close partnership with the executive team used process consultation to create shared vision, mission and values.

A key catalyst in the transformation was a two-day whole-systems event:

- The event brought employees from both organisations together to celebrate their history and envision their future.
- Employees participated in identifying and aligning key actions to support the new strategic direction.
- For full engagement of all participants, WorldsView drew on an old African method of ensuring that all voices are heard, called lekgotla (creative dialogue).

The lekgotla process helps individuals to be heard in groups, groups build a common point of view and become teams, and teams to pursue common goals. Diversity is celebrated and built on, as individuals practice the art of listening and building on each others views.

**Results**

- Trust, understanding and commitment to the integration effort were built.
- Values were examined and aligned; foundational change actions planned.
- The leadership team witnessed the beginning of a profound organisation transformation and renewal.

## CASE 2 : STRATEGICALLY TRANSITIONED HIGH TECHNOLOGY, GLOBAL COMPANY FROM HARDWARE TO SOFTWARE – PRODUCT TO SOLUTIONS PROVIDER

**Goals**

- Increase year over year percentage growth.
- Gain competitive advantage over emerging niche providers.
- Integrate hardware and software product set with custom services and support.

**Critical Actions**

- Developed integrated solutions strategy.
- Accelerated product development cycle; worked on transition from development to market.
- Accelerated cultural change; trained sales force/vendors/support in under 3 months.

**Results**

- Re-launched software and services integrated solutions in under 6 months.
- Increased profit margins.
- Expanded client base with entry into customer loyalty/management market.

## CASE 3 : ENABLED A SMALL RURAL SCHOOL DISTRICT SERVING A PREDOMINANTLY POOR AND HISPANIC COMMUNITY TO RAISE STUDENT PERFORMANCE BY CREATING A CULTURE OF HIGH EXPECTATIONS AND COLLABORATIVE ACTION

**Goal**

- Increase student achievement under tightened state and federal accountability standards. In 2001, only 5% of tenth graders met performance standards in mathematics; 21% met standard in writing and reading.

**Critical Actions**

The Whole Scale™ model was used to lead participants through a basic change formula in which they:

- Fostered urgency by working with data to highlight dissatisfaction.
- Considered a shared picture of more desirable futures for students.
- Determined next steps.

People were seated in diverse groups to foster new perspectives. They gave them structured time to restate information, find common ground, and weigh in on ideas through public voting.

Challenges included language barriers and a community that consistently doubted the capacity of its children to achieve academic success.

**Results**

Leadership learned to focus the entire district and community on essential outcomes for students.

- Increases over four years in percentage of students meeting standards of 39% in reading, 29% in writing, and 31% in mathematics.
- 96% of the 2004 graduating class went to college and were still enrolled fall 2005.
- 82% of the 2005 class went to college, with none requiring remediation.

## CASE 4 : ENHANCED TEAM EFFECTIVENESS TO FACILITATE GROWTH IN A LEADING FAMILY-OWNED HEALTHCARE MANAGEMENT CONSULTING FIRM

**Goals**

- Further develop senior leadership.
- Implement new management structures, HR policies, and business practices to better support local and remote staff.

**Critical Actions**

- Designed and implemented customised leadership development programme; facilitated series of workshops on leadership skills.
- Provided one-on-one coaching and additional support to the president and other management team members.
- Designed and facilitated customised "Consulting Skills 101" programme to share strategies and techniques for managing client projects and improving team communications.
- Prepared competency-based performance assessment tools for evaluating both management and professional staff.

**Results**

- Implemented new policies and procedures to standardise business operations and better align them with best practices for remote work
- Created new strategies and established specific communication protocols for management to support and further develop local as well as remote staff
- Enabled the firm to come together as a more cohesive unit; positioned them to take future actions to ensure ongoing growth and success

## CASE 5 : HELPED THE NEW CEO TURN AROUND A SOFTWARE COMPANY TO POSITION IT FOR BUSINESS SUCCESS

**Goals**

- Pinpoint the core purpose, values, and strategies for the company. The new CEO knew that turning the company around would take more than just restructuring : "I wanted to look introspectively to determine fundamentally who we are, what is important to us, and where we want to go."

**Critical Actions**

- Work began with a plan to get the executive team to think creatively about the company and its future.
- The executive team identified the core purpose, values and strategy for the company.
- Realising that the entire company needed to accept their work in order to implement it successfully, the leadership team engaged managers in defining actions needed to achieve the strategy.

- The leadership team presented their work to all employees in an energised, creative town hall meeting.
- The leadership team cascaded the strategies through the entire organisation so all employees saw how their goals contributed to the core purpose of the company.

## Results

Said the CEO, "This initiative has been an unqualified success. We have a clearly defined strategy and the management of the company is more energized than I've ever seen them. We have built the foundation to be a truly great company."

## CASE 6 : ENABLED PUBLIC COLLEGE IT DEPARTMENT TO IMPROVE QUALITY AND DELIVERY OF SERVICES THROUGH REORGANISATION AND TEAM DEVELOPMENT

### Goals

- Align IT department with college strategic and academic goals.
- Clarify department roles and responsibilities.
- Set department priorities.
- Improve communication with colleagues and clients.

### Critical Actions

- Worked with senior IT executives to introduce a new organisation structure.
- Supported department operations through intensive results-oriented team development and coaching of IT staff.
- Assessed how staff perceived their work unit's internal dynamics and external relationships with other work units.
- Based on this assessment, developed and delivered a series of facilitated two-hour sessions focused on improving teamwork and internal communications patterns. The timing, content, and duration of sessions were tailored to meet the needs of each team.

### Results

- Tangible improvement in the quality and effectiveness of IT staff services.
- An approach to organisation change that, in the words of the Chief Information Officer, could serve the college as "both as a model and a catalyst for modifications in existing decision making processes and management operations."

## CASE 7 : ORGANISATION DEVELOPMENT IN A "GOOD TO GREAT" ORGANISATION : ORGANISATION CHANGE AT ABBOTT

This project, part of an ongoing change effort at Abbott, illustrates a collaborative effort between corporate and university OD programmes. It received the Silver Bowl Award from the OD Institute for Best Corporate OD Project of the Year 2006.

**Goal**

- Culture change to realign corporate culture with strategy, mission, and changes in the external environment.

**Critical Actions**

The project consisted of a number of interventions guided by an action research process, which involved a continuous cycle of evaluations to help us learn from, modify, and strengthen the interventions. Interventions included :

- Culture surveys and feedback
- Small group interventions
- Organisation design interventions

**Results**

- Measurable changes toward the desired culture ranging from 10% to 50% percent positive change depending on the dimension of culture.
- Measurable increases in performance, with an overall positive change of 43%.

## CASE 8 : ORGANISATION DEVELOPMENT

**Situation**

One of the nation's leading insurance companies desired to socialise a new vision, and the strategies by which they planned to achieve their vision, across their entire employee base.

**Process/Methodology**

AIM Consulting Associates conducted a series of vision socialisation workshops that engaged every employee in the "operationalisation" of the vision. The workshops empowered employees to define the employee behaviours that were essential to the Company executing its strategy. The output of the workshops was an agreed upon set of behavioural competencies that were celebrated at a companywide "launch event." The competencies, which define "a new way of doing business" at the firm, have been incorporated into the performance appraisal and leadership development systems. Additionally, a new set of customer service standards have been developed to further promote optimal customer interaction.

**Results**

The effort was so successful that within the first quarter following the launch event, the company realised an astounding and unprecedented 11% growth in overall profits.

## CASE 9 : STRATEGY DEVELOPMENT AND METRICS

**Situation**

A large behavioural healthcare provider required a strategic plan that addressed future growth as well as the major managed mental health care challenges in its industry and locale. The organisation had recently merged with several small agencies to form a large non-profit behavioural health care organisation providing a wide array of services to adults, children, and families.

**Process/Methodology**

They applied their methodology to create a 5-year business plan and establish an executive set of measures that allowed the company's leadership team and board to monitor progress on the plan. The organisation was led through a well-structured strategic planning effort, and then followed this with the development of a "Balanced Scorecard" system of metrics (based on Kaplan and Norton's methodology).

**Results**

In the seven-year period since the consulting intervention began, the organisation has consolidated two new behavioural health care organisations, an outpatient drug rehabilitation centre and a youth intervention programme into one company. In addition, the organisation has more than doubled its size, from a $25 million to a $60 million enterprise. The organisation has also grown from 150 employees to 750 and now includes 23 locations.

## CASE 10 : LEADERSHIP

**Situation**

Following the terrorist attacks of September 11, 2001, the need for preparedness-focused leadership programmes arose in many state and local agencies in the USA. AIM Consulting Associates became extensively involved in the design of several programmes to foster inter-agency cooperation, build relationships, and hone leadership appropriate for homeland security specialists and first responders.

**Methodology**

The effort produced a three-tiered programme designed to meet the needs of the various agencies. The Regional Programme consists of two multi-day training sessions and includes team building, multidisciplinary problem-solving, inter-agency collaboration, project management, change management, crisis leadership, emotional intelligence, contingency leadership, and negotiation. Students also participate in a multidisciplinary project designed to demonstrate the use of leadership skills acquired in the programme. An Advanced Programme is available to all graduates of the Regional Programme, and dives deeper into preparedness leadership principles. The day-and-a-half Executive Programme reinforces inter-agency leadership skills important to State agencies involved with preparedness and counter-terrorism task forces.

**Results**

From 2003 to 2007, the programmes have produced over 100 graduates from a range of organisation levels. The programme is known to promote the value of working relationships between all levels of government and to reinforce the importance of open lines of communication.

## CASE 11 : CONFLICT MANAGEMENT AND NEGOTIATIONS

**Situation**

A Fortune 500 manufacturing firm faced major contract negotiations with a union representing thousands of its hourly employees. The company's global competitors enjoyed huge cost advantages, including lower retiree medical burdens, lower wage scales, less current-employee healthcare costs, and newer and leaner manufacturing facilities. The company knew it faced a hard bargain with a strong and prideful union.

**Process/Methodology**

The company engaged AIM Consulting to develop and execute a negotiating strategy. Over an 18-month period, they participated in intensive deliberations with corporate executives and various other outside partners. They helped launch a comprehensive process that enabled the company to achieve a major shift from its historical bargaining position. They developed a bold strategy that would enable the company to lower its costs, improve its manufacturing capabilities, and reassure financial markets. Bargaining proved difficult and challenging, but their painstakingly developed approach enabled them to achieve significant gains.

**Results**

Once agreement was reached with the union, the company could rightly claim that it had gone a long way toward saving manufacturing operations in North America. It had restructured its labour costs, substantially reducing its retiree health care liabilities. It had also achieved wage and plant-adjustment flexibilities to improve its financial position. The agreement negotiated set a significant precedent for employers in other manufacturing industries.

## CASE 12 : ORGANISATION CHANGE IN HEALTHCARE

The organisation is a healthcare and financial services organisation, founded in 1940. In December 1997, the company was bought by Guardian Royal Exchange, which has in turn been bought by the AXA group. The programme began in September 1996 during a period of considerable organisation change. SML (Self-managed Learning) was specifically chosen as a management development strategy to facilitate that change. The programme was provided initially for 120 senior managers and is now used in all areas and at all levels of the business.

**Aim**

As identified in the handbook given to managers at the start of the programme :

- To promote continuous development.
- To link personal development to the needs of the business.
- To encourage individual ownership of personal development.
- To facilitate cross functional support and networking.
- To promote a cost effective approach to development and training throughout healthcare.

**Process**

- Obtaining the buy-in and support of the CEO and HR Director.
- Design and development of the programme.
- Restoration and equipping of Learning Resource Centre.
- Development of internal Learning Group Advisers with external support to ensure organisation capable to continue to support learning.

- Half-day introductory briefing session covering: the principles of the programme.
- Three-day residential workshop including: formation of learning groups, mapping on organisation context.
- Learning Group Meetings held every six weeks over a period of nine months.
- Endorsement event where Learning Groups present their achievements to the CEO, HR Director and members of other Learning Groups.

## Evaluation Methods Implemented

- In-depth interviews with senior managers.
- Focus groups with participants.
- Interviews with key stakeholders including the Chief Executive Officer.
- Questionnaire based survey of participants.

## Achievements

- Increase in confidence of Senior Managers to take action.
- Created culture of working collaboratively and inclusively.
- Many measurable improvements to business performance – e.g.
   1.   New product development; fresh approach to market research.
   2.  Radical new way of creating and documenting Customer Service processes.
- Management Development is now business focused, flexible, able to meet the changing needs of individuals and the organisation, fun, innovative and cost effective.
- Created a life-long capability of managing own learning.

## CASE 13 : LIFELONG LEARNING IN ERICSSON LIMITED

Ericsson Limited is the UK subsidiary of the Sweden based Ericsson Group. Ericsson is the world leader in digital mobile networks with over 40% of the market. There are 5,500 employees based at 5 sites in the UK. The first phase of the programme was started in May 1998 and the second phase in October 1998. The approach was chosen to facilitate a change of culture to lifelong learning in line with the organisation's strategic direction and local business strategy. It was initiated and run by senior line managers and presented as an opportunity for volunteers. The two programmes covered 114 participants across two divisions in the following roles :

- Senior Managers
- Project and Product Managers
- Group Supervisors and Team Leaders
- Software Designers
- Administrators and Secretaries
- Human Resource Officers

The approach now forms part of Ericsson's learning and development strategy in the UK. It is already an integral part of the company's two-year graduate scheme and is planned for the management leadership programme.

## Aim

Ericsson Group Strategic Direction:

- Ericsson has an environment of continuous learning and development that fosters lifelong learning for our employees.
- Ericsson has people who proactively take initiatives.
- Ericsson shall have a Research and Development organisation set for speed and flexibility.

## Local Objectives

- To encourage people to take charge of their own development so that they would avoid the situation where people were waiting passively for others to organise courses or learning activities.
- To get the most out of the time that people were investing in learning activities.
- To provide an approach to learning that people would enjoy, was collaborative, highly visible and where people would take a creative approach to identifying sources of learning.

## Process

- Designing and developing the programme.
- Briefing sessions.
- One-day off-site workshop.
- Six Learning Group meetings over a period of 10 months with external Learning Group Advisers.
- Half-day reflection at the end of the programme.

## Evaluation Methods

- Focus groups with participants.
- Questionnaire based survey of participants.

## Achievements

- People working with others to pursue learning goals: 88% of respondents stated that set members had helped to generate ideas and solutions to problems they had encountered in their learning goals.
- People viewing their careers in terms of learning and development.
- People taking a proactive approach to their future direction.
- Evidence of a change in approach to responsibility for learning against mental habits:
  (a)  Honest assessment of success and failures, especially the latter.
  (b)  Aggressive collection of information and ideas from others.

    (c)    Propensity to listen to others.

    (d)    Willingness to view life with an open mind.

    (e)    Risk taking and a willingness to push oneself out of comfort zone.

- People focusing on longer term goals and objectives as well as 'day to day' fire-fighting.
- Increased networking, coaching and support between people.

## CASE 14 : TOP MANAGEMENT TEAM AT AMBICA GLASS CORPORATION

The Ambica Glass Corporation produces and markets plate glass for use primarily in the construction and automotive industries. The multiplant company has been involved in OD for several years and actively supports participative management practices and employee-involvement programmes. Ambica's Organisation Design is relatively organic, and the manufacturing plants are given freedom and encouragement to develop their own organisation designs and approaches to participative management. It recently put together a problem-solving group made up of the top-management team at its newest plant.

The team consisted of the plant manager and the managers of the five functional departments reporting to him: engineering (maintenance), administration, human resources, production and quality control. In recruiting managers for the new plant, the company selected people with good technical skills and experience in their respective functions. It also chose people with some managerial experience and a desire to solve problems collaboratively, a hall mark of participative management. The team was relatively new, and members had been working together for only about 5 months.

The team met formally for 2 hours each week to share pertinent information and to deal with plant-wide issues affecting all of the departments, such as safety procedures, interdepartmental relations, and personal practices. Members described these meetings as informative but often chaotic in terms of decision making. The meetings typically started late as members reached at different times. The latecomers generally offered excuses about more pressing problems, occurring elsewhere in the plant. Once stated, the meetings were often interrupted by "urgent" phone messages for various members, including the plant manager, and in most cases the recipient would leave the meeting hurriedly to respond to the call.

The group had problems arriving at clear decisions on particular issues. Discussions often rambled from topic to topic, and members tended to postpone the resolution of problems to future meetings. This led to a backlog of unsolved issues, and meetings often lasted far beyond the 2-hour limit. When group decisions were made, members typically failed to follow through on agreements and there was often confusion about what had actually been agreed upon. Everyone expressed dissatisfaction with the team meetings and their results.

Relationships among team members were cordial yet somewhat strained, especially when the team was dealing with complex issues in which members had varying opinions and interests. Although the plant manager publicly stated that he wanted to hear all sides of the issues, he often interrupted the discussion or attempted to change the topic when members openly disagreed in their views of the problem. This interruption was typically followed by an awkward silence in the group. In many instances when a solution to a pressing problem did not appear forthcoming, members either moved on to another issue or they informally voted on proposed options, letting majority rule decide the outcome. Members rarely discussed the need to move on or vote; rather these behaviours emerged informally over time and become acceptable ways of dealing with difficult issues.

## Questions :

1. How clear are the group's goals ?
2. What is the group's task structure ?
3. What is the nature of team functioning in the group ?
4. Which intervention should be applicable ? Why ?

## CASE 15 : JOB DESIGN AT CENTRAL UNIVERSITY

The Vidyasagar School of Business and Management (VSBM) at Central University was one of the largest business schools in the country and has the third largest part-time MBA programme. The school also provides graduate education aimed at different markets including an executive- MBA (EMBA), a presidential/key executive MBA and a specialised master's degree in organisation development (MSOD). The MSOD programmes' curriculum consists of 10 four-unit classes over 22 months. Eight of the classes are conducted off-site during 8-day sessions at both domestic and international locations. The MSOD programme office consists of a faculty director, a programme administrator and an administrative assistant. In response to cost-cutting initiatives at the University level, a proposal was being considered to alter the job designs of the MSOD programme.

The MSOD Programme Administrator, the focus of this application, was responsible for marketing and recruiting new students, managing the delivery logistics of the off-site programme, managing the student's registration and financial relationships with the university and maintaining relationships with the MSOD alumni. The marketing and recruiting duties involved working with the Programme Director and the Director of Marketing for VSBM to develop marketing tactics including advertisements, brochure, conference marketing and support, and other market development activities. The recruiting process involved explaining the curriculum to prospective applicants, overseeing the application process for each applicant, working with the faculty to have qualified applicants interviewed and managing the admissions process. This too had to be coordinated with the director and the administrative assistant. Once a class was admitted, the Programme Administrator worked with various off-site facilities to establish room and board rates and catering services; managed the faculty's travel and teaching requirements; managed various intersession activities including the final exam; managed the students enrolment and graduation processes including their interface with the university registrar and finance office and the school's financial aid office; and coached students through the programme. After graduation, the Programme Administrator served as an unofficial placement service, hooking up eligible graduates with prospective employers who called looking for MSOD talent, provided career guidance and worked with the programme's alumni organisation to sponsor conferences and other alumni activities.

Each of the above activities was somewhat programmable in that they occurred as specific times of the year and could be scheduled. However, because each applicant, student, class or graduate was somewhat unique, the specific tasks or actions could not always be specified in advance and there were a number of exceptions and unique situations that arose during each day, month and year.

The MSOD Programme Administrator has worked with the MSOD programme for over 15 years and was a fixture in both the MSOD and the general OD communities. Year over year, the Programme Administrator delivered qualified applicants in excess of available space although that task had become increasingly difficult in the face of tuition increases, increasingly restrictive corporate policies on tuition reimbursement and the ups and downs of the economy. He has handled both routine and non-routine administrative details professionally, displays and reports a high level of job satisfaction and commitment to the program and has been complimented formally and informally by the students in the programme. In fact, each cohort develops its own relationship with the administrator and he becomes a de facto member of almost every class. The alumni considered the Program Administrator a key and integral part of the MSOD programme. The set of duties described above has evolved considerably over the Programme Administrator's tenure. In particular, he has become more involved and responsible for marketing and recruiting activities and the alumni relations duties have been added in response to alumni requests that cannot be filled by traditional university departments.

In an effort to improve efficiencies and in recognition of the MSOD Programme Administrator's outstanding productivity, a proposal was being considered by VSBM administration to change the design of his job. The proposal suggested that the MSOD Programme Administrator continue to perform all of the current duties of the position and in addition, provide administrative support to two PKE classes from their initial class to graduation. The duties of administrating the PKE programme would be similar in nature to the delivery aspects of the MSOD programe, including working with faculty to support their teaching efforts, managing textbook ordering processes, and providing different faculties logistics activities. It would not include marketing, recruiting and alumni developing activities. He would receive additional compensation for the increased responsibilities and a title change. The new position would share, with the EMBA programme administrator, supervision of an assistant programme administrator, who would in turn supervise a pool of administrative assistants. The assistant programme administrator would also report of the EMBA Programme Administrator. The MSOD/PKE programme administrator would be shared between the MSOD programme director and a director of EMBA/PKE programmes.

**Questions:**
1. Is there a need for job redesign ? Why ?
2. How much feedback about results does the job contain ?
3. How much task significance is involved in the job ?

### CASE 16 : INTRODUCING A NEW MANAGER TO AN EXISTING TEAM

Lasa Development approach to Organisation Development is pragmatic and practical. They aim at enabling and stimulating positive change within an organisation. They focus on what works well for the organisation and on the future which the organisation can change to improve. The problems that are encountered in organisations are usually around the way people do things. They indicate patterns that have become stuck. From being stuck, people move on to judgement and resistance. A high-tech Corporation named Century Private Limited was their client.

The product management team of Century Private Limited had been without a leader for almost 9 months. A very experienced person (Mr. Ram) was hired. His team did not feel comfortable with him. He was also new to the organisation and didn't yet understand 'the way we do things around here'. Ram asked for help to get his team working better together.

Lasa consultant Mr. John designed an initial 3 day team workshop on the expectations between Ram and his team: basic communications skills; expectations; fun session (He took them for Jet Skiing, which no one had ever done before) for team building and finally worked on team vision and goals. The expectations session included working with team only and discussing all the team's complaints about Ram. He then grouped them. The team agreed on the message that was to be given to Ram; they listed 6 expectations they had of him.

Next, John gave Ram their feedback; shared the team's feelings and encouraged him to share with them what he felt. John also listed 6 expectations he had of the team. Back together, they shared with each other. Ram chose 3 expectations from the team's list, which he would commit to fulfil and they did the same for him. Then they all returned on a regular basis to review and work further on team development.

**Question :**
1. Which type of OD intervention was implemented by Mr. John ? Do you think it was the most appropriate intervention ?
2. What type of positive change can be expected in the organisation ?

### CASE 17 : THE CASE OF OD IN AN NGO IN INDIA - BY NISHA NAIR AND NEHARIKA VOHRA, IIMA, INDIA

Adhikar (which stands for human rights) is a mass-based organisation in the state of Jharkhand in India that started in 1985 with the aim of altering society's power base towards the poor and the marginalised. Since its inception, Adhikar has worked alongside socially marginalised communities – primarily the tribal communities and other landless labourers spread in and around Jharkhand with the intent to support organised action from within the community against any unjust distribution of wealth, resources or power. The founder Mr. Rajan Mishra sought to espouse the ideal of self-determination through organising people into unions and other collectives to fight for their rights. The organisation has grown from a few handful inspired by Mr. Mishra during the early days to over 200 employees. Mr. Mishra currently serves in a prominent position at the Centre in the Government of India. He has chosen to dissociate himself from Adhikar so that he is not perceived as aligned with any political party or he is not seen as doing favours to Adhikar.

## Scope of Work of Adhikar

The differing areas of Adhikar's are *Adivasi Sanghathan, Arthik Siksha*, Scholarship Programme and Emergency Relief. Adhikar first began its work through the *Adivasi Sangathan* created to organise the tribal people into unions. Under the umbrella of the *Adivasi Sangathan*, other unions like the Agricultural Labourers' Union, Land Rights Protection Committee and the Construction Workers Union have evolved. Along with the unions, Adhikar also works in the area of budgetary analysis and expenditure monitoring for the state government through its wing called *Arthik Siksha* which also conducts training programmes for other NGOs of different states in classification and analysis of budgetary information. In addition there is a Scholarship that seeks to fund and train local level leadership to raise issues and awareness at the village level. These individuals are funded by Adhikar and avail of a monthly stipend. They have the autonomy to form their own unions and serve as an extended network for Adhikar. The emergency response programme of Adhikar encompasses relief work at times of calamities and distress.

## Structure of the Organisation

Adhikar is structured along both geography and programmes. As the organisation has grown, the structure of Adhikar too has evolved. The various unions such as Construction Workers Union, *Adivasi Sangathan* and programmes such as *Arthik Siksha* and Scholarship programme are overseen by different coordinators all reporting directly to the Managing Trustee, Mr. Mishra. In addition, there are location coordinators in Chaibasa, Ghatsila and Saraikela, which are districts in the state of Jharkhand. There is considerable overlap between programme and region. The coordinator of Chaibasa region, Ms. Devi, was among the first few members of Adhikar and was the Director of Adhikar at the time of the intervention. She was appointed the Managing Trustee by Mr. Mishra a week before the intervention ended.

## Organisation Entry – Engagement with Adhikar

The engagement with Adhikar began when the first author contacted Ms. Pia Mishra, who is the programme director of Adhikar to seek permission for the engagement. Pia expressed interest in the project and welcomed the engagement. After the informal first meeting, a second meeting was arranged where both the authors met Pia at the Adhikar office to explain the nature of the intended engagement and seek permission for the first author to study the organisation, conduct interviews and apply OD as and when required. The intent was to enter the organisation, understand the nature of its work and functioning, collect data on the culture and other relevant information, and on the basis of the findings suggest some interventions for improvement or changes.

## Methodology of the Study

The primary methodology of the study comprised the following.

**Interviews :** The process followed was largely based on closed room interviews with each of the coordinators, usually lasting for 1-2 hours where the author first introduced herself and elaborated on the nature of her engagement and sought the views of those being interviewed regarding the organisation, its culture, areas of concern, and any suggestions or other comments pertinent to the discussion. All the respondents were assured of the confidentiality of their responses. It was made clear that the role of the author was to understand the functioning of the organisation with a view towards diagnosing issues and recommending areas of improvement.

**Field Visits :** The author also visited the field in Ghatsila where she interacted with the field workers and the regional coordinator, Mr. Dubey. During this visit, she sat in on one of the regional meetings following which she had interviews with the field workers in small groups of four or five. This was done to understand the organisation from the view of the fieldworkers and gain insight into its issues through their lens.

**Memos and Reports :** The initial familiarisation with the organisation and its activities came through a study of the various reports and manuals published. These included annual reports, budget analysis reports of *Arthik Siksha*, newspaper clippings on Adhikar and other documents relating to the organisation. All this information was available in the library of Adhikar. The author spent several hours in the library, familiarising herself with the organisation and its history.

**Observations :** In addition to the interviews, the author also observed the non- verbal cues, pattern of interaction and nature of relationships among members, indicative of the climate of the organisation during her visits to the Adhikar head office and the field visit. These observations continued beyond the course of the interviews to the time when she was sitting in on some of the meetings of the coordinators and her informal interaction with the members.

**Diagnostic Presentation :** Towards the end of the engagement, a session was held with all the coordinators present, where findings from the authors' engagement with the organisation were presented to the members in a closed room group meeting. This served both as a mirroring (feedback) activity as well as a forum for initiating dialogue and communication across the organisation members.

## Meeting with the Coordinators

The author first met with Ms. Pia Mishra who served as the point of contact throughout. Following this, she met with each of the coordinators in turn, to get their perspective on the organisation and the issues and concerns. Ms. Mishra (in charge of the Ghatsila region), Ms. Devi (director of Adhikar and in charge of Chaibasa region at the time of the intervention),

Mr. Pandya (coordinator for the Construction Workers Union), Mr. Singh (coordinator for *Adivasi Sangathan*), Mr. Dubey (coordinator for Ghatsila), Mr. Nath (coordinator of *Arthik Siksha*), and Mr. Sharma (coordinator of the Scholarship programme), were among those who were interviewed in detail. Most of the issues and concerns surfaced through the sessions with the coordinators. While most coordinators opened up freely to discuss their concerns and the issues facing the organisation, some like Ms. Devi and Mr. Sharma were less open and did not share much about their views on Adhikar and its functioning.

Most coordinators had been with the organisation since its inception. All of them echoed a strong sense of identification and commitment to the organisation and the cause it worked for. There was high regard for the founder Mr. Mishra. His daughter, Pia has had to prove herself in the organisation. There were still some issues around the acceptance of Ms. Pia Mishra by all the coordinators. She is professionally qualified and actively working but she was being tested for her commitment to the organisation and its work. However, what was interesting was also that during the author's meeting with Pia she never once mentioned the fact that she was the daughter of the founder, Mr. Mishra. The author came to know this only through others in later interviews.

The issues that emerged through the sessions with the coordinators were analysed. There appeared to be a lack of clarity regarding the structure of Adhikar in the minds of not just the staff but even the coordinators. Some clarity on the role of Pia was also sought by one of the coordinators at the time of the diagnostic presentation. The confusion over the structure existed primarily because of the organisation boundaries being both geographical and programme driven. The resultant matrix structure caused confusion in clarifying reporting relationships. Since the organisation is structured around programmes such as *Adivasi Sangathan*, Construction Workers Union, *Arthik Siksha* and Scholarship on one hand and around regions such as Ghatsila, Chaibasa and Saraikela on the other, with separate coordinators for each, there was confusion regarding reporting relationships and authority. Instances were cited during the interviews when this matrix kind of structure caused misunderstanding or confusion regarding reporting relationships or precedence of command.

To a large extent there was considerable autonomy and decentralisation at the coordinator level in the organisation. All the coordinators expressed their happiness in being given the responsibility and autonomy to work on the issues the way they saw fit for their differing units. The connecting link between them had been Mr. Mishra, the charismatic founder leader. In the absence of his regular engagement, there were gaps in communication and confusion over identity, operations, and means of operation. Some felt that the sense of responsibility and accountability that comes with empowerment was lacking in Adhikar. For example, Ms. Mistry echoed concerns regarding irregular reporting and documentation by some of the coordinators. The coordinating mechanisms such as periodic meetings among coordinators to make decentralisation effective were absent. In such a scenario, the differing units seem to be operating in silos with little coordination and total absence of centralisation at any level. The withdrawing of Mr. Mishra was seen as causing a vacuum of leadership in Adhikar. In the past his energy and vision had kept people tied, but in his absence there was not enough structure to bind the members of the organisation.

Largely there was agreement on the objectives of the organisation as rights based mass organisation striving to facilitate social change through mobilisation and advocacy. However, some coordinators felt that they needed to be also working towards the development of the tribals. They felt the organisation did not admit it but at many times was doing just that. The vision and future direction of Adhikar as either a rights based or both rights based and developmental or either of the two, did not have consensus among all the coordinators. The view posed by some was that it is time for Adhikar to foray into developmental work based on the understanding that much of the right based work had seen its culmination and the future lay in the area of developmental work. They felt it would make it easier for them to understand their own work and attract relevant resources if the purpose of the organisation could be clarified.

This is a theme that emerged as the most common through all the interviews. Almost all the coordinators thought that there was not enough coordination between them. Apparently the various units of Adhikar were performing their tasks well, but there was little sharing of information across the units. The high degree of decentralisation at the coordinator level had granted a great degree of autonomy but the coordinating mechanisms were absent. There had been a noticeable decline over the years in the number of meetings or occasions when all the coordinators met, and many cited this as a reason for the disconnect they felt with Adhikar as a whole. This lack of coordination coupled with the matrix structure led to confusion about authority and roles.

In talking to the coordinators some of whom had been with the organisation since its inception and some who were relatively new, there appeared to be some lack of trust between the two. The new in the organisation felt their growth or initiatives were blocked by the old who appeared to be guarding their turfs. The new also did not feel welcome by the old. On the other hand, the old members in the organisation felt that the new were ambitious and got right into the field without making an effort to understand the organisation. It was felt that though this was a concern with only a few, it had the potential to grow and create further conflict if not properly addressed.

There was no proper induction for new employees. Tied in to the seeming gulf between the old and the new in the organisation was the fact that the new entrants did not go through any formal socialisation process upon entry. This was cited by one of the coordinators, which also manifested in a feeling of not being welcomed into the organisation. Instances were mentioned when the new entrant had to go and seek information and figure things out for him/herself which further created a sense of dependence and feeling of isolation. The lack of a proper induction process appeared to have accentuated this gulf with the older members feeling that the new have been thrust upon them while the new were left with a sense of being unwelcome.

Ms. Devi had been with the organisation since its inception and enjoyed support in her region. She was however based off Chaibasa. Pia, the daughter of Mr. Mishra had been with the organisation for five years as the Programme Director of Ghatsila. Both Ms. Devi and Pia were potential future leaders of Adhikar. However, they independently echoed reservations as potential next leaders and mentioned their gender as one of the reasons. They felt that the other male coordinators and the community they served may not be ready for a female leader. They also felt that it was almost impossible to step into the shoes of the very charismatic Mr. Mishra. However, in discussions with most of the other coordinators, the authors got the sense that they were open to having a woman leader. They were keen to know who was going to be the next leader and wanted this to happen quickly. They felt that many of the coordination issues and problems would get addressed if a new leader was appointed.

Adhikar had a very charismatic leader in Mr. Mishra. A number of those who were associated with Adhikar had been attracted by his personal charisma and felt committed to him. After Mr. Mishra's active involvement in politics, his association with Adhikar on a regular basis had diminished. This created a leadership vacuum. Many in the organisation exhibited an inability to think beyond Mr. Mishra as their leader. The organisation seemed to be facing a crisis in terms of a leader who could command the same level of respect and following among the masses and the coordinators. There was a dearth of second level leaders in the organisation and Mr. Mishra still appeared to be the de facto leader, at least in the minds of organisation members at the time of the intervention. Even though towards the end of the intervention, Ms. Devi was appointed the new Managing Trustee, during the earlier meetings and in the eyes of others she was a shadow of Mr. Mishra and a surrogate leader for Pia, the daughter of Mr. Mishra. Pia appeared to be the chief decision maker. She operated from the headquarters while Ms. Devi preferred to work from her Chaibasa location. In our interactions it was felt that Ms. Devi was very committed to Mr. Mishra but lacked the vision, the energy needed to lead a highly motivated team and serve the interests of the entire community. She may have been a good worker but lacked creative abilities and an inclusive mindset. Ms. Devi had not been very forthcoming in the interview and was not too accommodating of the diverse views that were expressed during the diagnostic presentation meeting. The new leader appeared to be in stark contrast to the charismatic leadership of Mr. Mishra. The leadership issue is a classic problem (Ramos, 2007; Schnell, 2005) whenever a charismatic leader moves on and his/her shoes have to be filled.

Adhikar started out as a rights-based organisation. Most of the experienced and older employees chose to work for it due to their dedication to the original cause. Even the younger generation, which was better trained professionally, voiced concerns over the current remuneration and facilities. The newer employees were getting paid higher. The perks or facilities granted to some of the coordinators were perceived to be discriminatory and was a source of discontent among the older members.

Being a developmental organisation that has to depend on external funding many a time, the issue of job security and continued association with Adhikar was a matter of concern to some. With Mr. Mishra's lesser involvement there was a palpable fear that Adhikar may close shutters some day. The view expressed was that some form of assurance from the leadership for the continuity or clarity on the future of Adhikar may ease the sense of insecurity.

There were some concerns on the irregularity of reporting by some of the coordinators. That reporting and attending to administrative tasks serves as a helpful mechanism was not disputed, however, the tardiness of some coordinators to turn in reports on their progress was also tied in to the issue of leadership and authority. Most coordinators in the past had reported on a regular basis verbally to Mr. Mishra, who was able to fill in gaps of information whenever required for other coordinators. Thus the formal system of submitting and reading others reports had never been emphasised.

### Diagnostic Presentation Meeting

Based on the diagnosis and analysis of the issues, it was decided to have a mirroring (feedback) session with all the coordinators. Since one of the most important issues was the lack of coordination or communication between the coordinators, this meeting was also intended to be a platform to initiate dialogue and communication at the coordinator level. Pia arranged for the diagnostic presentation and informed all the coordinators about the session. Around this time, a change that took place in the organisation was the appointment of Ms. Devi by the board of trustees as the Managing Trustee in place of Mr. Mishra. The authors were informed of this change just prior to the diagnostic presentation.

The meeting was attended by five of the eight coordinators. In the beginning, the first author presented her findings (as have been presented in the earlier part of this case). The slide explaining the differentiation by programme and geography invited most comments, with organisation members unclear or divided in their interpretation of the structure. There was some ambiguity about the role of Pia too, with questions being asked if she was a coordinator or a region in charge. Although this line of discussion and debate didn't get resolved it pointed out to the group an area of concern.

However, there was an apparent reluctance on the part of the newly elected Ms. Devi to acknowledge the issues that were being presented. She engaged very little and when she did it was mostly to refute the existence of many of the findings even though they were being openly played out before her eyes at the time of the meeting, such as the lack of clarity on structure or poor communication and coordination across the coordinators. Further, there was a visible divide between the coordinators, with seating designed to separate and crystallise the distinction. Pia and Ms. Devi sat on one side of the room along with the authors and the other coordinators sat on the other side of the room. This was also indicative of the power distance between the two groups. The role of verbal and non-verbal exchanges in establishing and defining the boundaries of engagement and behaviour were also made obvious in this session.

What was also interesting was the lack of involvement of some of the coordinators during the session. Though they had been very open and vociferous during the individual meetings, when their point of view was presented or negated by Ms. Devi, they would not speak up. Rather they would also join in the say that the issue was not serious or it was non-existent. For example, poor coordination among the coordinators and the lack of meetings for dialogue and sharing at the coordinator level was an issue that almost all the coordinators cited in the individual meetings, but when Ms. Devi denied the existence of such an issue, it was not countered by any of the coordinators present. This could possibly be due to the fear of antagonising the power centres in the organisation or from a fear of being labelled the dissident camp. It could also be a function of high power distance (Hofstede, 1983) among Indians, resulting in a reluctance to be openly critical of superiors.

Though the meeting could not resolve any of the issues, this session to some extent was successful in bringing the coordinators together and sparking off discussion and debate in areas of concern and potential improvement zones. For an organisation where various groups had been operating in increasing silos with the divide never openly acknowledged and where the coordinators had not sat down together in years beyond the annual meeting, this itself was a beginning. While the authors were able to diagnose the leadership vacuum, there was little they could do given they were unable to meet with Mr. Mishra and Ms. Devi's refusal to engage effectively in the final presentation. Further, due to the limited time available for the engagement it was left to the organisation to follow up on the issues and findings. A report summarising the findings and observations was presented to the management.

This intervention presented a novel opportunity for the first author to enter an organisation of her choice and understand the issues involved and apply the learnings of OD to the field.

**Questions :**

1.  Explain the important lessons for the consultant ?
2.  Which organisation diagnosis model would best fit in this case ? Explain.